So Far, So Good

SO, THAT GOT WEIRD

AMELIA KINGSTON

SO, THAT GOT WEIRD

Dedication

To my amazing husband. You are my partner, my other half, the wind beneath my wings and all that cheesy crap. Thanks for being you. And thanks for loving me.

Chapter One

Elizabeth

Outside the restaurant after dinner, Jeremy seems as shy as I am, toeing the pavement with his hands in his pockets. Okay, maybe not *as* shy. He can make eye contact without blushing. He's the 'oh, isn't he sweet' kind of shy, while I'm more the 'oh, she has trouble functioning in society' kind. He seems my speed. Slow. Three-legged turtle on a glacier slow. He's nice too. Non-threatening. Safe.

Dinner was only mildly awkward, a raging success in the relative terms of my dating life. But it's the end of the night and this is the part I hate.

What do we do now?

Hug?

Kiss?

Shake hands? *No, that's weird.*

"I had a good time tonight," Jeremy chirps with an innocent smile on his lips. Meanwhile, my stomach is trying to turn itself inside out. *Calm down, Elizabeth.*

He's far from my dream guy, being barely taller than me at all of five foot nothing. He can only be considered 'in shape' if you mean round. He's never going to grace the cover of *GQ*, or even *Wired*. I don't care. I want him — anyone — to sweep me off my feet. I want to feel something — anything — other than this paralyzing fear.

My palms are sweaty. My heart's beating faster than if I'd run a marathon. My brain has unfortunately kicked into hyperdrive.

What if I have something stuck in my teeth?

What if my breath smells like onions?

What if my deodorant stopped working?

What if I'm a bad kisser?

What if I think he's going in for a kiss, but he's actually just going in for a hug and we do that awkward back-and-forth dance, resulting in knocking our heads together?

My stomach continues its acrobatics, tying itself into knots. I wrap my arms around myself, silently pleading for it to settle. I'm unaware of the pinched shape my face must've taken on when he asks with genuine concern, "Are you okay?"

I can't tell him I'm freaking out, so I lie. Admittedly, not something I'm particularly good at.

"Yeah, I'm fine." I try to pull off a nonchalant shrug and say the first thing that pops into my head. "Just a little gassy. You know, Mexican food…"

You did NOT just say that!

Jeremy's soft smile falls into a disgusted frown.

"Right," he says. He eyes his car in the parking lot, undoubtedly eager to get away from my train wreck of a personality.

"I had a nice time, too," I try to backpedal.

He gives me a forced smile. *Now who looks gassy?* This guy's officially lost interest. Can't say I blame him.

"Well, it's getting pretty late." He backs away with a wave, clearly avoiding any physical contact at this point. "Have a nice night, Elizabeth."

"You too, Jeremy." I return the awkward wave and make my way home, my head hanging in shame the whole way.

The second my front door shuts behind me, I beeline for my computer. I pull on my headset and stare at the video chat window, waiting for Jackie to answer. Jackie is my best—and only—friend. With bright red hair and a nose ring, she's also my complete opposite. She's a fierce and feisty woman, the human equivalent of a chihuahua. Small but bossy, Jackie is hellbent on conquering the world. So. Not. Me. I hate being noticed and try to fly under the radar. She loves being the center of attention and ends up bossing everyone around. I count on her for brutal, unabridged honesty.

"*¿Qué pasa, chica?* That's Spanish for *sup, girlie?* Thought you could use a little culture in your life." Jackie's megawatt smile and flaming red locks light up my screen. The smile fades when she sees the defeat stamped across my face. Or, is it *loser* stamped on my forehead? Or, maybe *twenty-one-year-old virgin*?

"Hey, what's with the sad face?" Her voice drags my brain away from contemplating facial tattoos to commemorate my failures and back to the real world.

"I had my date tonight with Jeremy."

She stares at me blankly. "Who the fuck is Jeremy?"

"You know, CommanderUxorious?" His username finally sparks recognition in her eyes.

"Oooohhhh, that geekalicious noob you've been chatting with for…" She pauses, taking an overly dramatic deep breath before adding, "Foooooreeeeeveeeer?"

"Shut up. It hasn't been *that* long. Only six months."

"That's three times the life expectancy of one of my relationships. So, was he hot?"

I try to think of a nice way to describe Jeremy. "He's kinda cute. In a hobbitish sort of way."

"Hobbitish? What the fuck does that mean? Like hairy feet and a fetish for second breakfast?" Jackie asks with a chuckle.

"Well, he's kind of short. And hairy. And chubby. He reminds me of a hobbit. Not in a bad way. Or maybe a guinea pig?"

"Sweet baby Jesus, stop. No. Just no. You can't be *hobbitish* in a *good* way. No one wants to fuck Frodo. Could you imagine screaming *Harder, Baggins, harder!*"

She makes crazy sex noises, moaning and slapping her desk à la Meg Ryan in *When Harry Met Sally*. I'm desperate to hold back my smile, but I can't. The second she sees me cracking, she goes full tilt.

"Oh, your feet are so big and hairy. Give it to me, baby! Take me to Mordor. Destroy that ring!" We both burst out laughing. I laugh until my sides hurt and my eyes are watering.

"My precious! My precious!" Jackie finishes with a flourish, leans back in her chair and smokes an imaginary post-coital cigarette. "So, what happened? Did you show him your hobbit hole?"

"Not exactly."

Jackie knows me well enough to hear the embarrassment in my voice. And, in true Jackie style, she calls me on it.

"Lizzy, what did you do?" She uses the nickname she knows I hate just to be a brat. Like I'm the family dog that got into the trash. She's disappointed, a twinge angry maybe, but in no way surprised.

This isn't my first colossal disaster of a date. Epic failure is kind of my thing.

"I-I..." I stutter, thinking of how to explain. "I might have told him I was gassy." I hide my face in my hands, sure I'm turning redder than Jackie's hair. She's still laughing when I finally peek through my fingers. Keeled over in hysterics, she nearly falls off her chair. Luckily, almost cracking her head open sobers her a bit.

With a few deep breaths, she composes herself. "What, and hobbits aren't into that? Guess you won't be hearing from him again any time soon."

"Seriously, Jackie, what's wrong with me?"

"So many things, my child. So very *many* things."

"I'm serious. We had so much in common. We spent two hours debating AMD versus Nvidia."

"Oh, gee. Graphics cards. What a panty dropper."

"I thought he was perfect. Respectful. Sweet. Mild-mannered—" Jackie's obnoxious fake snore interrupts me. "And even with him, I freak out and ruin it! Why am I so pathetic?" I drag my fingers through my hair and tug at the roots until it almost hurts.

"You're not pathetic," Jackie assures me, albeit with derision and frustration in her voice. "You spent six months building this spectacularly boring guy up in your head and you're surprised when he comes up short? Pun intended."

"Why can't I meet a nice guy and not freak out when it comes to the physical stuff? I can't even *kiss* a guy." I bang my head on my desk in classic toddler-meltdown fashion.

"Darling, sweetie, beautiful, light of my life, you know I love you, right? I mean in the strictly BFF way. I don't do Taco Tuesday."

"I love you too. And, eww."

"Lizbit, listen to your momma Jackie. You don't need a nice guy. You need a sexy filthy *man* who won't just pop your cherry—he'll obliterate it. You need to get fucked. Then it won't seem like a big deal."

I shake my head, almost losing my headset in the process. "It's not that easy."

"Yep. It really is." Jackie holds up one hand in a circle and moves the index finger of her other hand back and forth through it. *Classy.*

"It's not. Not for me. I get stuck in my head and overthink things. I get all panicked and say something stupid that ruins it. Like *I'm gassy!*"

Jackie lets out a quick chuckle at the reminder of my ineptitude. "That's because you're going out with hobbits! But yeah. Don't say that again. You need someone so fucking hot you turn your brain off and think with your pussy for once."

"What the hell does that mean?"

"It means dress slutty, go to a bar, find a guy who gives you a lady boner and ride him until he's dry." She gives me a shoulder shrug. "Easy."

"That's so not me. That's *never* going to happen." I shudder, panic trickling up my spine at the idea.

I don't do slutty.

I don't do bars.

I don't do *riding.*

"Well, I guess you'll be a virgin forever then. Is it too late to switch your major from pre-med to religious studies? You'd make an awesome nun."

* * * *

I hate Jackie. I mean, I love her, but right now I rue the day I ever accepted her stupid friend request. *'Just go to a bar and find a guy.'* It's that easy. I can walk right up to the bar and order one. I'll have a margarita and a sexy surfer. Beer and a muscled jock. Whiskey sour and a frat boy. Nope. I'll have a rum and cola—hold the rum—and an ever-growing sense of inadequacy. There's a bunch of guys here all right, but they're all chasing after the hot blonde in the short miniskirt. No one is lusting after my awkward smiles and self-conscious fidgeting.

My butt is asleep from being perched on this stupid bar stool for the past hour. I'm a complete loser sitting in this cramped campus bar by myself, sipping my soda and waiting for someone to ask me for a *ride*. The looks I'm getting aren't of the come-hither variety. They're more of the what's-her-deal kind.

Who comes to a bar alone on a Friday night? Weirdos. And serial killers, who I guess, by definition, are weirdos. Their own species, but same family. The point is, nobody approaches the creepy loner unless they want to be chopped into little pieces and buried in the desert. That's the level of weirdo I'm flirting with. I'm sitting alone. Strike one. I'm in a T-shirt and jeans, not a low-cut top and skin-tight leggings. Strike two. I came here to meet people, so Jackie made me promise not to stare at my phone. No selfies for this girl. Strike three. *Total weirdo.*

A group of girls take up residence next to me at the bar. I give them my token swear-I'm-not-a-psycho wave and get a lukewarm chin-raise in response. Sadly, this is the most positive interaction I've received from anyone tonight. What I wouldn't give to teleport back in front of my computer right now, safely swaddled in my footie pajamas.

A few more minutes go by and I'm trying not to be too obvious while eavesdropping to find an in on their conversation. It's about the Kardashians. Not my forte. I angle myself toward them so people might think I'm part of the cool crowd. Part of *any* crowd.

My mouth goes dry, my heart stops and my breath catches in my throat when the unthinkable happens. A guy — a hot guy — staggers up to me, gestures to my chest and says, "Cool shirt." He's talking to me! He's actually talking to me. Out of all the girls in this bar, he chose me. A wave of idiotic, giddy pride washes over me.

I blush, smile and glance down at my black T-shirt that reads 'There are only 10 types of people in this world. Those who understand binary and those who don't.' Jackie told me to wear something sexy. Black is sexy, right? Being funny is sexy too. This shirt is a twofer.

His eyes don't leave my chest while he sips his beer. He must be a slow reader. "Do you get it?" I ask him, trying to keep my tone un-insulting. He doesn't have to be a genius. I'm searching for my first time, not my soulmate.

He puts his arm on the bar behind me and leans in close enough that I can smell the alcohol oozing out of his pores. I have the urge to scream 'Personal space invasion!' but I bite my lip and keep silent. My back stiffens and I lean away as far as I can until it hits the bar behind me. He pushes his thumb inside the sleeve of my T-shirt, massaging my biceps intimately.

His hot breath is on my ear as he pants, "You know what'd make it better? If it were on the floor next to my bed."

Bile rises in the back of my throat and panic surges through my body. Sure, this guy is hot, but I don't want this. This isn't me. I pull my hands into my chest. "No, thank you." My voice is shaky and it comes out a question. That only seems to encourage him.

He moves his other hand to my knee. Condensation from the beer he's got pinched between two fingers seeps into my jeans. I feel violated by the cold, wet, unwanted sensation.

"What nice manners. I'd love to hear you say pretty please. On your knees," the stranger croons into my ear.

I want to tell him to fuck off. I want to shove him away. I can't. I'm frozen in place. He moves his hand up my thigh. My entire body goes rigid and my eyes go wide. I look to the girl next to me, silently pleading for help.

She sees the sheer terror on my face and snaps, "Hey, creep! Leave that poor girl alone."

"I'm just being friendly," the guy answers. He pulls away from me, a lecherous grin slashing across his face.

"Why don't you go make friends with your left hand? I think it's getting jealous," she quips.

The guy just holds up his hands in surrender, shakes his head and walks away.

Once I'm able to breathe again I turn to the patron saint of hopeless women and thank her for intervening.

She gives me a tight smile. "You know, if you don't respect yourself, no one else is ever going to respect you either."

"Ah, okay," I answer, not really sure why being harassed by an asshole at a bar is somehow my fault now. Trying not to seem ungracious, I add, "Thanks again." I give her a shaky smile and a quick wave. She just nods and returns her attention to her friends. I down the rest of my warm, flat soda before making my way to the nearest exit and into an Uber faster than I can say 'Friday night fail'.

"Jackie, you're an idiot," I tell my best friend as soon as I get home.

She rolls her eyes at me and sighs.

"No, I'm a genius. You're just doing it wrong."

"Oh, gee, thanks. I didn't realize there was a wrong way to get *molested* by a stranger in a bar!"

Jackie quirks an eyebrow. "There certainly is. And if you weren't enjoying it, then you were definitely doing it wrong. Was he hot?"

"Yes, he was hot. And he was also crass, overbearing, drunk and had a serious misconception of my personal space boundaries."

"Jesus, you and your Goldilocks vagina are impossible. *This guy is too shy. That one's too aggressive,*" she mocks in a high-pitched voice that is epically condescending. "They're boys, not bowls of porridge. Just pick one and dig in already."

I can't form a response. Creepy fairytale analogy aside, she's totally right. The guys I like are too shy to ever make a move and the guys who do make moves go too fast. It's the same every damn time. Either they run away or I do. Fizzle or explosion. I can't find a middle ground. My just-right Mr. Right.

It seems hopeless. I'm doomed to wander the earth untouched and unloved forever.

"I guess there *is* one other thing you *could* try." Jackie's tone has a familiar deviousness to it. She's waiting for me to take the bait. And, because I'm an idiot, I do.

"And that is?"

"Hire an escort."

An escort? That's crazy. Extreme. Ridiculous. Flat-out insane. *Isn't it?*

I pull up my web browser and type 'male escort' into the search bar. Big mistake. Huge. Massive. Throbbing. Mistake! I close the browser and try to purge the last thirty seconds of G-strings and gyrating-hip pop-up ads from my memory banks. Why do men think leopard print is sexy? I don't want to be mauled by your penis, thank you very much.

Dialing it down a notch, I have better luck searching 'college hookups.' The first few links are all *Maxim* magazine-type articles explaining the dos and don'ts of the college hookup. Spoiler alert, vomiting on a guy is a turn-off. I'll file that gem away for later reference. Halfway down the page I hit pay dirt.

Scoreyourscore.com.

It's a website designed for people to rate their sexual partners. You can sort by campus, age, gender, sexuality, kinks, etc. It's sexual Yelp. Too much nipple play. Nimble tongue. Sloppy kisser. Ridiculous stamina. Micro penis. Two-pump chump. Meat curtains. *Do. Not. Google. That!* It goes on and on. Men and women both detailing their exploits. This handy website is a goldmine of data.

I don't know how to read people, but data I get. Data speaks to me in a language I can understand. Right now, it's telling me, somewhere in all this hay, I will find my needle. That special someone to take my virginity. A brilliant if slightly deranged idea begins to form in my twisted brain. I don't need a professional — more of an experienced amateur. I open up a spreadsheet and go to town, more optimistic than I've ever been about taking the next step in my womanhood.

Chapter Two

Elizabeth

I've always hated my father's study. It's too big and it smells stale. It makes me feel insignificant. Decisions about my life were made in this room and I was never the one making them. Stepping across the threshold, I'm twelve years old again.

'Stop fidgeting, child,' my mother's stern voice calls out.

'Richard, are you listening to me? Your daughter has made me the laughing stock of Montgomery Preparatory Academy.' She taps her foot. It's her rattlesnake tail, warning that a strike is coming.

'How so?' my father asks, his eyes focused on the papers in front of him.

'Percilla Ellison ambushed me in front of the entire Council of Concerned Parents! She claims our daughter is a threat to the other children. That she is obsessed with the gruesome and morose.'

In biology lab, I told Becca Ellison a severed head can remain conscious for up to twelve seconds, which is both accurate and cool. Becca thought it was a threat. I don't know how to be normal, but for my mother, I try.

'I thought it was interesting.'

'Hush, child.' I hate when she calls me that, like I'm not hers. 'Why is she so odd?' my mother asks the universe. She looks me over with a sigh, her forehead wrinkling in disapproval. 'Posture, Elizabeth. Do you want to grow up a hunchback?'

I pull my shoulders back and stand up straight.

'Harriet, I have a conference call in five minutes.'

'I am withdrawing her from that school. I refuse to subject our family to gossip.'

'But I li – ' My mother silences me with a glare that could turn a saint's heart to stone.

'She can have tutors here at the house.'

'Fine, dear.'

'People will ask why she isn't attending school. I can't claim she is gifted. Perhaps she is ill? Too morbid. Delicate.' With one simple word, my life is changed.

Banished to my room for the rest of the night, I log into my computer and get lost in another world. A world where I have friends. Where I'm not a disappointment and a mistake.

"Loitering is unbecoming, Beth." My father's voice pulls me out of my memories. I step farther into his study, unsure of why I've been summoned. My father is sitting behind his desk, Mr. Phillips, our family attorney, in the chair facing him. I haven't seen him since after Mother's funeral. He came by with papers for Father to sign. When I introduced myself, he smiled, patted me on the head and gave me a candy. I was fifteen. It didn't occur to me to be offended at the condescending gesture. I thought he was a sweet old man.

"Sit," my father commands, gesturing to the seat next to Mr. Phillips. I do as I'm told, crossing my ankles and laying my hands in my lap, my shoulders back.

Mr. Phillips greets me with, "Good to see you again, Elizabeth. You have grown into a lovely young woman." I give a demure smile and blush slightly. "I understand you've recently had a birthday."

"Yes. I turned twenty-one last month."

"Lovely. That is actually why I'm here. Do you recall after your mother's passing, I mentioned a trust she left for you?" I nod, although I don't particularly recall the conversation. "Now that you are twenty-one, you have full access to the trust. I just need you to sign a few papers." He leans over and pulls out a folder. I don't bother reading any of the documents he lays out in front of me before I sign them. "Oh, and your mother left this as well." He hands me an envelope with my name written in Mother's delicate scrawl.

She wrote me a letter? Mr. Phillips continues, explaining to me how much is in the trust, how I access it and a bunch of things I should care about but don't. My mother took the time to sit down and write to me before she died. My hand is shaking and my eyes struggle to focus through the tears building in them. I clutch the letter to my chest, covering it with both hands, and stare up at the ceiling, willing away the emotion.

Mr. Phillips standing up beside me startles me back into the moment. We say pleasant goodbyes and I run up to my old childhood room, eager to be alone with my letter. I perch on the edge of the bed, wipe the stray tears out of my eyes and take a deep, calming breath. The anticipation of what my mother could have wanted to say to me before she died is causing my heart to race. I push down the nerves and peel open the back of the plain white envelope, being careful not to tear it. I pull out the single sheet of plain white paper folded into thirds and set the envelope down next to me on the bed. Opening the letter, I stare down at the beautiful, curling letters my mother's hand formed for me so many years ago. My heart sings and my chest is full. I read slowly, savoring every word because they are the last I will ever have from her.

Elizabeth —
Unfortunately, this money will not make you the woman I hoped you would be. When I am gone, remember the traits I struggled to engrain in you. Try not to be so odd. You carry my legacy into the world. Do not make a mockery of our family.
Always,
Mother

My uncontrollable tears soak the page, smudging the ink and blurring my mother's final words. It doesn't matter that they are no longer legible. They are forever carved into my broken heart.

* * * *

Familiar voices echo in my ear through my headset as I trudge through my game. What is normally my escape, my safe place, hasn't kept my mother's haunting words at bay. I'm following Jackie into battle, but my mind is somewhere else. My heart isn't in it.

"Lizbit, get your shit together," she snaps at me. I nearly sent my army into a crossfire. It's the third time she's had to tell me to focus.

"Sorry," I mumble. I struggle for another thirty minutes before we give up, failing to vanquish Jackie's latest in-game rival. We log out of the game, but she keeps our voice chat up.

Let the inquisition begin. "That's it. You're going to tell me what the hell is going on. You've been out of it all week and I'm sick of getting my ass kicked while you're off in la-la land."

"It's nothing," I deflect.

"Bullshit," she challenges. "Did you get a B on a test or something?"

"Nothing that traumatic."

"What then?" She waits for my answer.

My mother's words torture me in the silence. "I got a letter from my mother."

"I thought she was dead."

"She is."

"Creepy." Jackie isn't the most sensitive soul. "And?"

I sigh and pinch my eyes shut. The image of my mother's disapproving scowl confronts me in the darkness. "She basically said I'm her legacy, so don't be so weird."

Jackie laughs. Her cackles fill my headset. "So?"

"So? I'm a disappointment."

"Spoiler alert, babe. We're all a disappointment. My mom wants me to be her little clone. Just because she loves spending her free time barefoot in the kitchen, she expects me to be Betty fucking Crocker. No thank you."

I don't point out that her mom is also a successful real estate agent while Jackie has been a barista in her grandpa's coffee shop for five years and counting.

"She's right, though. I can't even have a conversation like a normal person. Maybe it's a sign. Maybe it's time I tried a change."

"If you want to change, then change. Be something else. Someone else. Just do it for you, not for her. She was a bitch when she was alive and she's still a bitch post-mortem. Who gives a shit what she thought?"

I do. I care. I need to make a change.

* * * *

I plop down in the seat across from him with a thud. The university library is so quiet the sound echoes through the nearly empty study hall. For someone so small, I'm surprisingly graceless. My mother's turning in her grave. It doesn't help that I'm so panicked to talk to him my knees practically gave out underneath me. I swallow down the lump in my throat, try to ignore my own awkwardness and press on with this crazy plan.

He looks up at me with a questioning expression. He doesn't even know who I am. But I know him.

Austin Jacobs, hot jock and sex god.

I've been sort of stalking him for a week now. There are no voodoo dolls or Photoshopped wedding photos in my apartment. I'm a little nuts and a lot weird, but I'm not full-on *Fatal Attraction* crazy. I trolled his social media and watched him studying here a couple of times. Nothing restraining-order-worthy. I might have also read every one of his scoreyourscore.com reviews. A few times. Maybe more than a few times. The boy's got skills and he's not shy about using them.

It was all data collection. For science. Or so I keep telling myself now that Austin stars in all my personal fantasies. Tedious hours spent poring over what Jackie has dubbed my 'devirginizer' spreadsheet all point to him as the ideal candidate. He's gorgeous, chronically single, selfless in bed, doesn't kiss and tell and is financially anemic. He's on a football scholarship, but has to work a couple nights a week too.

Five minutes ago, positive he's the one, I dove headfirst into the deep-end of my own stupidity. Now, with his inquisitive eyes staring back at me like I have a giant rhinestone dildo sticking out of my forehead, I'm drowning. I wish I were back in the shallow end of the social pool with the rest of the rejects, stupid yellow floaties on my arms and all.

This has got to be the worst idea I've ever had. And that's really saying something. I once cut my own bangs after watching a YouTube video. Lots of hats that summer.

My brain shouts at me to say something and I wonder how long it's actually been since I sat down. I think it's just a few seconds, but I space out when I get nervous. And sitting across from Austin is more than enough to make me as edgy as a frat boy at a DUI checkpoint on a Friday night.

Austin is six feet two inches of the all-American dream. Dirty-blond hair, crystal-blue eyes, pearly-white smile, lean muscles and a deep tan across his athletic body from all those football practices in the sun. He could have given Mother Teresa impure thoughts.

"Strategic Management Sixth Edition." At a loss for my own words, I read out the title of his textbook. "Good choice. I hear the first five editions were garbage. All strategy and no management," I deadpan, hoping to break the ice.

He doesn't appreciate the joke. He doesn't reply. He doesn't even move, but he's staring at me. Those baby blues are filled with wonder.

Wonder is too benevolent a word.

Not curiosity either.

Confusion.

Yep. That's it.

Maybe a bit of annoyance too.

I certainly know how to make a great first impression.

"That was a joke." I try to talk my way out of the discomfort his constant gaze and my continued idiocy are causing. "You know? Ha ha?"

Nothing.

He's watching me, his face stoic and unreadable. My heart is racing. I'm sweaty, but my mouth is dry. I look anywhere but at him. I would rather do the chicken dance naked in front of a full house at Carnegie Hall than be in this seat right now. I'm suddenly rethinking every life choice I've ever made that led me to this moment.

Abort. Abort. ABORT! Get out of there, Elizabeth!

"Oh, I thought jokes were supposed to be funny. My mistake," Austin quips back as a devilish smirk spreads across his lips.

He's funny. Who knew?

I'm stunned into momentary silence, but I can't control the smile that creeps onto my face. I'm nearing a panic attack, but his relaxed, easy manner makes me believe there's at least a small chance this won't end in a flaming catastrophe.

His eyes take in the five-foot-two tangled mess in front of him, from the frizzy brown hair on top of my head down to the baggy jeans and sneakers on my feet. He's trying to figure me out. *Good luck, buddy.* I've only ever managed to figure out what I'm not.

Not cute. Not tall. Not confident. Not brave. Not sexy. Not friendly.

Not normal.

"Touché. I guess comedy is in the ear of the beholder." I shift in my chair, determined to avoid making eye contact. He's so beautiful it's hard to look

25

directly at him. He's the sun and I'm asking to get burned.

"I'm Austin Jacobs." He reaches out his hand. It seems oddly formal.

My mind flashes back to Mr. Phillips patting my head. It's hard to feel like a woman when everyone treats you like a child.

"I'm Elizabeth Wilde." I reach my hand out. His hand engulfs mine, his fingers swallowing my palm entirely. His grip is gentle, but the visual is intimidating.

You know what they say about big hands?

I shake the thought out of my head. I can't go there. *Yet.*

"Nice to meet you," I say before a stiff pause consumes us. Panic is rising in my stomach. My lunch isn't too far behind. I don't think that chicken parm is going to taste as good the second time around.

"Oh, sorry. Guess you'll want your hand back now," I mutter, finally releasing his hand. Mine is cold and somehow seems smaller, foreign. I've never understood the phrase 'know it like the back of my hand.' I don't know my hands, couldn't pick them out of a lineup if they were attached to my wrists. Who stares at the backs of their hands anyway?

"That's how most people introduce themselves. Just for future reference." His voice rings in my ears, drawing me back to reality. His smug little smirk is back. It melts my insides while simultaneously making me want to smack it off his beautiful face.

"So, Elizabeth, is there something I can do for you?"

"I think there's something we can do for each other." I try to sound confident as I play the part I've written for myself. I launch into my speech. I've rehearsed it a million times, but with his blues piercing through me it's hard to remember. The tension around us is stifling.

If he feels it, it doesn't show. His forearms resting on the table and one side of his mouth hitched up, he seems calm and collected.

"I need a tutor," I spit out.

"I think the campus has a program for that sort of thing," he adds helpfully.

"Not that kind of tutor."

He's staring at me, one eyebrow raised.

"I have money but am lacking in certain life experiences. You, on the other hand, have a wealth of knowledge in those certain life skills." The words tumble out of my mouth in one long breath. The confused expression deepens on his face. I almost miss that smirk.

"Life skills?" His voice is playful and curious. I take that as a good sign and press on.

"I don't really know how to interact with people very well," I confess, already off script.

Damn it.

His inquisitive eyes are throwing me off. There's something about him that makes me want to confess my deepest secrets even though being near him makes my whole body tense harder than if I was standing on the tracks in front of a runaway freight train.

"Could've fooled me," he retorts.

This guy's got jokes.

I want to smack him again.

"Ass." The word slips out, under my breath, before it registers that I've said it. I've never called someone an ass to their face before. Out of all the times in my life I could speak up, now is the one I pick? With Austin Jacobs! *Kill me now.* My eyes shoot to his, trying to determine if he heard me.

He did.

Hello, smirk, my old friend. He stifles a chuckle. Suffice to say this isn't going how I planned.

I'm ready to get this over with and start word-vomiting, butchering the rest of my intricately thought-out speech.

"Look, I've heard your football scholarship only covers tuition. Not housing, food or books. And you have to work nights at some awful job that can't pay much more than minimum wage." My words wipe the smirk right off his face faster than any slap could. His eyebrows furrow and his mouth drops open. I've spooked him a bit, but I keep going anyway.

"You make, what, a grand a month? I'm offering you five times that. I'll give you five thousand dollars for a month of tutoring me three nights a week."

He tilts his head, his expression changing from concern to reserved interest at the mention of money. He's eyeing me with suspicion, tapping his pen on his still-open notebook. He's thinking about it.

"Tutoring you? In what, exactly?"

I'm relieved he seems to be more curious than creeped out for the moment.

"Teaching me some social skills."

"Like what? *Exactly.*" He isn't going to let me be vague. Subtle innuendo isn't going to work.

"Like flirting, touching, kissing. Like sex."

Confusion morphs into something else as his eyes go wide. I'm expecting shock or maybe repulsion. What I see is amusement.

"Did you just proposition me?" His voice is full of teasing. Of all the ways he could react, this is far from the worst. It stings a bit, regardless. He's laughing at me.

"I'm not propositioning you." I hear the defensive indignation in my voice. "I'm offering you a *business proposal.* I am *not* paying you for sex. I am paying you to be my *tutor.*" Even to me that sounds pedantic. "I'm dealing with unfamiliar material and I'd be willing to pay you for your expertise."

"Okay, where are the cameras?" he asks, glancing around the room. "This is campus hidden camera or something, right? Someone is going to pop out and..." The dead serious look on my face tells him it's not. "This *has* to be a joke. A prank. Who put you up to it? Drew?"

I shake my head and reply in complete seriousness, "I don't know a Drew. And I thought jokes were supposed to be funny."

"Holy shit. You're serious?"

His amusement is fading now. Apprehension rises in his expression. I've made him feel awkward. I think that might be my secret superpower.

Captain Awkward.

"Yes."

"You're going to pay me to have sex with you?"

"To *teach* me how to have sex." I continue to emphasize that point, unsure if the semantics matter to anyone but me.

"By actually having sex..." He isn't asking a question—he's throwing the bullshit flag.

"A certain amount of physical intimacy will be expected, yes."

He covers his face with his hands, shakes his head slowly and lets out a sigh. I can't tell if he's considering my offer or wondering how fast he can get a restraining order.

"I know this is an unusual proposition, but I think it could benefit both of us."

Almost immediately I'm aware of my mistake. His eyes lock on mine. They're filled with smugness.

"Bad word choice. Not a proposition. A business proposal."

"You can't be serious. Five thousand dollars?"

I can almost see the wheels turning in his head.

He's considering it.

My stomach flips. I'm not sure if this is terror or excitement.

"Five thousand dollars. Three nights a week for a month. I think we could really help each other out."

He traces his gaze up my body before coming to rest on my face. He's staring into my eyes, judging my commitment. For a brief moment I think I've got him, that this idea isn't crazy.

Then, the bubble bursts.

"This is getting a little too weird for me. I think you've watched *Pretty Woman* a few too many times," he says as he stands and packs up his books. He won't look at me.

"Is that a no?" I hate the amount of hurt I hear in my own voice.

"That's going to be a hard no. It was nice to meet you, Elizabeth." He reaches out his hand.

I don't take it. I scribble my number on the page of a notebook he hasn't put away yet.

"In case you change your mind." I slap the notebook into his open hand and watch him turn and walk away.

Well, that was a crushing defeat.

At least I got the last word. After I watch him leave, I take a few minutes to slam my head on the table, muttering to myself about how stupid I am. Once I'm satisfied with my self-inflicted punishment and before I gather too many stares, I make my way out of the library and back home to sulk in private at my humiliation.

* * * *

I've donned my give-up-on-love sweatpants, put on my favorite Disney movie and hunkered down on my couch for a quality pity party. I'm half a carton of ice cream into my wallowing when my phone rings. I don't bother to check the number before I answer it.

"Did you get me fired?" a vaguely familiar manly voice calls out across the line. No *hello*. No *how are you*.

"I think you have the wrong number," I tell the guy as I am about to hang up.

"No, I don't, Elizabeth. Answer my question. Did you get me fired?" His voice has taken a sharper tone than it had this afternoon, but I recognize it. My brain clicks the pieces into place and I sit up, almost falling off the couch.

"Austin," I screech into the phone. My heart is racing, knowing he's on the other end of the line.

"Elizabeth." He sounds annoyed, but more than that he sounds exhausted. "I really need this job."

"I didn't get you fired," I answer flatly.

"So it's a coincidence I got fired a few hours after you *proposition* me?" His voice isn't playful or teasing. It's angry and confrontational. I know I didn't do anything wrong and yet I'm combative.

"Yes. I wouldn't know how to get you fired even if I wanted to," I answer honestly, and yes, maybe I'm a *little* snooty.

"You certainly seemed to know a lot about me this afternoon."

I cringe, knowing I give off a quasi-stalker vibe.

"No more than anyone else with access to the Internet could find out. Maybe you should change your Facebook privacy settings and delete your Instagram account," I answer. Sure, I propositioned him a few hours ago, but I'm not malicious or manipulative. I don't want to trap him into going along with my crazy idea. There's a long pause while we both stubbornly refuse to say more. I don't know what to say, but for some reason I'm glad he hasn't hung up yet.

"I can probably get you another job. A real one, I mean," I finally offer, knowing I could get him a job as a night janitor or something in one of my father's buildings if I asked. It would be an awkward phone call—I've never asked my father for a favor before, so I'd have to face some questions—but if it stopped this churning in the pit of my stomach it would be worth it.

"And why would you do that?"

"Because you said you needed one." I let my tone add the implied *duh*.

"Seems counterproductive for you, given our last conversation."

"I don't want to be some guy's last resort!" I let out an aggravated sigh, pissed at myself for oversharing. "Do you want the job or not?" I snap at him. I'm annoyed and frustrated. And excited.

"Which one?" The teasing in his voice assures me he has that stupid smirk on his face. Picturing it makes my blood boil and my knees weak.

So, that's weird.

"Either."

There's a long pause again. He's thinking about what to say, what road to take.

"Tell me why." His voice is cajoling. For a minute, I have to physically shut my mouth to resist the urge to confess things to him. It's a strange feeling.

"Why what, Austin?" I ask, exasperated.

"Why do you need to pay someone to be with you, Elizabeth?" There isn't any disgust or accusation in his voice.

The question makes me self-conscious.

"I don't *need* to. I'm *choosing* to. There's a difference. I could find some random guy tonight if I wanted to." I know that's not true, but I say it without any doubt in an attempt to shut him up.

His voice is deeper. There's a new roughness to it as he says, "I'm sure you could." It makes my heart beat a bit faster, something I didn't think was possible at this point. "So, why are you *choosing* to pay someone?" He is gentle but insistent. He isn't going to let this go. I finally give in to the inexplicable desire to confess to him. I do it with a huff so at least he knows my words are unwillingly given.

"Because..." How do you tell a stranger all the insecurities your own inadequacies have created over a lifetime? "It's hard to explain."

"Try. I've got all night. Lost my job, remember?"

I laugh in spite of myself.

"Umm...have you ever been skiing?"

"No."

"Ugh. Okay. Well, I have. My parents took me on a ski trip when I was eleven. And, what you have to understand about me is, I'm kind of stubborn."

"You? I never would have guessed."

"Ass."

Somehow his teasing doesn't make me feel foolish. It makes me feel equal.

"I prefer to figure things out on my own. My parents told me the basics, then I strapped on a pair of skis and headed for the bunny slopes." I stop. I'm not sure if he's paying attention to my rambling story.

"How did you do?" He's listening. The thought makes my chest grow warm. It makes me feel powerful. Important. Special.

Weird.

"Horrible. I couldn't figure out how to keep my feet under me. I was awkward and uncoordinated. Some things never change."

He laughs at my self-deprecation. I swell with a bit of confidence and continue my story.

"When my parents found me, sulking in front of the fire, I told them I never wanted to ski again. Snow was now my mortal enemy. My mother spent the night lecturing me, trying to convince me to try again." My words trail off at the pinch in my heart from the memory of my mother.

"And did it work? Did you try again?" Austin's voice is tender in my ear.

He's *really* listening. I settle back into the couch cushions, relaxing a little for the first time since I picked up the phone. I pull the blanket off the back and curl up under it, getting cozy and comfortable.

"It worked. Her guilt trips always worked. But the next day was worse. The only thing I got better at was falling. I was bruised, so every fall was that much more painful." I hear Austin's soft laugh again and close my eyes to focus on the sound.

"On the third day, my parents realized I needed professional help. They hired a ski instructor who spent the entire day teaching me one-on-one. Wedge like a pizza to stop. Straight like French fries to go fast. Keep your knees bent and your weight centered. I made it down the mountain without falling less than three hours later." I finish my story and let silence dominate the phone line. I want to know if he gets it. Does he understand me?

"And you think sex is going to be like skiing?"

"Basically. I've crashed and burned the few times I've tried anything...*physical*." The embarrassing memories of past dates ending with genial buddy back-slaps overtake me. "Usually I'm good at figuring things out, but not with this. I can't read the *Kama Sutra* and teach myself how to do it. No pun intended." My voice is light despite my mortifying confession.

Austin laughs again. I'm beginning to love that sound.

"Don't get me wrong, I know what goes where. In general. I know how, I've just never been able to figure out *how*. Does that make any sense?"

"I think I get it. I can describe how to catch a ball all day, but there's no substitute for getting on the field and actually putting one in your hands," Austin adds his analogy. "The best athletes in the world can benefit from a coach who knows what they're doing. But why hire a stranger? Why not get a boyfriend?"

"A boyfriend, you say? Thanks! I've never thought of that."

He chuckles despite my snark.

"I've tried dating, but I always freak out. Guys seem to think I'm frigid instead of inexperienced."

"Then be honest and upfront with them."

"Oh sure, that's easy. Just confess my complete sexual inadequacy to the guy I'm interested in. Hi. I'm Elizabeth. I'm a virgin! Want to grab dinner some time? That'd encourage the creepers and send the few decent guys who're interested running for the hills. And being inexperienced only gets more embarrassing the older you get. Plus, going to med school? Forget about it. Besides, I have trouble talking to guys about the weather! Tell me, Austin, ever try to get a boyfriend when you can't even talk to a guy?" My response is flat, not hiding my annoyance.

Does he seriously think it's that easy?

I'm sure it is for him.

"Can't say that I have." He chuckles. I stifle a moan. First that smirk and now this laugh. I'm not sure I'll survive Austin Jacobs.

"But you're talking to me."

"Yeah, and I'm not sure why. It's definitely weird. But you're the first." Judging by the sudden silence cutting through the phone line, I'm not the only one who recognizes the significance of those words. I'm glad he can't see the blush burning across my cheeks. I pull the blanket up over my head, making a fort with my knees, just in case.

"It's an honor." His voice isn't sarcastic or teasing. It's soft and genuine. "I'll take the job."

"Which one?" I'm glib to try to hide my excitement.

"The one to be your first." His voice is low and sultry, with a hint of naughtiness. The sound of it makes my mind wander and my body flush.

"Okay," is all I can make come out of my mouth.

"Good night, Elizabeth," he coos into my ear and I melt into the couch cushions.

"Good night, Austin," I say before I hear him hang up.

I spend the next few hours on the couch staring at the ceiling, remembering the sound of his laugh.

Chapter Three

Austin

My shoulder aches as I toss my gym bag onto the torn passenger seat of my beat-up truck. Hitting the gym this morning before practice really kicked my ass, but I needed to clear up the rest of my night for Elizabeth's 'business proposal.' Meeting three nights a week means I'll have to shift my workouts to balls-ass early. It'll be painful, but on the bright side it means no more working nights. Plus, I get to keep my Fridays open.

I'm her tutor, not her boyfriend.

I stretch out each arm, enjoying the slight burn deep in my muscles, before I climb into the driver's seat. I punch the address Elizabeth gave me into my phone and the GPS tells me it's twenty minutes away. *Fuck.* I don't have time to head back to the house and change. I haven't showered yet. My cut-off tank top is soaked with sweat and my gym shorts are covered in grass stains, mud and a few small splotches of dried blood. Pretty sure it's not mine.

Fuck it. A sex tutor is the sweetest job I've ever had, but still a job. Nothing special. I throw the truck into drive and head out.

The closer I get to Elizabeth's place, the nicer the neighborhoods get. Most of the stuff around campus is pretty run-down. The dorms are all cheap mass construction to begin with and college kids aren't known for being good tenants. The football house I share with a handful of teammates should be condemned. It's got more bodily fluids on the floorboards than a hospital dumpster, but at least it's free. Elizabeth doesn't live in student housing. No, she lives in a brand-new high-rise apartment building. With valet parking. I opt to park on the street a few blocks over. *Wouldn't want to bring the property value down.*

I spot the elevators across the marble floor lobby but only manage to make it halfway there before the doorman blocks my path. Yes, a doorman. Elizabeth's apartment has valet parking *and* a doorman. I'm punching above my weight here. This dude takes one look at me, sweaty and dirty, before deciding I need to go.

"Can I help you, *sir*?" he asks, giving less than zero fucks about helping me.

"Nope," I answer, stepping around him.

"I'm sorry, but all guests need to be announced."

I can hear the pitter-patter of his loafer-clad feet in hot pursuit behind me.

"Then announce me," I retort over my shoulder without stopping. I press the Call button and thankfully one of the *six* elevators opens immediately. Jesus, what have I gotten myself into? "I'm going to the penthouse. Ms. Wilde's waiting." Elizabeth is on the twelfth floor. I have no idea if that's the penthouse, or if this building has a penthouse, but it sounded good.

I step into the elevator and turn back to face him with my arms crossed. He's scowling at me. I give him a knowing smile and a dismissive finger-wave as the doors close.

Fuck you, Jeeves.

I rock side to side on my feet in the elevator, trying to work out some of this nervous energy. I'm not having second thoughts. Five thousand dollars is a lot of money. I just don't get what I'm doing here. I have no idea why she picked me. This girl could afford a Hemsworth brother. One of the un-famous ones, at least. The whole idea seemed crazy when she first asked me in the library. I mean, a *sex* tutor?

That's insane. Saying yes was insane. There's a one-in-ten chance I'm walking into an it-puts-the-lotion-on-its-skin sort of situation.

I take a deep breath, hold it for a few seconds then let it out slowly as I roll my shoulders. I've had sex with girls for worse reasons, including simple boredom. When Elizabeth propositioned me, I was flattered, even curious, but more than anything surprised. Elizabeth isn't exactly a sex kitten, but she's not a hideous beast either. She's too conservative for my taste, but I'm sure nerds around the world would cream their jean shorts at the thought of getting into her granny panties.

I never would've called her if I hadn't lost my job. *Downsizing, my ass.* I got fucked over. They think I don't need the money just because I'm young and single? Fuck them. Everyone's gotta eat. Even with a scholarship, college is expensive as hell. When I was a kid, my mom couldn't pay rent, much less start a college fund.

I take another deep breath, hold it for a count of three and release it.

I called Elizabeth ten minutes after I got fired and was ready to murder someone. Somehow, after talking to Elizabeth, I wasn't so pissed. And the sex tutor idea didn't seem so crazy. She's a super-shy girl who needs a bit of a confidence boost. She needs help and I need a job.

We're a perfect pair.

A computerized voice announces the twelfth floor as the elevator doors open. I find my way down to Elizabeth's apartment, the last one at the end of the hallway. She opens the door almost before I finish knocking. The eager little beaver has been waiting for me.

She's wearing a loose T-shirt and jeans that are at least two sizes too big for her tiny frame, tragically managing to hide every inch of her figure.

Such a shame.

From the little I can see, she has potential. She wouldn't be half bad if she ever bothered to dress up. It was the same when I met her in the library. I wonder if she has any idea how frumpy she dresses.

Probably not.

This girl is beyond clueless.

She's frozen in the doorway, death grip on the doorknob, her petite body managing to block most of the entrance to her apartment. The only part of her moving are those chocolate eyes that keep getting wider. Her chest stops moving. I don't think she's breathing.

The way her mouth drops open makes me think she didn't believe I'd actually show up, though her five grand has already posted to my account. *Who pays upfront?* She's too damn trusting. Lucky for her, I keep my promises.

We can't stand here all night. I've got a job to do.

With a smirk, I wrap my arms around her waist, lift her and push us both into the apartment. I plant a kiss right on her pouty lips as I set her down. It's pretty tame, no tongue, but her hand shoots up to her mouth in disbelief. Those big brown eyes of hers get wider. *Didn't think that was possible.*

She's kind of adorable, in a lost-puppy sort of way.

"Mind if I grab a shower? I came straight from practice," I call back to her.

She doesn't say anything. I'm halfway down the hallway where I assume the bathroom is when I glance back at her. She's hovering near the door, a dreamy expression on her face. I must be a better kisser than I thought.

I don't take long in the shower, but I take a little extra care in scrubbing all the bits I might be using tonight. I'm a gentleman, after all. By the time I finish, she seems to have recovered from my friendly greeting and is banging around in the kitchen.

"Holy shit!" she screams when she sees me walk into the living room in nothing but my tight boxer briefs. She knocks over a cup of noodles on the counter and manages to burn herself splashing the near-boiling water.

"Ouch! Damn it, that hurts." She jumps around, shaking her hand in the air like a five-year-old.

This girl is absolutely ridiculous.

"Run it under cool water!" I holler at her.

She doesn't listen.

I cross over to her and take matters into my own hands. And by matters, I mean her body.

I come up behind her, grab both her wrists and push her over to the sink. I turn on the water and push her reddening fingers underneath it. She's caged in my arms and I have her body pinned against the counter. Her heart is beating fast enough that her pulse races in her wrist. She's taking deep breaths, trying to calm herself down.

She isn't worked up because of the burn. It's because of me.

"Does that feel better?" I ask, leaning down to her ear.

"Y-yes. I'm fine. Th-thank you."

Her body tenses as she tries to pull away from me. It's useless. I haven't given her any room to maneuver.

"I've got it now," she manages to whisper.

She shifts her hips back, angling to get away, but instead she manages to grind against me. She lurches forward again, throwing herself against the counter when I don't pull away. Too bad—I was kind of enjoying the grinding. I linger a moment longer, reveling in her awkwardness. It's kind of a turn-on that I can unsettle her so easily.

"Glad I could help."

I drag my fingers along her forearms as I let go of her wrists and step away. Goosebumps appear in the path my fingers traced and my cock perks up in my boxers.

Tonight's going to be fun.

"Why are you naked?" she asks, refusing to look at me. I clean up the noodle mess she made when jumping around like an idiot.

"I'm not naked," I assure her.

"You practically are," she snips.

She's an interesting dichotomy.

Dr. Timid and Ms. Feisty.

I wonder which version is the real her.

42

"Given what we've got planned for tonight's activities, what's the big deal?" I lean against the counter and dare her to meet my gaze. She does, but only for a second before wrapping her hand in a towel.

"We are *not* having sex tonight," she declares.

"We're not?" I try to sound hurt and confused, but mostly I'm teasing her.

"No!" She finally turns to face me, keeping her eyes safely above my shoulders. A pretty amazing feat given she has to be at least a foot shorter than me. "So, could you put some clothes on?"

"Sure." I saunter over to where I dropped my gym bag on my way to the shower. I throw on some shorts and a white T-shirt before turning back to her for approval. "Better?"

"Better. Thank you." She sighs with relief and I can't help but chuckle. "Well, my dinner's ruined," she says, tossing her ramen noodles in the trash.

"Ramen isn't dinner. It's a travesty. A damn food-hate crime," I tease her. "It's only acceptable in the dorms freshman year when a microwave and fifty cents is all you have to survive."

"I'm not much of a cook..." Her soft voice trails off. She wraps her arms around her waist and looks away sheepishly. Is she feeling self-conscious?

Because she can't cook?

She shifts back to timid so fast it makes my head spin. It scares me to think how easy it would be to break this girl. Suddenly, I feel shitty for mocking her.

"Then you're in luck. Cooking is one of my many talents. Let's see what we've got." I rifle through her kitchen cabinets, searching for something that could objectively be called food.

"I don't have much by way of cooking supplies," she mumbles behind me. I continue undeterred.

"Believe me, I've made epic meals with much less." It isn't a lie.

I've lived off some pretty horrible crap when I had to. That's probably why I enjoy cooking so much now. After years having to feed myself with whatever I could find in the back of the cabinets because my pathetic excuse for a parent hadn't been shopping in weeks, the freedom to make myself a delicious meal with fresh ingredients is a luxury.

I shake off the harsh memories of my childhood as I find some spaghetti noodles and marinara sauce.

"Ahhh! Perfect," I cheer as I turn to her with a wide grin. She's sitting on a bar stool on the other side of the kitchen but rewards me with a shy smile. We're quiet as I wait for the water to boil. I ask the question that's been driving me nuts since we met.

"So, you have to tell me. Why me?"

"Why you what?"

"You know what. Why did you ask me to pop your cherry?"

She cringes at my words. We'll have to work on that. I love talking dirty.

"That's not—"

"Yeah. Yeah. I'm the ski instructor. Whatever. Why did you choose me?"

She's quiet for a while, as if trying to decide what or how much to tell me.

"Have you heard of the website scoreyourscores.com?" she asks. I shake my head. "It's a website for people to rate the *experiences* they've had around campus." She watches me to see if I get it. I know the kind of thing she's talking about. People have been rating their fucks as long as they've been fucking.

"You mean girls rate the guys they've fucked?"

"Yes." Her voice is firm and she doesn't cringe this time, but her shoulders are slumped and she's wringing her hands.

"Including me?"

It's a rhetorical question. Obviously I'm on it or I wouldn't be sitting in front of her now.

"Yes," she answers quietly. She won't look at me and she's tracing the grout lines in the tile counter. She's clamming up, so I try to lighten the mood.

"Guess I got some good reviews then? Five stars. Two enthusiastic thumbs-up. Best I've ever had," I say in my best chick voice as I dump spaghetti noodles into the boiling water.

"There were no complaints in *that* department." Her response makes me curious.

"But there were in other departments?" I push her. I haven't slept with half the campus, but I get around. I've never left a woman unsatisfied that I know of. They all got a great night of no-strings-attached fun.

"I can pull up the site..." She turns around, gesturing to a computer desk that takes up a decent chunk of her living room. It's got three screens, some massive speakers, keyboard, mouse, joystick, a headset and a bunch of other gadgets and gizmos. Seriously, who needs *three* screens? I have a feeling she doesn't get out much.

"Nah, just tell me what they said." If she's struggling to say the words, she's going to have a hell of a time when we get to actions. And I definitely want to see this girl in *action*.

"Ummm." She's so uncomfortable, eyes darting around and off-the-charts fidgeting, I can't help but tease her more.

"I know for a fact every girl I've ever been with has come. At least twice. I'm a giver." I wink at her as I pour the water out of the pot and stir in the marinara. "Come on. It can't be that bad if I'm standing here."

"They aren't bad. The girls were very complimentary regarding your...assets...and...skills." The blush on her cheeks is adorable. No doubt she's remembering some of the more explicit posts. This girl is so innocent it's almost intimidating. "Their complaints were more about your hit-it-and-quit-it style."

"They all knew what they were signing up for," I say flatly. I have no doubt I was explicit with each and every one of those girls. "I don't date and I'm always clear about that. You should know that too, I guess. I don't want a girlfriend. No white picket fences or happily ever afters. I don't do forever."

"That's why I picked you. I'm not asking for forever, just a month. This is about figuring out what I need to know and moving on. No drama. No complications." Her words are as steady as mine.

Most girls hate it when I'm frank about our lack of a future. Elizabeth is different. She's like me, happily distant and detached. The only difference is I know how to fake a connection when I need to. I grew up being a chameleon, giving people what they want, hoping to be wanted in return.

"I think this is the beginning of a beautiful friendship," I say as I set her bowl of spaghetti in front of her.

"*Casablanca*," she says wistfully.

"What's that?" I ask through a mouthful of food.

She has a reminiscent smile on her lips. "It's the movie you were quoting. The last line from *Casablanca*. The beginning of a beautiful friendship..."

"Hmmm. I thought it was just a saying. Like raining cats and dogs. I've never seen it. Is it any good?" I manage to ask in between massive mouthfuls.

"One of my favorites. I think I have a copy. If-if you want to, you know, watch it." Her voice is hesitant.

Is she seriously nervous to ask me to watch a movie with her? After what I've already agreed to? I buy a few minutes shoveling spaghetti into my mouth. We eat together in awkward silence and I think about how I want to respond.

"Sure. I'm not going to be getting frisky any time soon after all those carbs." I drop my empty bowl in her sink, walk around to the couch and throw myself down into the cushions. She finishes her dinner and comes to fuss in front of the TV. She pops the movie in and sits as far away from me as possible while still technically on the couch.

The movie plays, but neither of us is actually watching it. She's sitting up, her back stick straight, her ass barely on the edge of the cushion. It has to be uncomfortable. I'm staring at her, waiting for her to scoot back and relax. She never does. I grab the remote and pause the movie.

"What's wrong?" she asks, her voice high-pitched and shaky as she turns to face me. I swear she only has one butt cheek actually on the couch at this point. She could be in the starting blocks at the Olympics, ready to sprint away at any minute.

"So, you've never had a boyfriend?" I ask her, already knowing the answer.

"I told you I haven't." She shies away, nervous as hell, but also a little sassy.

"And you've never slept with anyone?" I want to hear her say it.

"No. I told you I haven't." Her apprehensiveness borders on irritation. God help me, it's an alluring combination. She somehow manages to be innocent yet scrappy.

"But you've fooled around, right?"

"I guess that depends on what you mean by fooling around."

She's being evasive, but I'm not going to let her. *I play games for a living, sweetheart.*

"Ever given a guy head?" If she's going to be obtuse, I'm going to be blunt.

"No."

"Been eaten out?"

"No," she huffs.

"Fingered or hand job?"

"No."

She tries to slyly wipe her hands on her pants, but I catch it. I've got her sweating already. There's tension racking her shoulders as they hunch forward. Her fidgeting is worse, lacing and unlacing her fingers in her lap. She's keeping her face away from me to hide how red her cheeks have turned. She's refusing to meet my eyes.

"How about some under-the-shirt groping? Light nipple play?" I mock a little twist of my own nipples with a grin.

I get zero reaction.

"Dry humping?" I'm almost running out of things to ask. I'm pretty sure at this point no guy has ever so much as touched her, but I can't help myself from continuing to push her.

"No and no." Each time she says it, she's a little bit more defiant, and damn if it doesn't make my shorts tighter.

"Fuck. You've at least made out with a guy?"

She's quiet for a long moment, eyes darting around the room.

"Don't start lying now."

When her eyes find mine, they are filled with a raw vulnerability that unsettles me.

"No. I haven't kissed anyone. Before tonight."

Her final confession knocks me for a loop. No wonder she stood there frozen after I kissed her. That was her first kiss. I was her first kiss.

"How's that even possible?" I can't control my mouth. "What are you, twenty-one? Did you grow up in a cave or something? Are you some kind of religious freak?"

She jumps up off the couch and storms over to the front door, stomping her tiny feet and marching across the room. Timid Elizabeth is a distant memory. She's all fury and indignation now.

"I'm paying you to help me. Not to mock me. I've been honest about everything and if you can't handle it without being an ass, then this isn't going to work." She yanks the door open to punctuate her threat. One hand is curled in a tight fist at her side while the other grips the doorknob tight enough to turn her knuckles white. "You should go."

Her petite body is tense, electrified with rage. My attention is drawn to the hint of her pert nipples. Her shoulders are pulled back and her breasts strain against her cotton T-shirt with each heaving breath. Her face is flushed and her pouty lips are pursed. There's fire dancing in those chocolate eyes. *Damn.* Elizabeth Wilde is sexy as hell when she's pissed off.

I have a feeling this is a pattern, running away when she gets scared. *Not this time.* I cross the room to her slowly and confidently.

"There's no need to be so dramatic," I tell her as I pull the door out of her hand and close it again.

She crosses her arms and huffs at me.

"I'm sorry. I didn't realize where we were starting from," I placate her, my voice soft.

"Now you know."

I didn't know so much sass could come in such a small package. She's flipped a one-eighty from the apprehensive creature perched on the edge of the couch just a minute ago. She may not be comfortable with being sexy, but she sure knows how to be pissed.

"Now I know." I encroach on her personal space, curious to see if she'll switch back to the scared kitten from before if I turn up the heat. "I feel bad. If I'd realized that was your first kiss, I would've made it a better one. Can I get a do-over?"

I don't wait for a response before I wrap my arm around her waist and pull her body against me. I glide my other hand behind her neck and snake my fingers into her hair. Her body goes rigid against mine, but I don't let her pull away.

Ms. Feisty is reverting back to Dr. Timid as she deflates in my arms, the anger seeping out of her like a balloon.

I brush my lips against hers, teasing the sensitive skin. I wait for a minute, giving her the chance to tell me to stop. She doesn't.

"You're holding your breath," I murmur against her lips. A deep, ragged moan is her only response. Having this effect on her is intoxicating. I press my lips against hers, tracing with my tongue and sucking her bottom lip into my mouth.

She doesn't kiss me back. She doesn't do anything.

Panic radiates off her. I pull back and take her in. She's terrified. Her eyes are clenched shut and every muscle in her body's got to be constricted, like this is electroshock therapy. It's not sexy. Not the same ballpark as sexy.

"Relax," I tell her. "Get out of your head."

"I can't!" she snaps back at me. She's irritated but doesn't pull away.

"Open your eyes," I beckon, taking a step back and interlacing her fingers with mine at her side. Her face is a picture of angst and frustration, lips pouting, forehead furrowed, cheeks aflame.

What am I going to do with this girl? I need to get her to relax and calm down. It's just a kiss, for fuck's sake.

"You're psyching yourself out. Shake it out, okay? Let go of all that tension." I do a full-body shimmy, blowing out a deep breath as I do, showing her what I want her to do. She stares at me as if I'm insane. I do it again, shimmy and exhale, before motioning to her. She half-heartedly mimics me, giving me a sigh and a shrug.

"Again. Like you mean it this time," I demand.

"This is stupid."

"Yep. It's stupid. And awkward. And embarrassing. That's the point. Loosen up. This isn't serious. Believe it or not, kissing is supposed to be *fun*."

She rolls her eyes so hard she could star in *The Exorcist*.

"I want you to be my little loosey-goosey," I taunt her. She lets out an annoyed groan but gives it another try, shimmying and sighing at me.

"Say it. Loosey-goosey." I do another shimmy.

"Loosey-goosey," she mumbles.

"Shout it out. LOOSEY-GOOSEY!" I want her to feel a bit ridiculous. I want her to know it's okay to laugh at herself. I'm not going anywhere.

"Loosey-goosey..." she says in a mocking tone.

"Louder. LOOOOOSEY-GOOOOSEY!" I continue. We're both doing near constant full-body tremors at this point. I'm sure I look like I'm having a seizure, but I couldn't care less.

"LOOSEY-GOOSEY!" she shouts at me.

"Again! LOOOOOOSEY-GOOOOSEY!" I bellow. There's a tinge of a smile on her lips and I know I've almost got her.

"LOOOOOOOSEY-GOOOOOOOOOSEY!" she shouts at the top of her lungs with a full-body shake before she busts out laughing. It's a light and joyful sound. Her laugh is contagious. I throw my head back and laugh with her. I can't remember the last time I've laughed this hard. It feels good. Really good.

"Listen, Goose," I say as I get control of myself again. "Kissing is easy. It's just a little give and take. Relax your jaw, soften your mouth, tilt your head and follow my lead. Okay?" I put her hands on my pecs.

"Sure thing, *Maverick*," she chides with a playful smile.

I tilt my head and cock an eyebrow at her.

"You know...from the movie...*Top Gun*?" she mutters.

"Yeah, I've seen it." I give her a playful smirk in approval of the nickname.

I step into her, pressing my chest against hers. I slip my hands into her hair and stroke her neck. Her body is stiff, muscles coiled, as I kiss her again. At first, she only responds by mimicking my movements robotically. She's holding back, studying me. I decide to push her further.

"Open your lips," I whisper and she does without question. She's an obedient student. I tilt her head and slide my tongue into her mouth. It's soft and warm.

She tastes delicious.

I kiss her long and hard, caressing her tongue with mine. The longer we go, the more confident she becomes, swirling her tongue against mine. She sinks into the kiss, finally getting lost in the sensation of my lips against hers. I have to say, for a first-timer, she's damn good. When I'm satisfied she's had an adequate first kiss, I pull away. She doesn't resist.

"Not bad for a first kiss?" I ask with a smile. She rolls her eyes in response. I take her hand and pull her toward the couch. "Come on, let's watch this movie."

I'm not much for cuddling, a little too intimate for my taste. But it might be necessary for this job. I'm sure as shit not going to let her run away to the nether reaches of the couch again. She needs to get used to having her body pressed against mine. I pull her down into my lap and hold her there.

"Cozy?"

"Not really," she answers. I don't put much stock in her words. Actions speak louder. People show their true selves eventually. Instead of pulling away she shuffles her body around in my lap before pulling the blanket off the back of the couch and draping it over us.

"Good." I reach forward, grab the remote and press Play.

Chapter Four

Elizabeth

The rhythm of Austin's steady heartbeat is relaxing, like listening to ceaseless waves gently crashing ashore. *Bum-bump. Bum-bump. Bum-bump.* There is comfort in the consistency. I don't know if I've ever been cozier than I am tucked into his hard chest, feeling it rise and fall with every breath. I want to lose myself, to live here in the safety of his arms.

But I can't.

Sitting in Austin's lap is as unnerving as it is delightful. *Casablanca* is one of my favorite movies, but I'm completely incapable of focusing on it. I spend two hours chasing the thoughts running through my head, my brain preoccupied with calculating my next move. I'm so far out of my element I'm not on the periodic table anymore.

Maybe I'm too heavy. His legs must have fallen asleep by now.

Is he comfortable?

Is he just being nice when he really wants to shove me off into the other corner of the couch?

Was I supposed to move on my own?

Should I move now?

He doesn't seem to want me to move. He keeps me wrapped tightly in his arms. Maybe I'm supposed to make some sort of move. I wouldn't mind kissing him again.

Or forever.

He knows in excruciating detail how inexperienced I am now. I can't believe I told him I've never been kissed before. I should've taken that secret to my grave. He can't seriously expect me to put the moves on *him*. That's the whole point of this stupid deal. I have no idea how to do this. I can't relax. As good as it feels to be cradled against his warm body, my muscles are tense and my heart is racing.

I'm terrified.

These two hours are serene torture.

As the credits roll, my body goes stiff. I'm frozen in place, scared of making the wrong move. Austin doesn't seem to notice as he easily moves me off his lap and stands up.

I mourn the loss of his arms around me.

"What time is it?" he asks as he stretches and yawns. I drag my eyes from the tan abs he exposes to check my watch.

"Quarter past ten." I stare straight at the TV screen as if I find the movie credits riveting. I'm waiting for him to decide what's next.

"I've got to be in the gym early tomorrow. I should get going," he says as he holds his hand out to me.

I take it and he pulls me up into him. He tilts his head to the side and my eyes are instantly drawn to his lips.

He's going to kiss me again. The corner of my mouth curves up in a nervous smile. Our chests are touching, an almost imperceptible graze. The connection is electrifying.

He hasn't let go of my hand.

I'm both petrified and thrilled. He parts his mouth and glides his tongue across his lips. I want to feel those lips on mine again. I wait for it, seconds dragging out into eternity. But he doesn't move. I drag my eyes up to meet his. They are sparkling with a mischievous challenge as he stares down at me. He's daring me to do something.

Kiss him!

I want to. More than anything. But I can't.

Not cute. Not tall. Not confident. Not brave. Not sexy. Not friendly.

Not happy.

"Okay then," he says finally with a light chuckle. He drops my hand and steps away, leaving a pang of regret deep in my chest. That was a test and I failed. He grabs his bag off the ground and walks toward the door. I follow after him.

"Guess I'll see you tomorrow." Halfway out of the door, he pauses for a minute, those deep blue eyes studying me. His examination makes me feel stark naked.

Nope, fully clothed.

I look down at myself, suddenly scared I have something in my teeth or toilet paper stuck to my shoe, or something else embarrassing and oh-so-Elizabeth. I use one hand to smooth down my wrinkled shirt and the other to pat down the flyaways in my hair. Yep. I'm a mess.

"What?" I ask, exasperated.

He licks his lips before plastering on a familiar smirk. That smirk. Be still, my heart.

"Of all the libraries, in all the universities, in all the world, I'm glad you walked into mine," he says before turning and walking away.

A wide, goofy smile spreads across my face. Warmth flushes over my entire body as I watch him strut down the long hallway to the elevators. I want to go after him, jump into his arms. Kiss him. Instead, I shut the door before he catches me ogling him. I manage to close it just before I swoon.

I *literally* swoon.

A tingle rushes down every one of my limbs before my body goes limp. I fall back against the door with a dramatic sigh. Sliding down to the ground, I let out a delirious madwoman cackle. I press my hands to my cheeks and they're on fire.

You better watch yourself! This isn't love. This is business.

My heart sinks at the realization. This feeling isn't real. This connection *can't* be real. I barely know him. And we're polar opposites. I let myself get caught up in the moment. The feel of his arms. His lips. His words. His everything.

Get a hold of yourself.

I shove down the emotions and push myself off the floor. My knees are weak as I stumble to the kitchen on shaky legs. Relief washes over me as I spy the crusty spaghetti sauce on the pan he used to make us dinner. Sweet distraction. I try to focus on anything besides Austin's lips as I scrub.

I dissect the night, studying it harder than my neuroanatomy notes, trying to think of all the things I need to remember. How he told me to open my mouth, how he tilted my head to kiss me deeper, how he arranged my body in his lap. I try to make a checklist of what to do next time.

Next time.

He's going to be back in my house tomorrow and I'm not sure how to handle that.

I didn't lie to Austin when he asked me why I chose him. I started with research on scoreyourscore.com. What I didn't tell him is that he personally stars in all my X-rated fantasies. That I think he's the sexiest man I've ever seen.

Who wouldn't?

He's six feet of chiseled, tan masculinity. He's the poster boy for sex appeal. When I saw him in only his boxers, I about lost my mind. I knew he was in shape, but I hadn't expected trim muscles to cover every inch of him.

I'm hoping desire is stronger than panic and the unbelievable attraction I have for him will get me out of my head. After tonight, I'm not so sure. Yeah, I want to jump Austin every second I see him, but he's so intimidating I can't seem to put a complete thought together. I can't deny there's something about him, something that makes me want to be with him. To keep him. I fall asleep wondering if I can go through with this.

Can I spend the next month getting close to Austin Jacobs?

Will I be able to walk away at the end of it?

I have no doubt he will.

* * * *

Since waking up on this uneventful Wednesday, my hours have been consumed with trying—and categorically failing—not to think about Austin. From the second I opened my eyes, I've had a mental clock ticking down in my head until I see him again.

Shower and finish breakfast, eight hours and six minutes until I see Austin.

Grab a coffee on my way to class, six hours and seventeen minutes until I see Austin.

I take my usual seat in the front row of the lecture hall for advanced biochem, five hours and fifty-seven minutes until I see Austin.

Get a hold of yourself!

I may be more distracted than usual, but I diligently take notes once the professor covers the new material. This class is a lot of painful memorization and excruciating hours poring over my notes before every test. I don't do it because I love the subject. I do it because I know I'm going to need this stuff—and an A in this class—to get into med school. I won't let daydreams of Austin distract me.

Too much.

I'm scribbling furiously, desperate to catch what Professor Haynes is saying about lipids and membranes, but her voice is washed out by the incessant giggling behind me.

What could possibly be funny about non-polar solvents?

It's beyond aggravating. I want to be able to learn in peace. I don't sit with friends, not that I really have any, other than Jackie. And she lives five hundred miles away. If I did have friends, I wouldn't waste my time by joking around during lectures.

I want to turn around and admonish the peanut gallery. I want to rant about how they're wasting their time and interfering with my education. I want to tell them to grow up. I want to scream at them to shut up.

I don't. I never will. Instead, I lean in farther and strain to hear Professor Haynes.

I keep my head down, do my work and study my ass off. So far it's earned me the good grades I'll need to get into my top choices for med school. If I could get my degree without ever having to come to class, without having to deal with the gigglers, I would.

"And now for the moment you've all been anxiously waiting for." Professor Haynes pauses for effect before pulling a handful of papers out of her bag. "Returning your last exam. Some of you have shown improvement. Others have a lot of work ahead of you if you want to pass the cumulative final. And we had one unprecedented perfect score."

Oh, God. Please, no.

I know immediately Professor Haynes is going to call my name. When our eyes meet, she's smiling. I shake my head lightly, my eyes silently pleading with her not to do this. My Jedi mind trick fails.

"Ms. Wilde, well done." She even gives me a quick applause. No one else claps. Every eye in the lecture hall turns to me. I lean forward in my chair, hang my head low and scribble gibberish in my notebook to avoid drawing any more attention.

Professor Haynes sets my exam down on my desk, a giant red *100% Nice job!* clearly visible to the peanut gallery behind me that has now fallen silent.

There's your silver lining to this shit cloud.

I snatch the exam and shove it haphazardly into my backpack. I'm proud of my grades. I'd happily celebrate them in private. Alone. By myself. I don't need the sneers. The judgment. The sideways glances and rude comments.

Ass-kisser. Kiss-ass. Kiss-up. Suck-up. Lackey. Flunky. Bootlicker. Goody Two-shoes. Apple-polisher.

I've heard them all. My scholastic achievements have never earned me anything other than scorn from my fellow students.

As I'm packing up to make my escape, a guy's voice calls out from behind me, "Hey, teacher's pet." A classic.

I ignore it. A quick getaway is my only desire in life right now.

"Teacher's pet. Brown-noser." His words are accompanied by a tapping on the back of my chair this time. I freeze, caught off guard by his proximity.

"Yeah, you."

I turn slowly in my seat, taking in the sight of this massive guy. The row behind me is slightly elevated and he's looming over me. He has broad shoulders and lean muscles. If we were standing up, I'm sure he'd tower over me. He leans forward, trying to be intimidating. It's working.

"You know you and your little perfect score just fucked the rest of us, right?" he taunts.

His arms are crossed and there is a scowl on his otherwise delicate face. I stare at him. I don't know how to get out of this, to get away from him. I want to run away, but I'm glued to this stupid plastic chair.

My blank stare and lack of response seem to irritate him further. His nostrils flare. "Haynes grades on a curve."

What exactly is he expecting me to do? Apologize? For being smarter than he is? Yeah, I don't think so.

"I'm sorry?" It comes out as a question, my meek voice undermining the intended sarcasm. Something tells me he wouldn't have gotten it anyway.

He drops his voice slightly. "How 'bout you pump the brakes for the rest of us next time?" He flashes me a flirtatious smile. The girl sitting next to him, who I'm assuming was the source of most of the infuriating giggles for the past hour, lets out an annoyed sigh while crossing her arms.

He's either completely obtuse or doesn't see my involuntary eye-roll, since he continues, "You know, if you ask nicely, I might let you give me a *private* biology lesson." He rakes his eyes over my body in a way that makes me feel self-conscious and a little dirty. He licks his lips and my skin crawls.

"Pass," is my one-word rejection as I grab my bag and walk out of class. The girl next to him exchanges her giggle for a snide cackle.

"Stuck-up bitch," he mutters just loud enough for me to hear. I pick up my pace and scurry off to the library to study for physics.

After my classroom encounter with the King of the Douchebags, I'm happy to be back in the safety of the library. I pull out my notes and try to focus. It's no use.

I look across the study hall and replay the first time I talked to Austin. When I *propositioned* him. My heart flutters. I was so scared. He was so sexy. I bite my bottom lip to keep the smile off my face.

Two hours and forty-five minutes until I see Austin.

Get a hold of yourself, Elizabeth!

I shake the images of Austin out of my head and focus on physics.

Two hours and forty-four minutes…

* * * *

Down to the last few minutes, and I try to steel myself for the moment. It's pointless. My knees go weak when I hear him knock. My heart stops when I open the door and meet his smiling blue eyes.

"I've come prepared this time," he says, holding up a shopping bag as he breezes into the apartment. I'm amazed how he always seems so self-assured.

Does he ever get rattled?

Is he ever scared?

Intimidated?

I must be staring, because he stops unpacking groceries. Our eyes lock.

"What's up?" He looks me up and down, assessing me again. What I wouldn't give to know what he sees.

"What's for dinner?" I brush off his question, not feeling like confessing tonight.

"Nothing fancy. Just chicken and broccoli."

"Sounds good." I have no idea what to talk to him about.

Time to make awkward small talk with Austin Jacobs as he cooks dinner!

It's surreal.

"So, what's the plan for tonight?" he innocently inquires.

"What do you mean?" I know what he means, but I have no idea how to answer.

"I *mean*, what do you want to be *tutored* on tonight, Goose?"

I blush at the sound of my nickname.

"Well, *Mav.*" I'm trying to annoy him, but secretly I relish the idea that it's something only I call him. Maverick. It suits him. "I made us a schedule, actually." My voice has more uncertainty in it than I was hoping.

I hand him the carefully thought-out schedule I crafted over the past few months.

"Of course you made a schedule," he quips with a laugh. His smile only grows as he reads. "You made us a sex syllabus, a *sex*-abus."

I groan. He continues undaunted.

"Four weeks, four topics. So, we round a base a week. This week's kissing. Next week is touching, groping, fondling. Then oral. Giving and receiving. Last week we hit a few home runs," he offers.

Sex with Austin.

I get lost in my thoughts of what these next four weeks might bring. My body flushes and I cross my legs, fighting the building warmth between my thighs. I've pictured all this before, but now I'm realizing it's actually going to happen.

You are going to lose your virginity to Austin Jacobs!

"You seriously think we need a whole week dedicated to kissing?" he challenges.

"It's important to build foundational knowledge in a new subject before advancing to more challenging material."

Oh my God, you're such a nerd.

"Come here." He saunters around the kitchen island and I stand up to meet him. He steps right into my body. I lean back, but he grabs my hands and puts them around his neck. The gesture highlights our height difference. I can barely reach without him having to bend down.

He slides his fingers over the delicate skin of my forearms and down my sides, causing an effervescent tingle across my whole body. He wraps his arms around my waist, pulling me into him. I'm so small in his embrace. It makes me feel dainty and weirdly feminine.

"Kiss me," he demands.

"Now?" I swallow down my panic.

"Now would be good."

I don't do anything.

I just stand there.

Kiss him!

Just do it!

He's right here and he is asking you to do it!

My heart races and my stomach flutters. My throat gets tight. My mouth goes dry. I spiral into panic. Those beautiful blue eyes are bearing down on me, burning into me. I close my eyes, count to three in my head and do it. I push forward on my tiptoes and peck him on the lips. Peck is a generous term for the limp-lipped travesty that is my first attempt at a kiss.

"There," I declare in placid triumph.

"Damn, I must be a horrible teacher. Is that what I showed you last night?" he says in mock disappointment.

I stare at his chest and shake my head, feeling like a kid who got caught sneaking candy before dinner.

"How did I kiss you last night?" It isn't a rhetorical question. He wants me to answer.

"Deep," I say without thinking. "A-And long," I add with a shaky breath and a blush. That's the only way to describe his kiss. Other than being simply amazing.

"Hey." He lifts my chin up so our eyes meet again. "I know you're nervous, but you shouldn't be. This isn't a big deal. I know you can do this." Great, now Austin's giving me a pep talk. *Hello, Self-esteem. Meet All Time Low.*

Closing my eyes, I try to think back to his kiss last night. I take a deep breath and this time I pull him down to me. He leans down without resisting. I run through the checklist I made last night. I brush my lips across his as I tilt my head to the side. I place my lips on his, lightly teasing his bottom lip with my tongue.

"Open your lips," I whisper against him.

"Yes, boss," he quips. I stifle an annoyed sigh and slide my tongue into his mouth. He lets out a soft moan and eases his hands down to my butt.

Holy shit! You just made Austin Jacobs moan!

The sound fills me with a keen sense of womanly power. I relax into the kiss, sliding my fingers into his hair, grabbing a handful, and moaning myself. I flick my tongue around his mouth. I'm lost in our intertwined lips, our bodies pressed together and our hands exploring each other. If I had to try to name this feeling it would be *bliss*. I only pull away when I'm breathless.

"How was that?" The cockiness makes my own voice sound foreign.

"Damn, you're a quick study," he jokes. "But practice makes perfect," he teases, placing a chaste kiss on my forehead and a light slap on my butt before returning to the kitchen and starting our dinner.

"Have you ever had an orgasm?" he blurts out, pulling me out of my daydream and giving me conversational whiplash.

This guy must be a riot at dinner parties.

"Yes." I don't balk at his intrusiveness. I'm riding high on my new sense of empowerment from that kiss.

"Toys or fingers?" Thankfully his back is turned, so he doesn't see me blush with embarrassment.

So much for sexual empowerment.

"Both." My voice shakes, but I hope he doesn't notice it.

"Watch porn?"

What is this, X-rated twenty questions?

He's so blasé. He could be asking if I've seen the latest Marvel movie instead of categorizing my complete sexual history. I have *never* talked to anyone about this stuff. I'm so far outside of my comfort zone, I might as well be on Pluto!

Calm down. If you can't talk *about it, how are you going to actually* do *it* in four weeks?

"Some. But I prefer books."

"Books?" He startles at my response, as if the thought of an erotic book has never occurred to him.

"Yeah, romance novels…" I answer, embarrassed at my confession.

"Oh, I know what you mean. I had a foster mom who read some of the smutty stuff with jacked shirtless dudes on the cover." He dismisses the idea.

"It's better than porn. At least there is a plot and you're invested in the story," I retort.

He chuckles. I swear, that sound is connected to my stomach. And other parts.

"Hey, no judgment here. To each their own. Just don't think I want to read two hundred pages about a pirate and a princess before I get to jerk off."

"Sometimes things are better when they're hard," I quip, feeling philosophical.

Austin laughs. I bite my lip and resist the urge to rip his clothes off. Yep, I definitely have a thing for his laugh.

You're such a weirdo.

"Yeah, yeah. Ha ha. What are you, five? I mean some things are better when you have to wait for it, work for it. Then you know how badly you want it. The buildup, the anticipation — that's half the pleasure."

I'm lost in my thoughts, rambling more to myself than to him at this point. My monologue isn't unusual, it's just usually internal. For whatever reason, I can't seem to keep my mouth shut around Austin.

"That's pretty deep. I'm just talking about getting off, and believe me when I say I *always* know how badly I want it," he teases.

Blushing and ready to change the subject, I ask, "Foster mom?"

"Caught that, did you?" He only half turns toward me before focusing back on the chicken. "I spent a couple years in foster homes before ending up in a group home in high school."

I can't stop myself from asking, "What happened to your parents?"

"Never knew my dad, and my mom died when I was eleven," he answers.

"I'm sorry."

Why the hell did you ask? This is none of your business.

"Why? You didn't put me there."

"Yeah, but it must've been hard."

"It was what it was. I'm here now." He doesn't turn around. The muscles in his back are tense. I take the hint and happily drop it.

In the quiet I think about eleven-year-old Austin, alone and scared. I never would've guessed his past. He never seems to have a care in the world, to let anything bother him. Unflappable. I guess he's had to be. I want to reach out to him, but I don't know how.

I snap back to reality, racking my brain to think of something safe to ask Austin. What could we possibly have in common?

"How long have you been playing football?" I decide on a topic I know he must be interested in.

"Since high school." He doesn't seem very chatty. I can't blame him after my last catastrophic attempt at small talk, but I keep going anyway because I'm a glutton for punishment.

"Must be nice, to be part of something. A team."

"Depends on the team, I guess." He shrugs. "Don't confuse teammates with friends. Some of the guys are pricks, some are decent. But we're definitely not all tight."

"Oh." That's a surprise. From the outside, they're one big family. "Have you always been a...a..." I know his position, but I'm struggling to remember the name of it.

"I'm a cornerback." He fills in the blank. "And yes, I've had the same position since high school. I've got great hands and legendary stamina." He turns to show me his giant hands, wiggling his fingers with a glint in his eyes and a smile on his lips. I drag my mind out of the gutter, where it would've been happy to dream up activities for Austin's fingers all night.

Trying hard to ignore his sexual innuendo despite my blushing, I ask, "You must be good to get a scholarship. Is your family proud?"

"Orphan, remember?" he says with zero emotion.

"Shit! I'm such an ass." I facepalm, shaking my head in disbelief at my own utter stupidity. "You said...*literally* a minute ago!" I throw my hands up in the air in disgust. "I was listening, I swear. I'm just an idiot." I bury my face in my hands, hiding the shameful blush on my checks. "I'm sorry. I'm such an ass." It's a surprising amount of word vomit I manage to get out considering I've got both feet crammed in my mouth.

"Don't worry about it." He seems oddly indifferent. "It was a long time ago."

"My mother died six years ago," I confess as a penance. I know the pain in my heart is painted across my face. In some ways, it feels like I just lost her yesterday. In others, I never had a mother at all.

"I'm sorry," he apologizes sincerely, making sure his eyes meet mine before turning back to the stove.

"Thanks." I try to shake off the emotion in my voice. "We weren't close. But, you know, she was my mother."

"Yeah, I know what you mean."

I can see his head nodding, though his back is to me.

I'm too happy to move on to a less dramatic topic, but nothing new comes to mind. I'm almost willing to go back to the awkward questions about my porn preferences. We're both quiet until the food is done.

"Dinner is served," he announces and we eat quietly sitting next to each other at the kitchen counter. He eats fast and finishes before me again. This guy has an insatiable appetite and now he turns his hungry eyes on me. It's making me self-conscious.

"Why do you dress like that?" he questions.

"Because I'm comfortable. Why do *you* dress like *that*?" I retort defensively, gesturing to his standard attire, gym shorts and a plain T-shirt. It happens to be sexy as hell on him, T-shirt snug on his broad shoulders and shorts low around his hips, but I don't mention that part.

When my mother was alive, I used to dress conservative and feminine for her. Pearls, pencil skirts and cardigans. I hated it, it wasn't me, but for some reason she thought it was important.

'You never know who you are going to meet in life. It's important to always be put together,' she would say. I never saw the point. Why should I be uncomfortable all day just to give someone the right impression?

"The same reason, I guess. It's comfortable." He laughs, ignoring the snark in my question. I've never felt so comfortable being confrontational with someone. *Is this what intimacy is?*

"So, what do you wear to feel sexy and confident?"

"I don't know." I have no idea how to answer his question. I've never thought of myself as sexy. And I'm sure as hell not confident. Nothing I've worn has ever changed that.

His eyes are full of lust and I'm taken aback. I've never had anyone look at me the way he is now. And I can't get enough. "No lingerie? Nothing black and lacy in the closet?"

"Nope."

"That's a shame."

"And why is that?"

"You should have something around that makes you *feel* sexy. The sexiest asset any woman can have is confidence," is his honest reply.

"So you're saying I'm screwed?" I deadpan. He laughs, his shoulders shaking with the deep, sweet sound. I can't help but smile back at him. I'll never get sick of that sound. Making him laugh makes me feel good.

"Well, confidence and a great rack. One out of two ain't half bad." His voice is sultry as he lowers his eyes down my body to my chest.

I let out a small gasp and instinctively cover myself with my arms. I wear large T-shirts to make sure they aren't pulled tight across my chest. My mother used to lecture me on how unladylike it was to be busting out of my tops. As if it were my fault that my genetics resulted in being comically well-endowed compared to the rest of my tiny frame. I've had a complex about my large chest most of my life, constantly doing what I can to downplay it.

Judging by Austin's face, it hasn't gone unnoticed.

"I have an idea," he exclaims, jumping up. "Wait here," he calls back to me as he walks out of the front door. He's gone long enough for me to finish my dinner and move on to cleaning up. He saunters back in, without knocking, carrying a white button-down dress shirt on a hanger. He holds it out to me.

"Here, put this on." He has a huge smile on his face.

"Is that even clean?" I wrinkle my nose and don't take it from him.

"Mostly." He smirks. I have no defense against that smirk. "We dress up for away games. It's been hanging in my truck since our last one."

I don't take it from him. I stand there, staring.

"Come on. Trust me. You're going to look sexy as hell."

"Seriously?" With some hesitation, I take the stupid shirt.

"Seriously. Go." He takes me by the shoulders, spins me around and gives me a gentle shove toward my bedroom.

"Fine. No need to push," I snap back at him as I reluctantly head to the bedroom.

"All I do with you is push!" he shouts as I close my bedroom door.

I hold Austin's button-down in front of me and picture him in it, smart and sexy. It smells like him, a mix of his spicy sweet cologne and his salty skin. I bury my face in the shirt and breathe him in deeply.

Weirdo.

I pull off my T-shirt and toss it on the bed. Sliding into the oversized shirt, I make sure to do up each and every button for maximum coverage. I stare at myself in my bedroom mirror. I'm sexy. I look like a kid playing dress-up. With my arms at my sides, the sleeves come down well past my fingertips. The breast pocket is halfway to my belly button. I'm wearing a circus tent. I'm a clown. A joke. A mistake.

I throw my arms up in defeat, storming out to the living room to prove Austin wrong.

He takes one look at me and shakes his head.

"Why are you wearing pants?" he asks with a quick laugh.

"Why wouldn't I be wearing pants?"

Apparently I'm hilarious, because he laughs harder.

"Because we're going for sexy here."

"I'm not taking my pants off."

He crosses the room to me until his chest is inches from mine. My entire body tenses at his proximity, and I freeze in place. He tucks one finger into the waist of my pants and pulls my hips forward, colliding with his. Our bodies connecting and the fire in his eyes cause me to gasp. He leans down, and his lips brush against my ear.

"Either you take your pants off, or I will."

I close my eyes and take a deep breath to prevent the ensuing panic attack. I bring my hands up against his chest and try to push him away. He doesn't budge, so I take a step back instead, completely overwhelmed.

"We need to slow down. I'm not ready for this." I keep my eyes closed and continue to focus on my breathing. He covers my hands with his, pressing them lightly into his hard chest.

"Elizabeth, look at me."

I don't open my eyes. He lifts my chin with a finger.

"Elizabeth." The pleading in his voice breaks my will and I peer into his deep blue eyes.

"I know you're nervous, but this is about trying new things, right? That means you're going to be uncomfortable. I'm going to push your boundaries."

I nod, not saying anything.

"I need you to be brave. And I need you to trust me."

I don't answer. I stare up at him for a moment, taking in his words.

He's right.

And I hate him for it.

"Fine." I shove him, turn around and storm back to my room.

"And lose that bra too!" he hollers after me. I respond by slamming my bedroom door.

So mature.

Back in the safety of my room, I stand in front of my mirror again, examining myself. The shirt is way too big on me. I roll the sleeves up to the middle of my forearms. *That's better.* It's kind of a baggy shirt dress now. Or, it would be if I took my pants off. With a defeated sigh, I unbutton my jeans and let them fall down my hips before kicking them off entirely.

I stare at my reflection in the mirror. The bottom hem reaches my mid-thigh. It isn't as revealing as I thought it would be. My short, stubby legs are actually pretty cute peeking out from the bottom of the shirt. I feel a little naughty, one of those girls who has to steal a guy's shirt for the morning walk of shame.

I undo the top few buttons and pull the collar open, exposing the top of my chest. I smile at my reflection. Embracing the adventure, I reach up the back and unhook my bra, pulling it off through the sleeve. The shirt isn't quite see-through, but without a bra you can see my hard nipples peeking through the fabric.

I toy with the last few buttons at the bottom, debating unbuttoning them.

Why not? Just see how it looks?

I've come this far, I might as well go for it. I undo all but the three middle buttons over my chest, exposing my stomach. My skin is pale, but against the white of the shirt it's almost creamy. I run my hands down over my stomach and up along my neck, taking a moment to marvel at myself. I'm not a kid playing dress-up. I'm not a joke. I'm a woman.

I feel good. I feel sexy. I feel confident.

Austin is going to be insufferable.

My stomach twists as I think about walking out into the living room. It's one thing to feel sexy in private. It's something completely different to stand exposed in front of Austin Jacobs. I can't believe I'm doing this. This is only our second night and I'm going to be strutting around in almost nothing.

"You coming out or am I going to have to send a search party in after you?" His voice pulls me out of my reverie. I shake my entire body, trying to purge all the nervous energy that's building up in my limbs. God help me, but I actually repeat 'loosey-goosey' to myself a couple of times, quietly enough that I'm sure Austin can't hear me.

I crack the door, peeking out into the living room. Austin's sitting on the couch, his back to me. I slink out of the bedroom and tiptoe toward him. I pause halfway, debating running back to my room and never coming out again.

Don't be a chicken.

I take a deep breath and step into the living room, hoping for the best. As soon as I come into view, Austin snaps his gaze to my bare legs then up my body, devouring me. The caress of his stare is on my thighs, across my stomach and up my chest.

"Fuck. Me." The craving in his voice makes my heart race. "You look amazing. I told you you would." The I-told-you-so almost ruins the moment.

Almost.

He stands, stepping right into my personal space again.

Is he doing that intentionally?

Does he have any idea what it does to me?

Of course he does.

"How do you feel?"

"Naked," I reply with an eye-roll. I refuse to admit he's right.

"Not yet, you're not. All in good time, Goose."

My breath catches in my throat at his callused hands sliding up the outside of my thighs. He trails under the hem of the shirt until his hands rest on my naked hips. The tickle of his rough fingertips is divine. I put my arms around his neck as he lowers his lips to my exposed collarbone and peppers the soft skin with kisses. The sensation of his wet lips on my body nearly drives me mad.

He walks us both back toward the couch, pulling off his shirt before he sits down. I take in the glorious majesty that is a shirtless Austin Jacobs. Would it be creepy if I asked to take a picture of him right now?

Yes, it would. Don't you dare!

Right. Guess I'll just save that mental image instead.

"Come here," he implores, putting his hands back on my hips, trying to pull me down on top of him. "I want you to straddle my lap."

Oh God.

Oh God!

OH GOD!

I climb onto the couch in what has to be the most uncoordinated and awkward way possible. He's huge and I'm tiny. I don't know if I *can* straddle him. I put one knee up on the couch, pressed against his thigh, but I somehow get caught and twisted in the shirt as I try to bring up my other leg.

I'm pretty sure I kick him in the shin.

To his credit, Austin doesn't cringe at my very cringe-worthy performance. This man has the body of a devil but the patience of a saint. Why isn't he running for the hills yet?

Because you're paying him.

Thanks for that subtle kick to the ego, brain! Want to remind me of that time I tripped at the opera, fell down the stairs and landed in full view of the orchestra pit with my dress over my head? You know, just to make *real* sure every ounce of self-confidence I have is utterly dead and buried?

Eventually, I get both legs on either side of him and stop flailing. Austin keeps his firm grip on me and positions me in his lap. I let out a frustrated sigh. Any confidence I had was sapped by my ridiculous display. I am hopeless.

"Relax. We've got all night." The words are soothing in my ear. He brushes my hair off my shoulder, wrapping his fingers around the back of my neck.

"Kiss me," he entreats. I'm hesitant but eager to meet his lips.

I lean forward, pressing my chest against his, the thin fabric of my shirt the only thing separating us. My nipples harden with the friction. My lips brush his as I slide my tongue into his mouth and kiss him deeply. His moan is my reward.

His strong hands pull me down against him as his hips rock up to meet mine. Matching the rhythm he's setting, I move on my own, grinding against him. The power of him underneath me sends tingles across my body and heat builds between my thighs.

"That's perfect. Just like that," he praises with another moan.

I love that sound. Emboldened with a surge of confidence, I slip my fingers into his hair, tugging gently as I continue to kiss him. I press my body against his, aching for more contact. He moves a hand up the back of my shirt, spreading goosebumps across my entire body. He wraps his fingers around my shoulder and pulls me down hard onto his lap.

I lean back and gasp as I feel his hard length under me.

"Oh my God, you have an erection," I blurt out before I can help myself.

Smooth, real smooth.

My cheeks burn with embarrassment and I slap my hands over my face. Austin chuckles. I move my fingers enough to get a glimpse of him.

"That's usually what happens when a sexy half-naked woman's grinding in my lap," he offers with a mischievous grin. My heart swells at the easy compliment.

"I've never — *you know* — given a guy one before," I confess.

What a dork.

"Silly little Goose," he quips before dropping his full lips to my collarbone, licking and sucking, driving me crazy. "I guarantee you have. I'm just the first one who didn't bother hiding it." He pulls me back into him and kisses me hard, his tongue wet and demanding.

I sink back down onto him, desire pooling between us. I swivel my hips, luxuriating in the sensation of his thickness against my thigh. I feel so deliciously naughty. Nothing but my panties and his thin gym shorts are separating us, but it's too much.

I get lost in him. My whole world consists only of Austin's lips and hands. We're locked in each other's arms, our bodies colliding in a natural rhythm, for what seems like hours. My lips are raw and my legs are exhausted to the point of trembling. I never want to stop. I could live in this moment.

Our kisses are only interrupted by our heavy breathing and heady moans. Tension builds between us, but not enough for a release. I need more. Every inch of my skin aches for his touch. Austin grants my unspoken wish and glides his hands up the outside of my thigh. He hooks his thumbs into the sides of my panties and pulls them down slightly. He trails kisses as far down my chest as he can reach. I arch my back so he can reach farther.

"Austin," I moan shamelessly.

"Fuck." Austin lifts me off the couch as if I don't weigh a thing before flipping us over and crashing back down. The swift movement knocks the breath out of my lungs. He's hovering over me, his large body poised between my legs. My panties are low on my hips, barely covering me, and my shirt has ridden up to my chest. My heart pounds as he examines my body.

The hunger in his eyes fills me with terror.

The gravity of the situation hits me full force, yanking me out of my lust-filled haze. I cross my arms over my chest as the voice in my head screams *'Not yet. I'm not ready yet!'*

Nothing manages to cross my lips other than a whimper. I don't need to say a word. When Austin's eyes meet mine, he pulls away, leaving me emotionally relieved and physically unsatisfied. I ball my hands into fists at my side, digging my nails into my palms to avoid screaming in frustration.

"I'm running out of self-control here," he confesses as he stands up. He lays the blanket from the back of the couch across me before he adjusts himself in his shorts. "I need to go home and take the longest cold shower of my life."

I can't help but laugh, the tension easing out of my body. He doesn't seem as amused.

He picks his T-shirt up off the floor and puts it back on as he heads toward the door. With the blanket wrapped around my shoulders, I follow him. He pauses for a minute as if he's second-guessing his abrupt departure. Part of me wants to beg him to stay.

"What do you want for dinner tomorrow?" His voice has an unbelievably sexy rasp to it. My passion-soaked brain is struggling to remember what dinner is.

Food. He's asking you about food.

"P-pa-pizza?" I manage to stutter, more asking for confirmation that it is in fact a food item than it's acceptable for tomorrow's dinner.

"Too easy. Hope you're always this easy to please," he teases with a smirk. That smirk should be trademarked, replicated and sold to millions of lonely women around the world. No. On second thought, it's mine. Just mine, for now at least.

"Wait, do you want your shirt back?" I open the blanket, showing him the shirt and my body underneath it. He takes me in again and lets out a ragged sigh.

I know the feeling.

"No, keep it for next time."

I'm relieved he doesn't want it back. It's my new favorite outfit.

"But you should find something for yourself. Something that makes you feel sexy all on your own."

"Something black and lacy?" I ask, remembering his earlier comment. He nods but doesn't answer. I want to think he's getting worked up picturing it. A girl can dream, right?

"Good night," he croaks before heading down the hallway toward the elevator.

"Good night," I mutter as I close the door. I know exactly what I'm going to do, and it's not taking a cold shower.

Chapter Five

Austin

"You can't be fucking serious," Devin scoffs in disbelief as he spots me bench pressing.

I can't keep the smile off my face. "As a heart attack. Chick asked me to be her sex tutor," I answer between reps. I keep my voice even, casual. Being a sex god comes naturally to me.

"So, instead of stocking shelves at two a.m. you're fucking some coed for cash? Please tell me she's a troll at least."

I re-rack the bar with a chuckle.

"Sorry, man. She's not an under-the-bridge dweller." I push aside thoughts of Elizabeth's perky nipples in my shirt last night. Don't need a semi at the gym. "She's kinda sexy, for an uptight nerd."

"You're the luckiest little shit I've ever met. First, you get that fucking scholarship when you can't catch for shit—"

"Fuck you!" I interject.

"And now you're getting paid to get nasty with some chick," Devin quips in mock indignation. My luck is relative. He knows more than enough of my fucked-up past.

We swap places and he lies down on the bench. "So, is she into the super-kinky shit or what?"

"Nothing like that." I laugh at the thought of 'kinky' Elizabeth. "She's just shy as hell. Super inexperienced. She needs a little help."

Devin pauses with the bar on his chest and glares up at me, his face morphing into a terse scowl.

"What?" I ask, despite having a pretty good guess at what's coming.

He's got that big-brother look on his face. He's going to spout some nonsense and call it wisdom.

"Nothing. Just thought you'd outgrown this savior bullshit." He shakes his head disapprovingly.

"What are you talking about?"

"You know...what I mean..." he says between presses. "You're...little fucking...Bo Peep...with your...damaged...little lambs."

"I think you mean lost lambs, fuck nut," I deflect.

"Nah, you want the damaged ones." I cross my arms, waiting for him to continue. "When we got new foster kids at the home, the first-timers, you were always the one to hold their hand, tell them it was going to be okay and all that cheesy shit. You love fixing the broken ones."

"Come on, we all did that. Fuck, you did that shit for me. You're a big fucking softie." I shove him playfully. No one would ever think it looking at the giant, tattooed, brooding asshole, but he's got the biggest heart of anyone I've ever met.

"I helped you. Once. And only because I had to share a room with you and you smelled nasty. Couldn't even figure out how to use the damn shower by yourself!"

"Fuck off. I was only six."

"You were seven. And you wouldn't stop crying for your momma. So, yeah, I took pity on your pathetic ass. But you? You did it. Every. Fucking. Time. It was a sick fucking game for you, some test we all had to pass." Devin re-racks the bar, only completing half his set.

He sits up on the bench and turns to face me before continuing. "You'd play big brother, let them get all attached. Then, you'd shit all over them just to see how much they'd swallow before they'd walk away."

Before my mom died, I needed to know if people were worth it, worth loving. Turns out they aren't.

"I was just bored. I didn't mean shit to those kids. And they don't mean shit to me."

"Sure they didn't."

I shove him out of the way and take my spot on the bench again.

"And I don't give a shit about this girl either. She's just an easy paycheck."

"Sure she is," he grumbles. "Don't come crying to me when you break her and she walks away."

I grunt, avoiding giving him the satisfaction of admitting he's right.

They always leave.

* * * *

I have an armful of groceries, so I don't bother knocking on Elizabeth's door. I know she doesn't lock it anyway. I really should tell her how stupid that is, doorman or not. She lives in a nice neighborhood, but those are usually the ones that get robbed. She's too trusting. She obviously hasn't been sucker punched by life yet.

"Hey," I announce my arrival as I make my way to the kitchen and put the groceries away. Devin's voice echoes in the back of my head.

You love fixing the broken ones. You let them get attached.

This is different. The food is for me, not for her. Five thousand dollars is burning a hole in my pocket. I've never had that much money in my life. So, I bought all the nice stuff I never have the money for. I don't have to scrimp on the meat, fancy spices or fresh produce. And if I keep this stuff at my place, my douchebag roommates will eat it all.

It's not romantic. It's practical.

Here I can make dinner without having to share. Except with Elizabeth, but she's tiny. How much is she really going to eat anyway?

"Whatcha up to, Goose?"

She's sitting at her computer with her back to me, but I can hear her talking to someone.

"He's here. I gotta go. Yes, that's him," she says into some sort of headset. She's dwarfed in the giant office chair that looks more like a racecar seat. I bet it cost more than my entire truck. She's video chatting with someone. My curiosity is piqued when I realize she must be talking about me.

"No, that's not happening... Because it's weird! That's disgusting. Grow up...that is *none* of your business!" I can only hear one side of the conversation. She sounds playful but irritated. It's a combination I'm already intimately familiar with. I can't help but snoop. I sneak up behind her, keeping an eye on her screen.

I bend down beside her, grazing her soft neck as I pull back her headphones and brush my lips against her ear. "Who you chatting with, Goose?" I put my other hand above her knee and tickle the inside of her naked thigh with my long fingers.

She almost jumps out of her chair. I can't help but smile. While she composes herself, I unplug her headset. On her screen is a young, petite woman. She's got thick-rimmed glasses, a nose ring and fire-engine-red hair. Something tells me this girl doesn't take shit from anyone.

"Fuck me sideways, Lizbit, he's hot. The guys you pick are usually such goob troopers." The woman's voice rings out through the computer speakers.

"Sideways? Not my favorite position, but I'm sure I could be convinced to give it another shot," I chime in. Elizabeth pulls off her headset and traces the cord to the plug in my hand. She yanks it from me with a huff.

"Bye, Jackie!" Elizabeth growls, slamming a few keys, causing the screens to go black before Jackie can respond.

"What the hell is a goob trooper?" I stand and gaze down at her as she spins around in her chair, noticing for the first time that she's wearing my shirt again. Or, maybe still? She's as sexy in it as she was yesterday. Standing over her, I can see down the shirt to the curve of her full breasts.

I can't wait to have my hands on her again.

"Cross between a goober and stormtrooper." The timbre of her voice is enough to add the "*duh, idiot!*" to the end of her definition. "You're early." The annoyance is written all over her flushed face.

"You're welcome," I retort.

"And you didn't knock."

"My hands were full." I gesture to the grocery bags sitting on the kitchen counter. "And that's what you get for not locking your front door. Any sort of mischief can stroll right in." I smile down at her.

"Fine." She sighs, hopping up from her chair. She marches over to the front door and locks it.

"I have to be on the other side for that to work," I tease as I sit down in the office chair she just vacated. *Fuck, this thing is comfortable.*

"So, who's Jackie?" I play with her mouse to wake up her computer.

"A friend." She stalks back over to her desk.

"Don't touch that!" she orders, standing over me, trying to be intimidating. Her hands are on her hips and there's a scowl on her cute face. She's about as intimidating as a teddy bear.

"She seems like a character." I spin away from the desk and face her, answering her challenge.

"She's a firecracker," she mutters, dropping her hands off her hips and fidgeting. She's burned out the fire inside her for now.

"Firecracker?" I ask as I place my hands on the outside of her naked thighs. Her warm skin under my palms confirms that she's only wearing a pair of panties under the shirt.

"Nothing," she whispers. Her body is already tensing under my touch and she's pulling away. I'm not in the mood to let her.

"Nothing?" I stand, running my hands under the shirt, resting them on her hips. She steps back. I step forward, a weird sort of dance.

"Nothing," she sputters again as she takes yet another step back from me.

I'm tired of playing cat and mouse. Chasing her is fun, but catching her is better. I tighten my hold on her hips, turn her slightly and have her back pinned against the wall before she's able to object.

"You're wearing my shirt," I growl.

I pull her leg around my waist with one hand and continue my journey up her body with the other. I slip my fingers under her shirt, teasing the soft skin on her stomach. Her abs clench as she shudders against me.

"I was trying to explain it to Jackie and it was easier to just put it on." Her words are breathy in my ear.

"I think you like wearing it," I whisper against the delicious skin on her neck before dipping my mouth to leave a trail of kisses down to her tits. "I was right. It makes you feel sexy, doesn't it?"

"Do you think I'm sexy?" Her voice is timid, her eyes closed tightly. She can't pull away from me, but she's trying to hide. She brings her trembling hands up to rest on my shoulders.

"What do you think?" I pull her other leg up around me, lifting her off the ground completely. I pin her to the wall and rock my hips into her so she can feel how hard I am. She tightens her legs around me and a soft moan escapes her pink lips.

Damn, that's a sexy sound.

I'm already on the edge of losing it to my craving for her tight little body. Knowing I have to wait makes me want her more than I've ever wanted anyone before.

She's my forbidden fruit.

I skim my hands over her ribcage, brushing against the underside of her tits. I lift the swell of each to meet my eagerly awaiting lips. I kiss the soft exposed skin and her nipples get hard against my chest as I continue to rock my hips into her.

I line my cock up with the apex of her thighs. Her thin panties do little to hide how turned on she is. She smells like sex. I get lost in her moans in my ear, her warm skin under my fingers and lips. The air is charged with sexual tension. I grind into her against the wall, fucking her over our clothes. The friction is driving us both crazy, but it's not enough to push either of us over the edge. I need more.

I want her right here.

Right now.

"First base!" she screams as I ease my fingers inside her panties.

Despite how badly I want to keep going, the trepidation in her voice washes over me, freezing me faster than a bucket of ice water. I tear my hands off her body and slap them against the wall on either side of her. I have her pinned, my body pressed against hers, but I'm stopped dead in my tracks. I bring my forehead to hers and let out a deep sigh.

"First base," I reply in acknowledgment.

"Thank you," she whimpers.

She slides her legs back down to the ground, supporting her own weight again as we both try to catch our breath. I shove off the wall and run my fingers through my hair.

Old people doing jumping jacks naked on a windy day. Fat rolls. Wrinkles. Jiggling.

I turn around and face her again. Her cheeks are flushed and she's breathing heavily, the exaggerated rise and fall of her chest straining the buttons on her shirt.

My shirt.

I'm fucked.

"You need to change. And we need to get out of this apartment," I command. "Now."

"What? Why?" she asks.

"Because I haven't been this close to jizzing in my pants since junior high," I confess.

She lets out a soft giggle. That sound is as much of a turn-on as hearing her moan. She needs to realize what the stakes are right now.

"We can either get out of here or I find out if your pussy tastes as good as it smells. Your call."

Her grin drops as she sees the fire in my eyes. I'm two seconds away from taking her in ways her little sex-abus doesn't begin to cover.

She sets off for her bedroom at a jog, which is enough of an answer for me. While she changes into what I hope is a shapeless muumuu, I finish putting away the rest of the groceries and desperately try to think about anything but having her naked body under mine.

"I'm ready. Where to?" She pops out of her room in a few minutes. I've never known any girl who can get ready as fast as she can. Then again, she's the no-frills type. I appreciate that about her, among her other assets.

She's in her standard attire, baggy jeans and a formless T-shirt. It's better than seeing her in my shirt, but somehow knowing the curves she's hiding under that hideous excuse for an outfit keeps me pretty revved up. We can't get out of this apartment fast enough.

"Since I'm not cooking, I guess we're eating out. Come on." I grab my keys off the counter and we head down to my truck.

I take her to a small diner across town. The place isn't fancy, but the food is good and it's a cozy family-run joint. More importantly, it's far enough away from campus we aren't going to run into anyone I know. I haven't told any of my teammates about my new 'job' because it's none of their damn business. No one knows except Devin. I'm in no mood to explain why I'm out with Elizabeth.

I don't date, but if I did, she's definitely not my type. We're from different worlds.

I'd ruin her.

We order quickly, and now I'm sitting across from her, wondering what to do. We haven't spent much time talking, and I've purposefully engineered us into a situation where that's all there is to do. I didn't really think this plan through. She's fidgeting and avoiding eye contact.

Is she sorting the different types of sugar packets?

There's more awkwardness between us than there has ever been before, and that's saying something. Dating clearly isn't her thing either.

"Don't tell me you've never been on a date." It's a dick thing to say, but I can't help myself. I'm a little annoyed at her on behalf of my aching blue balls. Luckily she doesn't seem to take offense.

"No, I've had dates. But this isn't *really* a date. This is…" She pauses, studying me. "I'm not sure what this is, but it's not a date," she declares definitively. I have a feeling she's trying to convince herself more than anything.

"Business dinner? Right, boss?" I mock her. She doesn't respond, but the way she crosses her arms and stares out of the window lets me know she doesn't appreciate my categorization. She's quiet for another few minutes, refusing to look at me. It's obnoxious as fuck. This isn't awkward silence anymore.

This is intentional. I'm getting the silent treatment.

Being ignored by this woman has got to be one of the top ten most annoying things in the world. When someone decides they aren't interested, I decide I don't need them. I've made an art form out of not giving a shit when people blow me off.

Something is different with Elizabeth.

I want her attention, even when she's being a brat. I'll take her sarcastic mouth and snide comments over this silence.

"You weren't kidding about your lack of conversation skills." I push, trying to get her to engage with me. Her eyes finally meet mine, but instead of getting a rise out of her, she seems to retreat back into herself, slouching in her seat and wrapping her arms around her stomach. Mocking her isn't the best way to get her to open up. A twinge of guilt twists my stomach for being a dick.

"All right, I've got an idea. How about we add first date etiquette to that sex-abus of yours?" She shuffles in her seat and side-eyes me without answering. "Pretend this is our first date. Forget everything else. We're just two people trying to get to know each other." It's cheesy, but I'm okay with faking it through one dinner if it means we aren't sitting here staring at each other the whole time.

"I guess we could do that." Her voice is hesitant, but she seems a bit excited by the idea.

"It's nice to meet you, Elizabeth. So, where are you from originally?" I plaster a giant fake smile on my face and launch right into small talk mode.

"Nice to meet you, Austin." The shy smile on her lips matches the embarrassed tone of her voice. "I grew up in Atherton."

"Where's that?"

"It's up north. Couple hours' drive, maybe."

"How was it growing up there?"

"Nice. I guess. Quiet." I watch her, waiting for her to tell me more. She doesn't. I can't tell if she doesn't want to talk about where she's from or she simply doesn't know what to say.

"Small town?" I ask. Guess I'm going to have to carry most of this conversation.

"Decent size, I guess." She again doesn't elaborate, not seeming comfortable with talking about her past.

"Is that why…" I gesture to her, but she doesn't catch my insinuation. "The lack of experience. Not enough options at the stud buffet for you?" I ask with an eyebrow raise.

"Oh." She flinches as she catches my meaning. "No! I mean, maybe. The guys I've dated before aren't…" She gestures at me and I catch her insinuation. They aren't like me.

Is that a good thing?

"They've all been…" She pauses, bites her lip and gazes off into the distance for a minute. "Soft," she says tentatively.

"Soft?" I can't help but chuckle. "Does that make me hard?" I tease.

"No. Well, I guess. You're definitely different." The nervous fidgeting keeping her hands flying around doesn't distract me. My eyes are locked on hers and I am desperate to hear what she thinks makes me different.

"They were all apprehensive. I think they were as nervous as I was. I usually pick guys who are non-threatening. You're confident and bold. You push me. Scare me. In a good way. Mostly." She breaks our eye contact, obviously flustered. I'm starting to understand her. Understand why she needs me.

"Goob troopers." I try to keep a straight face and fail, earning myself the mother of all eye-rolls.

"Thanks, Jackie! Anyway, I was homeschooled mostly. Boys were kind of a non-factor."

"Homeschooled? Your family super religious or something?"

"God no." We both chuckle.

She's quiet and contemplative for a moment, weighing her words carefully.

"Growing up, I had two options. Be perfect or be invisible. The harder I tried to be perfect, the worse I failed. I've got being weird nailed, though," she quips, trying to keep her voice lighthearted. But the way she fidgets in her seat means she isn't too comfortable with the confession. "I was always doing something that would embarrass my mother. It was just easier to stay home with tutors."

Her shoulders are tense and her forehead is furrowed. She's exposed and vulnerable right now. While my curiosity is piqued, if I push her too hard, she'll shut down. She's been brave with her confessions tonight. I decide not to push her this time.

"What! You mean I'm not your first tutor?" My voice is full of mock incredulity. It makes her giggle, and tension releases from both of us.

"Not my first, but maybe my favorite." My chest swells at the teasing compliment, and I try to ignore it. What kind of pussy gets the feels from being called a girl's favorite tutor?

Watch yourself, Jacobs.

"Oh my, are you actually flirting with me? Well done, Goose." I give her a genuine smile.

"Thanks, Maverick." Her lips curve up into a coy smile. The sight is enough to make me want to drag her to the bathroom and pick up where we left off at the apartment. There's no way Elizabeth Wilde is going to let her first time be in a dirty diner bathroom. I clear my throat and think about root canals and oil changes.

"Where are you from?" she asks in the sexually charged silence.

"Orland." My voice is flat. I don't really want to talk about where I come from or my childhood. We have that in common.

"I've never heard of it."

"I'm not surprised. It's not worth knowing. Just a shit town a few hours east, full of fuck-ups and drug addicts," I reply sharply, trying to force down the memories. This is why I don't date. This getting-to-know-you small talk is bullshit. Talking about my childhood is about as much fun as getting my eyes carved out with a rusty spoon.

"Okay..." She glances toward the kitchen, eager for the distraction of our food.

I change the subject, asking, "What's your major?"

"Pre-med." Her eyes sparkle with her response.

"You want to be a doctor?" I can't keep the surprise out of my voice, unable to picture her bedside manner.

"Technically, I guess. But I am really hoping to go into medical research." She answers my question without me having to ask it.

"Why medical research?"

She balks at the question, picking imaginary lint off her T-shirt instead of answering me. I sit and stare at her until she answers with, "I've just always thought biology was interesting." I give her a *go-on* gesture and she meekly continues, "Humans are basically insanely complex machines that took hundreds of thousands of years of evolution to create. We're just beginning to understand that even though we're these complicated and sophisticated organisms, we're all so fragile and flawed." She stares at her hands in her lap, embarrassed by her own enthusiasm.

"That's almost poetic."

She shifts in her seat and says, "It's really lame, I know. I'm such a nerd, right?

"Don't do that." Her eyes snap to mine at the reprimand. "Don't belittle yourself or what you care about. The world is going to beat you down enough, you don't need to help it out. If you believe something, own it. Fuck everybody else." She blinks several times, holding back tears. She gazes at me like I saved a litter of puppies from a burning building. Now it's my turn to shift awkwardly in my seat. I'm no one's hero. "I just want to make money. Lots of it."

"There's a lot more to life than money."

"Spoken like someone who has a lot of it," I scoff. "Exactly how rich are you, anyway?"

"I'm not rich." She sounds almost offended. "I mean, my father has money, but—"

I interrupt her. "Same difference. You have lots of brothers and sisters?"

"No. It's just me." Her face goes squishy, eyebrows pinched together, lips scrunched to one side. Her eyes dart up and left, trying to see inside her own mind. She's working out what I'm getting at. It's hideously captivating.

"You're the only child of a rich man. I bet if you decided tomorrow you never wanted to work another day in your life, you wouldn't have to."

She seems lost in thought. I can't help but wonder if she's actually adding up her net worth in her head.

"It never occurred to me not to work. That's just what people do. But I guess you're right. If I didn't want to, I wouldn't have to work." She isn't bragging. If anything, she seems a bit self-conscious about being wealthy, as if it will make me see her differently. I'm surprised by her honesty.

"Yep, hate to break it to you, sweetheart, but you're rich," I confirm with a laugh.

"I've never really thought about it," she says, almost to herself. It's a revelation to her.

She's so naïve. She's never really experienced life, the good or the bad. She lives a sheltered beige existence, never knowing the brilliant shine of intense pleasure or the dark grunge of true suffering. She's only tasted a fraction of what the world has to offer. Her unassuming innocence is intriguing.

"About money? People who have lots of it rarely do." I don't mean it to be an accusation, but that's how she takes it.

"I'm not taking my private jet to our family's island in the Bahamas or anything." Her definition of being rich is enough to make me laugh. She's rich because she'll never have to work to eat.

"Maybe not. But you had five thousand dollars you parted with quite easily." It comes out harsher than I meant it to be. I'm frustrated that she doesn't understand what it's like for people with nothing.

People like me.

"It's from a trust. From my mother. After she died." Her words are choppy and disconnected, as if she isn't sure if she wants to keep going but somehow she does. *I'm an asshole.*

"I'm sorry…" I mumble. "I guess my small talk could use some work too."

She gives me a weak smile.

I'm not sure which one of us is more relieved to have our food finally arrive. We both let out an audible sigh at the sight of our approaching waitress, thankful for the excuse to be quiet as we each dig into our burgers and fries. Our eyes meet a couple of times as we're eating, and the awkward silence between us makes me desperate to say something.

But this isn't a date. I'm just feeding her. So, I take another mouthful of burger and keep my mouth shut.

"Thank you," she says to our waitress as she clears away our plates. Without the distraction of our food, we are back to uncomfortable silence. It's a little too close to an awkward first date for me.

"Did you like it?" I ask.

"It was delicious!" she says with a genuine smile. "I can't remember the last time I had a burger that good. And those fries!"

This time I'm trying to keep our conversation on the lighter side. "You save room for dessert?"

"Always." She gives me an innocent smile.

I order a slice of chocolate cake for us to share.

"Oh my God," she groans, a sensual moaning sound accompanying her first bite.

"That good?" I ask.

"It's awful. Don't bother trying it. I'm just eating it out of obligation," she claims with a playful grin on her chocolate-coated lips.

"You're so selfless." I laugh out loud as she shovels a second massive forkful of cake into her tiny mouth.

I manage a few bites before she consumes the rest of it. She reaches for the bill, but I grab it before she can manage. I shuffle out of the booth and help her up.

"It's my treat. I am rich, after all." She tries to grab the check out of my hand, but again I'm faster than she is. She's forcing a smile, still a bit insecure.

"That's not how dates work, Goose." I pull her against me. "The man buys his woman dinner."

"But I'm not really your woman, am I?" She stares up at me. I can't tell if she hates the idea. For the first time in a long time, I let myself wonder what it would be like to have someone. *What if that someone is Elizabeth?*

"Tonight you are." Before she can respond, I capture her mouth with mine. The kiss isn't gentle. It's possessive and hungry. I don't try to hide how much I want her right now.

"Not on the first date," she objects half-heartedly. There's the controlled passion in her voice, even as she's trying to push me away. I'm bigger and stronger and I'm not going anywhere.

"I can't help myself. You taste like chocolate." I give her another teasing kiss before paying and heading out.

I help her into the cab of my truck and shut the door behind her. The drive isn't long, but it's quiet. Too quiet.

"Let's play red light twenty questions," I say to her as I pull up to the stoplight.

"What's red light twenty questions?"

"When we stop at a red light, you ask me as many questions as you can before it turns green. You can ask me anything and I have to answer honestly. Next red light is my turn. Whoever asks the most questions wins."

"But it's already halfway through this red light," she objects.

"You better get going then," I quip. She rolls her eyes but plays along anyway.

"Middle name?"

"Peter. That's one."

"Favorite color?"

"Green. Two."

"Dogs or cats?"

"Dogs. Totally. Cats are assholes. Three."

"Uhhh…"

"Come on, is that all you've got? Clock's ticking, Goosey."

Anger flashes behind her eyes. She's a competitive one. I never would have guessed.

"Favorite movie?"

"*Scarface*. Say hello to my little friend." I do my best Tony Montana impersonation. She's unimpressed.

"Favorite holiday?"

"Holiday like vacation or holiday like Christmas?"

"Like Christmas and stop stalling, cheater!"

"Fourth of July."

"Really?"

"Yes, really. Beer, barbecue and explosions. What's not to love?" I skip the part where it's one of the few holidays that the world doesn't shit on people for having no family and no money. "But that doesn't count as a question. You're still at five."

"Biggest pet peeve?"

I know instantly what my answer is, but I hesitate. The last thing I want is for her to ask follow-up questions. I debate lying to her, but I haven't yet, so why start now.

"People who break promises." My hands tighten on the steering wheel, but she doesn't seem to notice.

"Biggest turn-on?" she asks.

"Watching a beautiful woman come." I peek over at her blushing cheeks. "I take that back. *Making* a beautiful woman come."

She bites her bottom lip and looks away when I wink at her. Images of her naked body writhing in pleasure under me flash through my head, and I get hard again.

"Green light." She points out of the windshield in front of us and refuses to meet my gaze.

"Lucky number seven. Not bad."

"Would've been better if I'd gotten my full time."

"Don't pout. You might get another turn yet. We've got a few blocks to go."

"I'm not pouting," she says.

With a pout.

"Of course you're not."

"Ass," she mutters. I can't stifle my laugh. This girl can't look me in the eye when I talk about making her come, but she has no problem telling me when I'm an ass. I decide to take the long way back to her place, the one with the most stop lights.

"Red light. My turn." I bring the truck to a stop and turn in my seat to face her.

"But you can't use any of my questions! That's cheating," she asserts incredulously.

"For someone who's never played, you sure enjoy setting the rules." A shrug is her only response. "Fine. Biggest fear?"

"Uhhh..."

"Hurry up, little cheater," I tease.

"Spiders." Her voice goes up an octave and I can tell she's lying. All the intimate things I've asked her, the confessions about her childhood, and this is what she chooses to lie about?

"Liar. New rule, you lie, you forfeit."

"Fine. Rejection. Ass," she retorts with a sigh and holds up her index finger. She's vulnerable and fierce. I love it.

"Favorite song?"

"*Stand By Me.*" She holds up a second finger. Goose loves keeping score. I'll have to remember that.

"Which version?"

"The Temptations. But that doesn't count as another question!"

"Favorite food?"

"Chocolate."

"Should've guessed that one. Least favorite food?"

"Escargot." She makes a scrunched face and shakes in her seat with disgust. We both laugh.

"Most embarrassing moment?"

"Getting rejected by you in the library. Thanks for that." She holds up a fifth finger and eyes the stoplight.

"Name something you can't live without. Other than me, of course." I smirk. She doesn't blink.

"The Internet."

"If you could go anywhere in the world, where would you go?"

"Paris." Dejected, she holds up seven fingers now, knowing I'm about to win.

"Favorite thing about me?"

"Green light!" she shouts triumphantly. "That's only seven."

"Nice try. That's eight. I finished asking the question before the light changed, so it counts. And you have to answer." The car behind me honks, but I don't pull forward.

"You better move. It's a green light."

"We're not going anywhere until you answer me." I shift the truck into Park, ignoring the increasing amount of honking coming from behind us.

"Please go."

"Just answer. And remember, you lie, you forfeit."

"God, you're obnoxious! Fine. You make me feel normal. Now move!" she shouts at me, crossing her arms and sinking into her seat.

"That wasn't so hard, was it?" I soften the taunt with a gentle squeeze of her thigh.

"Excruciating." She tries to sound annoyed, but there's embarrassment and vulnerability underneath it.

I pull the truck forward and we're quiet for a few blocks. "How do you feel usually?" I'm not sure why I want to know.

"What do you mean?"

"You said I make you feel normal. How do you usually feel?"

"Weird." She sounds disheartened.

"What's so wrong with being weird?"

"Everything." She stares out of the window, dejected.

"Weird isn't so bad. Weird is…unique. Interesting. Rare."

She interrupts me with a scornful laugh. It's a load of cheesy bullshit and we both know it.

Normal is acceptance.

Weird is rejection.

"Bizarre. Strange. Odd. Scary. Creepy." She pauses for a beat. "Lonely," she adds almost too soft to hear.

I know exactly what she means. I know the terror of not being enough, not being worth loving. If it were any other girl, I'd feed her a line about how being herself is enough. But we both know that's a lie.

Love is conditional.

Temporary.

The closest thing I've ever seen to that cheesy do-anything-for-you, can't-live-without-you Hollywood cliché was my mom's relationship with drugs.

That isn't love.

That's addiction.

We all play a role to get what we need. We hide the ugliest parts of ourselves, desperate to be wanted. To be loved.

"Trust me, everyone's weird. Some of us are just better at hiding it." Keeping my eyes locked on the road ahead of us, I reach across the cab and take her hand in mine, intertwining our fingers. This touch isn't about sex.

It's about connection.

Without speaking, she brings my hand up to her lips and kisses it softly. My chest tightens.

Don't get attached. Don't let her break you.

"You ready?" My words pierce the silence and sever our connection.

"For what?"

"To take back the lead." I pull up to the intersection, take my hand from hers and point at the red light in front of us. She launches into her first question without missing a beat.

"What superpower would you want?"

"Invisibility." I hold up one finger with a forced smile.

"Biggest regret?"

"Thinking people can change." I hold up a second finger.

"I win," she announces with a light smile.

"And you've still got time. You don't want to know anything else about me?" I arch an eyebrow in challenge. She bites her bottom lip, concentrating hard before she continues.

"Why are you here? With me."

"Because we couldn't stay in the apartment, remember?" My voice is dark and lustful as I remind her how close to the edge she had me. I try to sidestep her question, keep our game fun and light. She doesn't let me.

"I mean, why did you say yes?" She's holding her breath, her body is tense and her eyes are searing into me with sheer anguish. So much for keeping it light. "To this crazy idea. To me." She's gnawing on her bottom lip and she has a death grip on the seat. She's terrified of what I might say. It's brave to ask without being sure she wants to know the answer.

"Because I needed the money." I don't think about my answer, I just say it. She takes it like a punch in the stomach, physically recoiling from the pain. From me. I think she might actually vomit.

I'm a fucking prick. It's the truth, but not all of it. Sure, I need the money. But not bad enough to have signed up for her crazy sex tutor scheme if I didn't want to. That's my dirty little secret.

Part of me wants to be here with her.

But I'm sure as fuck not going to tell her that.

The hurt in her chocolate eyes makes me feel worse than if I'd kicked a puppy. I've got to give her something to keep her from taking a bath with her toaster tonight.

"Besides, for some reason I find your particular brand of weird irresistible." That does the trick.

A shy smile twists up her lips. "What are you doing tomorrow?"

I can't tell if she's playing the game or asking me out. That's a hell of a one-eighty. Time to let her down gently with a little reminder of who I am and what we are not.

"It's a bye week. That means there'll be a party at our house. Lots of drinks, lots of chicks, lots of hookups. You know, college at its finest." I answer with my most devious smile, eager to push her away.

"Oh." She sounds deflated. "Green light."

"I'd invite you to swing by..." I try to sound unenthusiastic. "But I'm sure house parties aren't your thing." I don't want to hurt her, but I need to be clear that we aren't dating. Some lines have blurred tonight and they need to be redrawn. In Sharpie.

"They're not." She's curt. I guess she got the message. "Don't worry, I wasn't begging for an invite. I was just playing your stupid game. Which I won, by the way." She crosses her arms.

She's so far away suddenly. She built an invisible wall between us. Part of me is relieved. And part of me is pissed at myself. We're both quiet for the last few blocks of the drive. Mercifully, we don't hit any more red lights.

"We're here." I pull in to her apartment complex. "Should I come up?"

"I'm done for tonight," she answers.

I'm not ready to let her go. I don't want to leave it like this. After a quick internal debate, I decide to hop out of the truck.

"Thanks," she says as I help her out of the cab. She turns to walk away without saying good night, but I don't let her just yet. We need boundaries, but I don't want this distance.

"Thanks for a weird night," I tease. She rolls her eyes, but I ignore it. Instead, I pull her against me, wrapping one arm firmly around her tiny waist. I plant a passionate good-night kiss on her, snaking my tongue through her parted lips and claiming her mouth. I remind her exactly what it is we're doing together. I don't stop until she gives in to the lust, digging her fingers into my biceps and pulling me closer with a soft moan.

My eyes locked with her, I tell her, "I'm not here to make you feel normal. I want to make you feel like the sexual goddess I know you are." She doesn't respond. She's speechless. There's a first. "Good night, Goose."

"Good night," she manages to squeak out as she walks away.

As her petite frame disappears into her building, I continue trying to convince myself she hasn't gotten under my skin with her artless charm.

I don't feel anything for this girl.

This woman.

This weird little goddess.

This is nothing but a simple business arrangement.

Keep telling yourself that, Jacobs.

Chapter Six

Elizabeth

"I know xXGodsGift69Xx is an obnoxious prick, but the trade deal's actually pretty sweet. He seems a bit desperate after getting sanctioned by The Federation for trading with Hellofaplace during the embargo. It's a gamble, since no one wants to touch him with a ten-foot pole, but I think I'll do it. What do you think?" I ask Jackie in our private video chat window while I check on the status of my small but mighty country in the background.

I'm hoping for some decent advice on the nation-building game we both play. We're each the proud owners of first-world nations in Rule Them All, an online game where players create and run their own country. I've been playing since it first came out seven years ago. Players interact with other countries, forming alliances and making trade agreements. Or, they can invade and conquer. Whatever floats their boat.

The game is how we met. Being a woman gaming online can sometimes make you a target for juvenile perverts, so I try to keep a low profile. Not so much in Jackie's case. Her player name is DominaTrix and she usually does just that, dominate. Her country is named WomansWorld. Subtlety has never been Jackie's strong suit.

My player name, Lizbit31415, and country name, Uforia, are both gender neutral. At least, so I thought. Jackie had a hunch I was a woman. What did Jackie do? She asked me for a picture of my tits, so I blocked her account. Turns out it was a fake account she uses to troll other gamers. She messaged me from her real account, claiming she knew I had to be a chick after I blocked her. A dude would have done a Google image search and posted the first pair of tits he could find before asking for some in return. Apparently, only dudes send titty pics.

Gotta love Jackie-logic.

It's hard to build up a country to first-world status. It takes an excruciating amount of time, skill and a bit of luck. I spend about ten hours a week playing. Then there's forums to read and my league membership responsibilities. It's more than just a hobby. Outside of school, this game is my whole life. One of the few things I'm good at. Jackie and I are two of only a handful of women who've managed it. I'm not going to say we're famous or anything. More in-game notorious, Jackie much more than me.

Jackie's kind of evil, in the game at least. She loves to say, "It's a man's world, but I run the bitch." It's fair to say I idolize her. But today she's getting on my last nerve.

"I think I know who wants to touch you with his ten-foot pole," she teases.

This is getting old. She's been at it all day, harassing me about Austin. I never should've told her about our fake date. Or about his party tonight.

"Jesus, can we talk about the game for once? You're obsessed." I want to talk to my best friend, play my game and zone out tonight. Jackie is having none of it.

"I'm not obsessed. Just an interested party. It was my idea, after all!" she reminds me casually.

Technically, she suggested an escort. I compromised with a sex tutor. The nuanced difference seems to be lost on Jackie. She's happy I'm going to finally 'get my freak on.'

I made the mistake of confessing my inexperience to her about a year ago. Months of merciless teasing culminated in a strip-o-gram on my doorstep. At least, I hope he was *just* a stripper. I never let him in to find out. I did give him a fifty-dollar tip to leave, though.

Never give a home address to strangers online, kids!

Jackie was pissed I wasted a perfectly good stripper and wouldn't stop hounding me about the idea of 'immersion therapy.' She said it worked for her cousin's fear of heights. It could work for my fear of cocks too. Her words, not mine. I don't use words like…*that*.

"Bee tee dubs, now that I've seen him, he's starring in all my wet dreams! I don't know how you haven't asked him to put it in you yet. I'd drop my panties in the first fifteen seconds for that man."

I used to blush when Jackie made lewd comments, but it only egged her on. She claims she's desensitizing me to it, and it's for my own good. I think she's vulgar to everyone. In any case, I've trained myself not to react to her. A talent I'm thankful for around Austin, who also seems to enjoy making me blush.

"First of all, stop having wet dreams about Austin. He's mine. Well, not *mine* mine, but you know what I mean." I'm not sure even I know what I mean. "And second, you know this is hard for me, so stop pushing! I've got four weeks." My response comes out more whiny than assertive.

"First, I bet he's hard for you too," she says in an extra-sultry voice. I roll my eyes, but she laughs. "Second, you can't control my wet dreams. The pussy wants what the pussy wants. And third, you only have three weeks now."

She's right. About the third thing, not the first two.

Ewww.

I only have three more weeks with Austin. When I first thought about 'immersion therapy,' four weeks seemed like plenty of time. It all fits on the schedule, my 'sex-abus,' nice and neat. Now, I can't believe the first week is gone already.

"Fine, three weeks is still a really long time," I claim, not really believing it myself.

I cringe at the thought of not seeing Austin again until Tuesday. It's been terrifying, but it's also surprisingly fun. He's so much more than I thought.

"Not at the pace you're going. You've barely even let the boy feel you up yet, for fuck's sake!" She grabs her own chest and gives herself a good jiggle. "Tell me again why you can't go to this party?"

"Because it would be awkward. We're business associates more than friends." I use Austin's analogy from our non-date dinner. I hated it at the time, but he's right. That's the closest description to whatever it is we are. Austin made it perfectly clear that he basically thinks of me as his boss. We're not dating. But sometimes, when he looks at me, I could swear there has to be something more between us. When he's not being an ass.

"First, it's not awkward unless *you* make it awkward. And second, he invited you. If anything, it's rude if you don't go." Jackie keeps using the same argument and it's slowly driving me insane.

"First, I'm *always* awkward. You know this. And second, he specifically *didn't* invite me. He said he *would* ask me to stop by, but house parties aren't my thing, so he *didn't* ask. And you know what? He's right. They aren't my thing!" I snap at her. It has zero effect. She's painfully pigheaded and ruthless when she thinks she's right. It's one of the things that makes her such a great dictator.

Stalin would be so proud.

"Please, that's just what guys say when they want to invite you, but they're afraid you won't show." Her dismissive tone grates on my nerves. My parents used that tone with me my whole life. It makes me feel about two inches tall.

"That's not how it sounded in his truck. It was very much a *dis*-invitation," I practically scream at her. I'm sick of her making me second-guess myself.

"And what did he say when you got out of the truck?" she asks, already knowing the answer. Why do I share things when she only ever uses them against me?

"That he wanted to make me feel like the sexual goddess he knows I am." My cheeks flush when I remember the heat in Austin's stunning blue eyes last night. Those words, that look, his kiss. Even just the memory undoes me.

Of course I want to see him again tonight, but I'm terrified he doesn't want to see me. I'm not his girlfriend. I'm not even really his friend.

Just this weird girl who is paying him for sex.

Jackie can read me like a book. The wistfulness in my voice is blood in the water and Jackie's a shark.

"That's an invitation to get fucked, sister."

"It *so* wasn't. I'm not going to show up there like some creepy obsessed fangirl."

"Then don't go for him. Go for you. It *is* a party. I'm sure there are plenty of other guys you can practice your new moves on." My heart revolts at the thought. I don't want anyone else's hands on me.

Or to see Austin's hands on someone else.

He doesn't belong to me. He could be with anyone he wants tonight. The realization makes my lunch want to make an encore appearance. Why am I jealous? He isn't my boyfriend.

But you wish he was.

Shut it, brain. No one asked you. Maybe Jackie is right. I can go to the party as practice. What's wrong with that? If I happen to see Austin, no big deal.

Liar.

"Maybe..." My willpower is fading.

"Good, we've decided you're going. Now, go put on that black dress I sent you for your birthday last year." Jackie pounces faster than a lion on a wounded gazelle.

"Jackie, no. That is not a dress. It's a glorified handkerchief. You can see my *everything*," I object strenuously, only half-aware that I've already conceded to going to the party.

"That's the point, sweet girl. You've got plenty worth showing and you should do it more often."

I don't budge, so she tries another tactic.

"Please go try it on. I just want to see it. I won't make you wear it if you don't want," Jackie cajoles.

I know this trick. I might as well get in a shady van with *free candy* spray-painted on the side. Still, I put on the stupid dress.

* * * *

This is a bad idea.
This is a really bad idea.
This is a really terribly bad idea!

After an hour of playing dress-up with Jackie, deciding how to curl my hair, putting on a bit more makeup and generally reminding myself I'm a woman, I walk up the driveway to the football house. And yes, I'm wearing the handkerchief dress.

What can I say? Jackie is good.

Music and people are overflowing from the open doors and windows, but I shove past with a few quiet "Excuse mes". No one responds and they only seem to get out of the way when I tap them on the shoulder. I guess common courtesy isn't big at house parties.

I'm not even in the door yet and I feel out of place and ready to leave. Jackie made me promise to stay a half-hour, long enough to have a drink and try to relax. Easy for her to say five hundred miles away, safely behind her computer screen.

I continue to make my way around people and through the house, on the hunt for something to drink so I can fulfill my promise to Jackie and get the hell out of here. There's a makeshift bar in the kitchen and I trudge through the crowd toward it.

"What can I get for you tonight, sexy?" a massive guy in a football jersey asks. He must be over three hundred pounds. I wonder if he has to turn sideways to walk through doorways. I step away to let the girl he's talking to behind me pass by, except there isn't another girl. There's just me. His eyes are locked on me and I swallow down the lump in my throat.

"Ummm..."

Words. This is where most people use words.

Nope, I'll just point to the giant punch bowl.

"Victory punch?"

I give him a quick nod. Who needs words, am I right?

"Nice choice." He gives me an approving nod as he hands me my cliché red Solo Cup filled with the unknown bright red concoction.

They wouldn't roofie a whole punch bowl, right?

Drink in hand, I make my way to a quiet section of the wall and begin my mental countdown. I get a few sideways glances, even an ogle or two, but when I shy away and don't return the interest, I'm mostly ignored. I've spent my life trying not to be seen. I'm a master at it now.

I'm halfway through my drink when I hear it. *Austin's laugh.* It isn't just the light chuckle I usually hear when I've done something stupid. It's a full belly laugh like the one we shared when I was idiotically screaming "Loosey-goosey" at the top of my lungs. I scan the room for him, wondering what made him laugh. Wondering *who* made him laugh.

Am I seriously jealous someone else got his laugh?

What was it I said about *not* being a creepy fangirl?

My eyes finally find him across the room. He's surrounded by a group of guys, other football players if I had to guess. One of them is gesturing wildly, in the throes of a super-engaging story. I let out a little sigh of relief.

Austin's sitting on the armrest of the couch, a beer in hand and an easy smile on his sexy lips. He is so casually confident, as if he owns the universe and everyone in it. He's drop-dead gorgeous as always, with his jeans that hug all the right places and a snug black T-shirt that shows off his amazing arms. I try to hide a shudder remembering how it feels when those arms are wrapped around me.

He is every bit the cocky athlete, but it's more than that. He fits in. He belongs. I've never felt that and I doubt I ever will. Last night, when he took my hand and said everyone is weird, I wanted to believe him so badly. But he isn't. He's everything I'm not. I'm both jealous and in awe of him. I watch him from the corner of the room for several minutes. Possibly without blinking.

Ease up, creepy stalker!

I try to drag my eyes away from him until I see a tall blonde bombshell lean against his shoulders. If I was trying to describe every man's dream girl, she'd be it. Her shapely tan legs seem to go on forever, only coming to an end at her firm butt and slender hips. Keep moving up and there's her tiny waist and flat abs, followed by a pair of perky boobs. And that's just her body. She also happens to have the face of an angel. If someone put a gun to my head, I wouldn't be able to say what's more stunning, her full red lips or the long lashes fluttering over her hazel eyes.

I know her type. Cheerleader. Cheerleaders are sugary sweet and lovably perky. They run on an endless supply of enthusiasm and hopefulness. Guys just want to put them in their pocket and take them home to meet their mother. That's not me.

She's touching Austin, so I hate her by default. But I'd be lying if I didn't admit to having a bit of a girl-crush too. She's that beautiful. Watching her massage Austin's shoulder, I drain the last of my drink and decide to grab another.

It's a party, right?

So begins my new drinking game. Barbie touches Austin's arms, I take a drink. Barbie smiles at Austin, I take a drink. Barbie laughs at Austin, I take a drink. Austin laughs at Barbie, I chug.

It's easy to keep them in sight while hiding. Even half-naked in Jackie's stupid dress, I'm nothing compared to the Barbie-esque women walking around. Austin hasn't glanced my way once. But then again, his Barbie has been keeping him pretty entertained. She's laughing again.

Take a sip.

Oops.

That's the end of that cup.

Better get another.

Is this the third or fourth?

How long have I been here?

I close one eye, trying to get the hands on my watch to stay still long enough for me to read the time. I huff and give up when the rest of the room spins as well.

I sway and grab what I think is the wall. I only notice the soft fabric gripped in my fist after it's too late. Luckily, the ground is there to break my fall. I pull the drapes right down on top of me, the curtain rod hitting me in the head with a comedic thud.

What a joke.

Even with the music turned up and the noise of the crowded house, everyone in the room turns to see the commotion I caused.

Everyone.

Including Austin.

Including Barbie.

Kill me now.

On the upside, at four drinks in I've kept my promise to Jackie and then some. As predicted, I came, I saw and I was conquered by my own awkwardness.

"Are you okay?" I hear a guy's concerned voice in my ear as someone's hand wraps around my arm, pulling me up off the floor. I don't know him, but he seems sweet and cute enough. He's shorter and scrawnier than Austin, but he's no hobbit. Plus, he's holding me and not Barbie, so I've got that going for me, which is nice.

As I get up off the ground, I slide my arms around his neck the way Austin showed me. Since he's shorter, it's much easier. I don't have to stand on my tippy toes to reach. To my surprise, the stranger doesn't pull back. He puts his hand on my waist to steady me.

Maybe it's the alcohol, or maybe it's the practice with Austin, but the contact isn't scary. It isn't anything. I wish it felt nice. Hell, I would take mediocre. I wish I felt anything other than regret for coming to this stupid party tonight.

"Yeah. I'm okay. Thanks. I got a bit dizzy there for a second." I try, unsuccessfully, not to slur my words.

"Elizabeth?"

And then I learn what regret really feels like. I catch Austin's blue eyes piercing into me as he stalks over to us in a few purposeful strides. I cling a little more desperately to this complete stranger. I can't read Austin's expression, but he definitely isn't happy to see me.

"What are you wearing?"

Damn you, Jackie!

"Nice to see you too, Austin," I reply with as much indignation as a drunk party-crasher can manage. He ignores my snark and exchanges glances with my stranger. The stranger pulls away, glancing between me and Austin. He's probably intimidated staring up at Austin, who has a few inches and more than a few pounds on him.

Austin looks aggravated. I try to defuse the tension by introducing them.

"Complete Stranger, this is Austin Jacobs. Austin Jacobs, this is Complete Stranger." Just as I finish my pleasantries, I spy Barbie over Austin's shoulder. Not wanting to be rude, I introduce her too. "And this is College Barbie."

Really, under the circumstances, I think I did quite well. My mother would've been proud of my attention to etiquette despite my inebriation. Of course, Barbie didn't seem to appreciate it. Although, I swear there was a flash of a smile on Austin's lips.

"Tommy." Complete Stranger holds his hand out to Austin, who shakes it with a mix of confusion and irritation.

"Elizabeth Wilde." Loosening my grip around Tommy's neck, I introduce myself too, giving him an over-enthusiastic shake before the world starts to spin again. I tighten my grasp on what I think is Tommy, but to be honest could also be the curtains again. A pair of large warm hands grabs my waist from behind with a familiar touch.

I lean back into him. "Austin, that feels nice. Did I say that out loud?" I ask nobody in particular.

Austin chuckles. The rumble in his chest against my back makes me moan. A wave of heat rushes over my body. The pleasure is short-lived as I have to shut my eyes to keep the world from spinning. Austin's touch is the only thing anchoring me. I hear the three of them talking.

"Do you know her?" Tommy asks.

"Yeah, I've got her. Thanks for the help."

Tommy lets go of me as Austin scoops me up in his arms. My alcohol-soaked mind rambles off something about brides, thresholds and wedding nights. I'm sober enough to pray to the party gods I didn't say any of it out loud.

"Jessie, can you grab a bottle of water?" I hear Austin ask.

Who's Jessie?

"Sure. She's pretty trashed." A surprising amount of concern laces Barbie's voice as she replies.

Of course she's got a cool name. Elizabeth is so lame. It's the name of a little old lady who knits ugly sweaters for her fifty cats.

"Jessie's her nickname actually." Austin's response confirms I no longer have an internal monologue.

That's just what this situation needs, an unfiltered drunk Elizabeth.

"Short for Jessica. And I think Elizabeth fits you." His velvet voice is in my ear, soft enough only I can hear it. It's intimate and sexy. And of course I tell him so, because I haven't had enough embarrassment yet tonight.

Screw it.

There's no recovering from tonight. I might as well go all in. I wrap my arms around Austin's neck and bury my face in the soft skin on the nape of his neck. He smells delicious, a rich spicy vanilla, sweet and intense. I'm overcome by the need to know how he tastes. Salty.

"Did you just lick me?" he asks with a snicker.

"Smell like dessert. Taste like ocean," is the excuse I give him.

That's not even an excuse. That's a random string of words.

My eyes fly open and I cling to Austin at the sudden sensation of falling.

"Don't worry, Goose, I've got you," he whispers, settling us into an overstuffed armchair. We're sitting back with his friends, where he was happily being manhandled by Barbie before I cannonballed into his evening. The same group I watched most of the night are now staring down at me and Austin. He's unfazed by the attention as he leans back in the chair and adjusts me in his lap, not letting go.

Three simple words. *I've got you.* And I'm at ease. I trust him completely.

When did that happen? Is it just the alcohol?

No.

The licking, yes.

That's entirely the alcohol's fault.

But the way I feel in Austin's arms, that's all him. I shamelessly snuggle into his chest. If I'm going to have to live with the regrets from tonight, I might as well take advantage where I can.

He tries to pull my tiny dress down over my exposed thighs. It's a sweet gesture, but it only serves to expose more of my chest, which is literally right under his nose.

"Not enough dress. Jackie's fault," I explain my wardrobe choice like a petulant five-year-old.

"Remind me to thank her later." His voice is playful. And, dare I say, lustful?

"Who's your new friend, Jacobs?" a guy's voice calls to us from the couch.

"People shake hands still," I mumble as my hand shoots out toward him. "Elizabeth Wilde." I shift forward, nearly falling out of Austin's lap introducing myself. I earn a laugh from everyone except Austin.

"Careful, or my teammates are going to get an eyeful of what I haven't even gotten to see yet," Austin warns as he tugs me back against him before his friend can shake my hand. I gasp, realizing what he means, and instinctively cover my chest with my arms.

"You clean up nice. Even got that brown spot off your nose," one of the guys chides with a sneer. It's King of the Douchebags from my biochem class. Great.

"Rude much?" I snap back. I'm never confrontational, but between the liquid courage coursing through my body and Austin at my back, I rise to the occasion. I'm used to guys like him. Bullies. There are a lot of jerks with huge egos in my pre-med courses. Some of them seem to have a problem with the fact that I don't talk to anyone and usually ace the class. I'm not an elitist, but that's how it seems from the outside. Sometimes I wish I could get over myself and make friends.

Be normal.

If it hasn't happened after twenty-one years, it's not going to. So, I'll stay painfully shy and unimaginably awkward and deal with jerks who draw the wrong conclusion about who I am.

"Calm down, Princess. You aren't in that ice palace of yours anymore. Your sweet little ass is in my house now." He isn't playful like Austin. He's mean.

"You got a problem, Montgomery?" Austin's voice is harsher than I've ever heard it before.

From across the room, I thought Austin was surrounded by his friends, laughing and loving life. Sitting here with him now is different, like he's on stage. We're putting on a show. These are his teammates, not his friends.

"No problem. Just surprised at your new piece. She acts like she's God's gift. But clearly she's lowered her standards if she's picking up strays now."

Austin's body goes rigid with anger underneath me.

Montgomery leans in and whisper-shouts, "Heads up, though, she's probably a rug muncher, being Haynes' favorite and all."

"Chill out, Monte," one of the other guys sitting with us says, giving him a little shoulder shove. Austin gives the other guy a slight nod in recognition. I've exhausted my bravery and sink into Austin.

Desperate to take the attention off me, I spot Barbie-Jessie coming back across the room and decide to be nice and continue my introductions.

"And this is Barbie!" I exclaim enthusiastically.

"Barbie?" a few of the guys call out and laugh. I didn't mean to get her name wrong. I don't think.

"Here." She shoves a bottle of water into Austin's chest. I don't know Barbie-Jessie, but even I can hear the anger in her voice.

"Drink this. Slowly," Austin demands, handing me the bottle. I sip it, as directed.

"I'm heading home," Barbie-Jessie adds with a pout.

"Fine," Austin responds without even looking up. I feel bad for her. I honestly do. I know how it feels to be the center of Austin's attention. It's like stepping out of a cave and feeling the warm sun after a long, cold winter. It's living instead of just surviving. Losing it is to step back into the darkness. I could easily be in her shoes, being summarily dismissed by the sexiest man alive.

"Sorry, Barbie." I mean it genuinely, but the use of her nickname, which I can't seem to stop saying, makes it sound passive-aggressive and super-bitchy. Barbie, I mean *Jessie*, slinks off without another word.

"Damn, new girl. That was cold," the guy who defended me earlier quips.

"Told you. She's the ice queen," Monte adds. Suddenly my stomach doesn't feel so good.

"Shut the fuck up, Monte," Austin snarls. Monte huffs and sips his beer.

"I didn't mean…" I try to explain, but I can't find the words.

"That's enough." Austin stands in a single motion, holding me to his chest as if I'm light as a feather. I'm nauseated from the movement, but the simple demonstration of how powerful he is still turns me on. I can't help myself from moaning in his ear as he carries me back to his room.

"Easy," he warns. "Nothing's happening tonight."

Nothing did, and I'd be lying if I said I wasn't disappointed about that.

Chapter Seven

Austin

It's early as fuck to be calling it on a Friday night, but between Monte trying to start shit and Elizabeth drunk off her ass, I'm fucking done. I make Elizabeth drink some water, peel her out of that ridiculous excuse for a dress and put her in one of my T-shirts. I lay her down in my bed and she passes out almost immediately, dead to the world.

I flop down next to her, too pissed to sleep. Pissed she's wasted. Pissed some other guy was touching her. Pissed Monte was staring at her tits.

She fucking licked me.

I chuckle softly, gazing at the crumpled mess beside me, snoring like a grizzly bear. In hindsight she's a pretty adorable drunk, despite the havoc wreaked on my home decor. I wrap my arms around her so I can tell if she wakes up. Nothing romantic or sweet, I just want to make sure she doesn't throw up in my bed.

Somewhere in the night, my hold on Elizabeth goes from puke patrol to spooning. It's not even really spooning, more of a blanketing.

That's a first.

I've had girls stay over a few times when I'm too drunk or too exhausted to kick them out, although I try to avoid it. When a girl gets comfortable sleeping in a guy's bed, instead of just being fucked in it, she gets comfortable everywhere else in his life too.

My sleepovers are minimal and I sure as fuck don't cuddle. Except with Elizabeth, apparently I do. Having her warm body wrapped up in mine definitely seems like cuddling.

Fuck.

We might even be snuggling.

I'm practically lying on top of her, covering most of her back with my chest. Our arms and legs are a tangled mess. Her tiny body is stretched across half the bed, limbs spread out in every direction. For such a small thing, she sure takes up a lot of room.

It's surprisingly nice. She must think so too. I know she's awake, but she hasn't pulled away.

Don't get used to it, Jacobs. Don't get attached.

The sun streaming into my bedroom is enough to tell me I've slept in way too late. Time to end this babysitter shit and get on with my day.

"I know you're up." The lack of her chainsaw-level snoring is proof of that. She doesn't acknowledge me. "Should we play sexual chicken to prove it?" I ask, as I glide my hand up the back of her thigh.

She doesn't flinch, but her breathing gets shallow.

I slip my hand under the hem of her T-shirt, tracing the curve of her tight little ass, giving it a firm squeeze.

My cock twitches in my boxers as I resist the urge to give her soft cheek a firm slap.

She's perfectly still.

It's a valiant effort, but her body is tense against mine.

I dance my fingers around her hips to the sweet heaven between her legs, applying enough pressure to know she's wet. My heart rate spikes, desperately pumping all my blood south, but I keep my body relaxed.

She holds her breath.

You're a terrible faker, Goose.

I dip my thumb inside her panties.

She jolts upright, panting heavily.

"I win," I confirm before rolling away from her onto my back.

She doesn't answer. She tugs the T-shirt back down and rakes her hands through her disheveled hair. Her embarrassment is replaced with the unmistakable look of nausea.

"There's a bucket next to the nightstand. Don't puke in my bed."

She closes her eyes and takes a few deep breaths before she moves again. When it seems she's back in control of her stomach and its contents, she turns toward me.

I'm lying here in nothing but my boxer briefs. I don't even try to cover my morning wood. She traces over my naked chest and I can tell the second she sees my hard-on by the way she snaps her gaze anywhere but on my junk.

"See anything you want?" I goad her. She blushes and pulls the covers up over herself.

I don't care. I'm not feeling very charitable toward her this morning. I couldn't get her out of my head yesterday, but I didn't invite her over because I knew it would end badly. Instead of the quick fuck I was aiming for, I had to take shit from my teammates and play nursemaid all night. I didn't even get laid for my efforts.

"Bathroom?" she squeaks. My anger fades at her frightened voice. I know she's never woken up half-naked in some guy's bed before.

"Across the hall. You can't miss it." I keep my eyes focused on the ceiling. She gets up quietly and walks across the hall.

"Stop being such a dick," I tell myself after she's gone. I throw on a pair of shorts and head to the kitchen to grab Elizabeth a bottle of water.

"Your junk get frostbite popping the ice queen's cherry?" Monte chides with a nasty sneer as soon as I turn the corner into the kitchen. The obnoxious fuck must've been waiting all night to use that line.

"What did you just say to me?" I spit back at him. I'm in no mood for this asshole's shit this morning. He's a prick in general, but worse with me since I destroy him on the field.

"We saw her do the walk of shame to the bathroom," Drew, the team's best running back, adds. "Not like you to let them stick around 'til morning."

"Why don't you two mind your own damn business?"

"I told you. No way did he tap that last night. Pay up," Monte declares victoriously. Drew studies me.

My arms crossed, shoulders tight, scowl firmly in place, I might as well have *sexually frustrated* stamped on my forehead.

"Damn it." Drew hands him a twenty. The pricks bet on if I fucked Elizabeth last night. Even if she hadn't been wasted, it's a pretty messed-up bet to make.

"Dude, I could've told you the frosty little princess was going to give you the cold shoulder." He beams with satisfaction at his stupid pun. I want to punch his teeth in, but instead, I grab a water from the fridge and a protein bar from the cabinet, telling myself he isn't worth it.

"Go fuck yourself, Monte."

Don't let them get to you.

"I'm just saying, there are easier ways to get your rocks off, man. That chick don't want no dick. Believe me, I've tried."

"So that's what this is about? You made a pass at her and she said no? That makes her like the other ninety-nine percent of the girls on campus, too smart for your dumb ass," I quip with a genuine smile, loving that Elizabeth said no to the egotistical little shit.

"Whatever. Just trying to be a friend. Keep wasting your time if you want. I know you enjoy a challenge, but no way that frigid bitch is worth it." His comment stops me dead in my tracks.

"Call her a bitch again and I'll fucking end you." There isn't an ounce of humor in my voice. Rage fills my veins. I don't know where it came from.

"Take it easy. Jesus, she's just another Friday-night fuck," he remarks.

Big mistake.

I cross the kitchen in a few long strides, grab a fistful of his shirt and shove him against the wall before it even registers to him what's happening.

"She's not *just* another *anything* to you. As far as you are concerned, she's *my* girl. So, shut your fucking mouth or I'll shut it for you," I growl in his face.

"All right, Jacobs. I think he's got it." Drew puts his hand on my chest and pushes me away.

I give Monte a final shove, enjoying the sound of his head hitting the wall behind him. I grab the water and protein bar, wanting Monte to try to have the last word. He doesn't. *Guess the asshole isn't so stupid after all.*

I turn the corner back toward my room and almost knock Elizabeth over. I wrap her up in my arms, keeping her from falling. How long has she been standing there? Long enough. She's in nothing but my T-shirt and her underwear.

"You putting on a show, Goose?" My voice is sharp from the tussle with Monte, causing her to cringe slightly. I tower over her, looking down into her wide brown eyes. I never noticed the light golden flecks in them before.

"I couldn't find my clothes…" Her timid voice trails off as she tries to pull the shirt down to cover more of her milky thighs.

I'm pissed at Monte for being a dick. I'm pissed at her for causing drama in my life. And I'm pissed at myself for acting like some possessive boyfriend. But all that anger isn't what's making my heart race right now. It's her tight little body pressing against mine. I'm not so angry anymore. Now I'm scared. Of her. Of what she does to me. How did I let her get so close so fast? I let her go and take a step back.

"Toothbrush?" she asks.

"Sure." I grab her hand and take her into the bathroom. I snag one of the many unopened spares from under the sink and hand it to her. She examines it. I know the question she wants to ask.

"The guys have a lot of guests. We try to be hospitable."

"The guys?" She gazes up at me, wanting me to give her some reassurance. I can't. Wouldn't want her getting too comfortable.

"Yes, Elizabeth. Occasionally, our female visitors spend the night after we fuck their brains out." I might be a bit harsh, but we aren't playing house here. She needs to know who I am. I can't have her thinking she's special. "Do you need to read my reviews on scoreyourscore.com again?" I don't wait for her to reply before I leave.

I toss the water and protein bar on my desk before lying back down on top of the covers. She tiptoes back into my room. It's the lion's den and she's trying not to wake the beast. She's scared of me. It's shitty, but necessary.

"I'm sorry. About last night. I shouldn't have…" Her voice is shaky. Embarrassment is pouring out of her. She's tugging at the bottom of my shirt, pulling it as far down her thighs as the fabric will stretch. Her eyes are locked on her feet that are drawing little circles on my carpet. I prop myself up on my elbows and face her. She freezes in place, a deer in headlights.

"You shouldn't have what?" I ask without an ounce of forgiveness. "Come to my party? Gotten shit-faced? Ripped my curtains off the wall? Almost flashed my teammates? Slept in my bed?"

She cringes at my words.

"Right. Sorry about all of that." She darts her gaze around the room, anywhere but on me.

"Your dress is on a hook in the closet." I motion to the small closet door across the room. She grabs her dress and the sneakers on the floor next to it. She walks backward toward the bedroom door, afraid to turn her back on me.

"Going somewhere?" I ask, sprawled out on the bed.

"To the bathroom. I'll change and get out of your hair."

"The bathroom?" I ask with a laugh. "You realize I'm the one who put you in that shirt last night, right? You can lose the modesty. I've seen it all before."

That pisses her off.

I can see the change in her entire demeanor as Ms. Feisty comes out to play. Her eyes go wide and wild. Her nostrils flare. She pulls her shoulders back and stands tall, putting her tits on display. My dick appreciates the show.

"Fine," she declares as she rips my shirt off over her head and throws it at me. I'd already seen her last night. I'd even had my hands on the luscious curves of her body. But she was drunk, basically passed out. It wasn't sexy. It was almost clinical.

Standing in her matching pink bra and panties, hands on her hips, defiant, she is beyond beautiful. I don't move, pretending she has no effect on me, as my heart races and my cock gets hard. She pulls her dress on, struggling to zip it up behind her back but refusing to ask for help. I don't offer. I stare at her, enjoying the view.

She pulls on her shoes.

Who wears tennis shoes with a dress?

It's very Elizabeth. Weirdly sexy. I like a woman in heels as much as the next guy, but Elizabeth makes sneakers alluring.

Our eyes lock for a few heartbeats and we stare at each other in complete silence. She's waiting for me to fold, to apologize.

Don't hold your breath, sweet cheeks.

"Thanks for the help last night," she snaps at me before leaving, slamming the door behind her. I grab the shirt she threw at me and take a deep breath of her scent.

This girl is killing me. Death by foreplay.

The second she's out of the door I jump in the shower and jack off to the image of her. Her creamy legs wrapped around me, her curvy hips rocking into me, her huge tits in my mouth, the fire in those brown eyes as she comes on my cock.

It takes all of two minutes to shoot my load. I haven't come that fast since high school. I cut myself some slack considering she has been torturing me all week. I'm hoping indulging in the fantasy will get her out of my head.

It doesn't.

Getting her out of my head is a lot harder than getting her out of my bed. A single shower rub-n-tug isn't enough of a release. I'd planned on blowing off some steam with Jessie last night, but Elizabeth is an epic cock block. I rinse off and hop out of the shower, already getting another chubby thinking about Elizabeth in my lap last night in that dress and her stupid damn sneakers.

Thoughts of her plague me all day. Some aren't even X-rated.

Most are.

As I make myself scrambled eggs, I wonder what she eats for breakfast, given her complete lack of culinary skills. Has she ever had s'more Pop-Tarts? Bet she'd like them, being a chocolate fiend and all. Rich people probably don't eat Pop-Tarts. They eat those fancy toaster strudels. Then again, she does have a pantry full of ramen noodles. My mind drifts to thoughts of bending her over her kitchen island, which I suspect is the perfect height, and pounding into her from behind.

At the gym, I wonder how she keeps her trim figure. Is she a runner? Yoga maybe. Please God, let it be pole dancing classes. Fuck me. Now my dick is hard in a room full of sweaty dudes.

Flipping through TV channels after dinner, I pause on some black-and-white flick and wonder if she only watches old movies. She didn't react to my *Scarface* impression. Maybe she's never even seen it. Maybe we can watch it at her place while I fuck her on the couch. Then eat some Pop-Tarts.

I may have been thinking about her all day, but I'm proud to say I resist the urge to text her. She's probably still pissed anyway. I was kind of a dick. I jack off again before bed, picturing taking off her little pink cotton panties with my teeth. I wake up the same way I fell asleep, smelling her on my pillow and yearning for the warmth of her. I jerk off a third time in twenty-four hours to dreams about what I want to do to her body. This is getting downright pathetic.

Nothing seems to work. Lying in bed Sunday morning with my heart racing and my cock still sticky, she's all I'm thinking about. This is fucking weird. I've never been this hung up on a girl before. Of course, my dick's never been stuck in purgatory this long before either. Absence may make the heart grow fonder, but abstinence makes the cock grow harder. When I agreed to this stupid sex tutor shit, I didn't realize how much of a fucking torture the tease would be.

I need to fuck Elizabeth before I go insane. I'm a starving man staring at his favorite meal, luxuriating in the aroma of what I can't have. I remind myself that I'll fuck her soon enough then it'll be fine. That's all this is, a momentary obsession. Fuck Devin and his Bo Peep bullshit. I'm not that kid anymore. Soon she won't hold any more allure than any other girl I've fucked and walked away from. I just need to have my fill of her first.

I give up trying to hold back and shoot her a text. Maybe we can add sexting to our trip around the bases.

Me: *How's that homework i gave u coming?*

Goose: *Homework?*

She responds quickly. A good sign, even if it's just one word.

Me: *Something black and lacy...*

I wait for about twenty minutes, but she doesn't write back. Against my better judgment I double-text, hoping she doesn't read the desperation between the lines.

Me: *Shoot me some pics and i'd be happy to check your work ;)*

Nothing. Guess she's pissed. I refuse to write again. Two unanswered texts is bordering on loser territory, but three is straight up pathetic. I can't help myself from checking my phone every five minutes like some ridiculous teenage chick, hoping for nudes. Around lunch I cave and text again with something she'll have to respond to.

Me: *We still on for Tuesday?*

She doesn't write back. For hours. It's six o'clock now and I'm angry. Maybe I was a dick yesterday, but that's no reason to play these games. I'm not putting up with three more weeks of her pouting just because I don't play the doting boyfriend. I'm not her boyfriend. She can't say she's fine with that then flip out. I grab my keys and head to her place, determined to either get her to talk to me or quit this charade.

I don't knock, waltzing right into her apartment like I own the place. Why give her another chance to ignore me? She's standing in the kitchen and our eyes lock immediately. Her face flashes with the same panicked expression she always gets when I push her boundaries. I cross my arms and give her my most devious smirk in response. I'm surprised when she rushes toward me instead of her usual running away and hiding.

"What are you doing here?" she grumbles, as if my presence is an insult. I don't bother answering. I reach out and grab her, palming her ass with one hand and pulling her against me. I kiss her hard. Fisting her hair, I tilt her head to slide my tongue between her open lips and deepen the kiss.

This isn't like our PG-13 make-out sessions. It's possessive and dominant. I'm claiming her mouth and telling her I will not be ignored. It's a war, her body our battlefield and my tongue the invading army. She's rising to my challenge as our mouths crash against each other, fighting for breath. I'm lost in the passionate struggle when the sound of someone else stirring in the room rips her attention from me. She pulls away and my eyes search for the source of the distraction. It's a man. I'm instantly defensive.

Elizabeth turns her back to him as she tries to calm the flush of her cheeks. Whoever this guy is, he has Elizabeth discomposed, and not in the fun way I do. Her face is a mix of shame and terror. Without thinking, I step between them, shielding her from his sight. *No one gets to make Goose uncomfortable but me.*

The guy is older, maybe late fifties judging from his gray hair and the prominent wrinkles on his forehead from what I assume has been a long life of scowling. He clears his throat as he stands from the couch and buttons his suit jacket.

"Good evening," he says with a professional detachment.

"Evening," I answer.

"And may I ask who you might be?" He is polite enough, but I recognize the stern challenge in his eyes. We're like predators stumbling on each other in the jungle, deciding if the other is a threat.

"Austin Jacobs, Elizabeth's boyfriend." The words come out in one steady breath, without hesitation.

Why did I fucking say that?

I don't need to tell this guy anything about my relationship, or lack of one, with Elizabeth. For some reason I have the urge to lay claim to her with some sort of title, and 'girlfriend' seems about as good as any.

I've never called myself someone's boyfriend before, although I'm sure I know a few girls who have. I usually avoid labels more than sorority girls avoid carbs. Labels come with expectations, which I inevitably never meet. What's the difference what I call myself if it's all fake anyway, right? Judging by Elizabeth's sudden death grip on my forearm, it matters to her.

"And you are?" I ask the well-dressed stranger.

"Richard Wilde, Elizabeth's father." He lays his own claim on her as he holds out his hand to shake mine. No wonder Elizabeth is blushing. Her dad just watched her mouth get tongue-fucked by her boyfriend. Or whatever the hell I am.

"Nice to meet you, Mr. Wilde." I pry my arm free from Elizabeth, who is hiding her face from both of us, and give him a firm handshake. Time to climb out of this hole I dug us into.

"Likewise, Austin. And please, call me Richard. Elizabeth did not mention she was involved with someone." Both of us turn our focus to Elizabeth at my side. This is the most timid I've ever seen her, and that's saying something.

"I…" Her soft voice trails off and she peers up at me with pleading eyes.

She's struggling with the lie, even with just the idea of continuing the lie. But telling her father she hired a 'sex tutor' isn't an option here. I can't help but take pity on her. Unlike Elizabeth, I have no problem lying. I'm quite good at playing whatever role I need to. Time to put on a show. I slide my hand into hers and give a little squeeze.

Don't worry, Goose. I've got you.

"It's new. I'm not entirely sure she's used to the idea yet." I make sure my tone is wistful and sappy as I lean down and give her a chaste kiss on the temple. "I'm sorry for barging in on your evening. I didn't realize you had dinner plans, sweetie." The adorable confusion on her face is priceless. I don't even have to fake my broad smile.

"I would've mentioned it if I thought you were planning on dropping in." Her tone is clipped. She must be struggling to get into character as my little woman. I'll help her with that.

"I missed you too much. Couldn't stay away," I coo, bringing our interlocked fingers to my lips to kiss the back of her hand. Her skin is smooth and warm against my lips. I remind myself to keep the PDA father-appropriate, despite wondering how those smooth hands would feel wrapped around my cock.

"I tried texting…" I shoot her a knowing glace.

Maybe next time don't ignore me.

"I didn't—" she begins, but her father cuts her off.

"I am afraid that is my fault. No phones during family time. A rule of my late wife's we honor." At least that explains why she didn't answer.

"And a good one, I believe. Sometimes being too connected to the entire world makes us lose the connection to those most important to us." I smile down at Elizabeth in time to see her roll her eyes. Thankfully, Richard didn't catch it. I'm laying it on a little thick, but her dad seems to be buying it. Plus, it's always fun messing with my little Goose.

"I didn't mean to intrude on family time. I should leave you two to your dinner plans." I stare at Richard, waiting for the offer I know he'll make.

"Nonsense. The more the merrier. I am sure Beth agrees." We both turn our attention to her again.

I can see the wheels turning in her head. She'd rather I not stick around all night, but I get the feeling facing questions from her father alone right now isn't too appealing either.

"Of course. Only the reservation at La Rouge is for two. And their dress code is quite" — she gives me a quick sideways glance as if in a tacit apology — "quite strict." All three of us take an appraisal of my outfit. I'm not wearing my usual gym shorts, but my jeans and T-shirt combo are hardly black-tie.

I take in Elizabeth's outfit for the first time and realize she's dressed up too, sporting a khaki skirt and an argyle sweater rather than her usual baggy jeans and circus-tent-sized T-shirt. To top it all off, she's got a delicate string of white pearls around her neck. She's wearing a costume, a caricature of herself.

Elizabeth lets go of my hand and starts in with the fidgeting, the telltale sign that she's nervous. Or feeling guilty. Or both. *Think you're the first one to tell me I'm not good enough, Beth?* Not even close. *Think you're going to hurt my feelings?* My skin is thicker than that.

You couldn't hurt me if you tried.

"Oh, nonsense. I am sure we could work something out with the maître d'," Richard chimes in unconvincingly.

He's politely going through the motions of trying to include me, happy in the knowledge that it isn't actually going to happen. I'm not going to trek all the way downtown to some fancy restaurant just so some snotty waiter can turn up his nose at me before sending me away. Fuck that.

"No, Richard. I'm afraid Beth is quite right." I use her father's nickname for her, but don't like the way it feels in my mouth.

She may be his Beth, but she's my Goose.

"I'm ill-prepared for dining out. But please don't let me spoil your plans with my rude interruption." I've always hated this fake-politeness shit, but that's the game we're playing. I take her hand and give a squeeze to let her know I'm admitting defeat, but not without a parting blow.

"Give me a call tonight, would you, sweetie? So I know you're home safe? You know how I worry." Her eyes are closed and she almost appears pained. Does she seriously feel bad for me right now? I place another gentle kiss on her temple, expecting to see a victorious smile or a smug glint in her eyes, but I don't.

"Pizza!" she shouts randomly while her hands shoot up in the air like she just won a game of bingo no one else knew we were playing. Richard and I both turn to her, completely confused. "You could make us pizza. We have all the ingredients you brought last time." She's talking to me, but looking at her dad sheepishly, as if embarrassed to admit I've been in her apartment before.

"Pizza?" Calling Richard's tone unenthusiastic would be calling the Mona Lisa a little doodle. Understatement of the fucking century.

I'm only slightly less enthusiastic myself. "Pizza is a poor substitute for La Rouge." I have no real idea since I've never been, and I do make a pretty damn good pizza. But something tells me Richard's tastes are a bit more discerning than my normal dinner partners'. There's no way in hell I'm signing up for that critique.

"Please?" Elizabeth's brown eyes are the size of saucers.

I'll admit it, the worry in her eyes does something to me, makes me want to take care of her. She looks at me like there's something her rich daddy can't give her, but I can. It's bewitchingly endearing. Her hand finds mine again, interlocking our fingers and squeezing. Every ounce of resistance I have crumbles. I swear, I'm not usually this much of a pussy.

"All right. If that's what you want." I drop my forehead to hers with a sigh. This isn't part of the game anymore. I didn't say it out of fake politeness or because of her father. Right now, in this moment, all I care about is making the woman holding my hand happy.

"Thank you." Her words are almost a whisper, but I hear the strength with which she means them.

Chapter Eight

Elizabeth

I asked him to stay.
Why did I do that?
I'm pissed at him for being a jerk yesterday morning.
You kind of had that coming.
Fine. So, I'm not pissed. Maybe just a little hurt. But my father finding out what's going on between us has got to be at the top of my over-my-dead-body list of things I *never* want to have happen.

Two parts of my life, of myself, colliding together is dangerous. I should want him to hit the road. Instead, I begged him to stay. And, weirdly enough, he did!
Why did he do that?
Unfortunately, I don't have time to puzzle out an answer. Austin's touch brings me back to the real world. His simple squeeze of my hand has an unnerving ability to center me.

"One condition," Austin answers with a smile. "You're my little kitchen helper tonight."

"Deal," I agree quickly, pulling Austin into the kitchen before he changes his mind.

My father isn't what you'd call a pizza kind of guy. It's fair to say he frowns on finger foods in general. I can tell neither he nor Austin is too excited about my change in our plans for this evening. After basically telling Austin he isn't good enough to eat at La Rouge, I couldn't stand the thought of eating at the hoity-toity restaurant without him.

I don't care about Michelin and its stupid stars. Yeah, I'd sell my soul for a decent crêpe, but duck confit with Perrier water on elegant table linens and fancy waiters isn't exactly my style. Austin and his hand-made pizza in my kitchen are my style.

"How did you two meet?" my father asks, begrudgingly taking a seat on one of the bar stools on the other side of the kitchen counter. Austin pulls the premade dough and cheese out of the refrigerator and I pull the sauce and spices out of the cabinets.

"In the library." I stick to the truth as much as possible. I'm a terrible liar. Maybe that's why I keep my mouth shut around my father so much. There isn't much I have to say that we agree on.

"Elizabeth needed a tutor," Austin hints with a mischievous glimmer in his eyes as they meet mine. I stifle a gasp.

"A tutor?" my father inquires with a disapproving lilt. "I thought all your studies were going quite well, Beth."

"Oh, don't worry, they're well in hand now," Austin teases and I blush. He's playing a dangerous game and I'm cursing myself for asking him to stay.

I attempt to change the subject. "Austin is one of the university's star athletes!"

"Is that so?" my father muses. "In which sport?"

"Football," Austin and I answer in stereo. "But I'd hardly call myself a star," Austin adds.

"Talented enough to have earned a scholarship," I retort.

Am I bragging about Austin? I am. I want my father to like him.

That's weird.

It shouldn't matter what my father thinks of Austin. He's never going to see him again. Still, he's the first boyfriend my father has ever met. Actually, he's the first boyfriend I've ever had. Well, I guess he isn't even that. He's more an employee than anything else.

Don't blow it all out of proportion.

Austin Jacobs is pretending to be my boyfriend while he makes dinner for me and my father.

No biggie.

"Plus, you've maintained over a 3.75 GPA each semester too. It really is impressive, Austin," I add, unable to keep myself from talking him up. Austin gives me a sideways glance. Creepy stalker warning alarms must be going off in his head. Guess he doesn't realize the Dean's List is published on the school website each semester. I know because my name's on there too, near the top.

"That is an achievement. What is your major?" My father's tone is almost impressed. Academics are more his forte than sports.

"Business," Austin and I sing out in chorus again, causing us both to chuckle. Austin has already finished prepping his pizza and slides it into the oven. I copy him with my pizza. It's just spreading sauce on dough, then covering it with cheese, but I feel accomplished in my contribution to our meal.

"I'll be entering an MBA program next fall, if I'm lucky enough to get another scholarship, that is." Austin puts my pizza in with his before turning back toward my father with an easy confidence. I've always seen Austin as strong, but juxtaposed to my father, he's both young and powerful.

My father has a way of making me feel small, in both stature and importance. I'm dwarfed in comparison, somehow perpetually the eight-year-old little girl who needs to learn not to interrupt the adults. But Austin commands the room with the simple way he carries himself. For the first time in my life, I see my father not as some unquestionable force, but as what he is. Just another man. It's oddly empowering.

"I have no doubt, if you continue in your dedication to your studies, you will receive one," my father acknowledges.

I gloat at the understated compliment.

Before long, the three of us are digging into our pizzas. It's good. I've always been more of a deep-dish girl, but Austin's simple thin crust is delicious.

"This is amazing!" I profess with a slight groan of delight. Even my father can't deny it.

"Quite good indeed," he adds, a roaring endorsement as far as my father is concerned.

"I'm glad you both enjoyed it." Austin has a humble but satisfied smile. It's beautiful on his handsome face and I desperately want to kiss him. *Really* kiss him, the kind of kiss that isn't appropriate in front of my father. I bite my lip to resist the urge and Austin catches me. I don't hear him laugh, but the shake of his shoulders tells me he's holding one back.

I clear the plates in front of us after we finish eating, not believing the night has gone by so quickly. The three of us have made happy small talk all throughout dinner with my father and Austin casually chatting about business, both Austin's classes and my father's experiences. I don't think they'll be going out for beers any time soon, but it seems as if my father approves of Austin, at least as much as my father ever approves of anyone.

Austin is charming. His easy confidence never falters. Grown men are usually intimidated by my father, but not Austin. He's discussing the benefits of a market economy, capital expenditures and managing operating expenses. He makes being sexy seem as easy as breathing.

Austin steps behind me and places a hand on my hip as he deposits the rest of the dirty dishes in the sink. Throughout the night he has treated me to these soft, innocent touches here and there. A hand on my knee, a brush of my hair behind my ear, a gentle kiss to my temple. Each time they spark a sweet heat in my chest that radiates in waves throughout my body, making me flush. A week ago, a man touching me, even innocently, in front of my father would have freaked me out. Now, I yearn for those fleeting touches. Austin has already conditioned my body to respond to the simplest of caresses.

"I am afraid we are not being the best dinner companions." My father's voice interrupts my enjoyment of Austin's proximity. "Beth has never had much interest in business."

Austin places another soft kiss on my temple. "Sorry if we're boring you, darling." The slightest undertone of sarcasm is just enough to tell me he's teasing me with the term of endearment. I hate them and I think he knows it. Every pet name he's used tonight—darling, sweetie, honey, dear—all leave his mouth with an annoying hint of condescension. I like when he calls me Goose. It isn't some generic platitude to show people we are special to each other. It's just for us.

"It has been a lovely evening, but I am afraid it is getting rather late. I should be heading home," my father declares, standing and grabbing his suit jacket off the back of his chair. I hadn't noticed he'd taken it off. He rarely does, even at home. The sight fills me with pride, knowing that my father actually relaxed and might have even enjoyed his evening in with me. With us. Usually our 'family time' leaves me with the feeling that our visits are a chore for him, just one more in his long list of responsibilities. Tonight was different. Because of Austin.

"I'll walk you out, Richard," Austin calls after him.

The door shuts behind them and in the quiet of my empty apartment, a rush of happiness washes over me. I was terrified when Austin blew into my apartment like a hurricane, but he made my evening. For the first time in my life, I think my father actually likes me. Tonight, with Austin by my side, I almost felt normal. One dinner with my boyfriend—or whatever he is—and the way my father sees me is changing. I'm a person and not a walking mistake. Maybe it's because around Austin I'm finally starting to feel like a woman. *God, how cheesy is that?* But it's true. Austin makes me feel powerful, sexy, worshiped. Maybe he's right. Maybe somewhere inside me there's a sexual goddess.

This moment must be celebrated. I turn on my stereo and crank my favorite oldies station. Mel Carter's *Hold Me, Thrill Me, Kiss Me* flows out of my speakers and I can't help but close my eyes and sing along as I dance in my living room. I'm belting out the second verse when I hear Austin's snicker and nearly jump out of my skin. I don't hesitate to grab a pillow off the couch and throw it at his head. He catches it without even flinching, which just makes me angrier. *Damn him and his athletic reflexes.*

"I thought you left!" I screech.

"I gathered as much. Please, don't stop on my account."

I respond only with a scoff, so he sings in a cheesy dramatic tone as he struts up to me. He wraps his arms around my waist when he reaches me, singing, "Kiss me." So I kiss him, fusing my lips to his. His singing gets softer as he kisses a trail along my jaw and we sway to the music. In an instant the atmosphere in the room changes. This isn't pretend anymore.

The playful air is clouded by a thick fog of unspoken emotions. He continues to sing softly in my ear, pleading for me to never let him go. The words of the love song become a promise. He pulls me into his arms and it feels like home. It feels like forever.

"Make me tell you..." The whisper dies in my ear. He doesn't finish the lyric — *I'm in love with you.* He leans back and all I see are his eyes peering down into mine. The rest of the world melts away and the two of us are all that ever has been or ever will be.

He isn't singing anymore and we stopped swaying. I'm seized by the electricity surging between our bodies. The sound of our racing hearts fills the room. His lips crash onto mine and I can feel his fervor and devotion, his heart reaching out for mine.

This is the moment, the one I will never recover from. My life is now divided in two. There is before this kiss and there is after. I cling to the now, to this blissful moment, scared to face the new world and the possibilities it holds.

Too soon the song ends and our moment is over. Austin steps away quickly, not even looking at me. I'm desperate to see his face, to know he's as affected as I am. But he doesn't let me.

"Well, it's late. I'm gonna head out." He's at the door before I can even object. He turns back to me for the briefest of seconds. "Sorry again about crashing your night. Guess we're even now." His smirk is locked in place, but his eyes don't hold the same fearlessness. For the first time, I see Austin Jacobs flustered.

Chapter Nine

Austin

Shit.
Damn it.
Fuck!

I bolt out of Elizabeth's apartment knowing I fucked up. I fucked up bad. I got caught up playing boyfriend with her. It was stupid to sing along to that damn old song she had playing. It didn't mean anything.

She doesn't mean anything.

Just a job.

Except, Elizabeth isn't *just* anything.

She looked at me like I was her everything. I've never had anyone see me that way. Plenty of girls stare. I get eye-fucked on the daily. I'm an ice cream on a hot summer afternoon, a quick, easy treat. A momentary distraction from whatever shit is weighing on them. With Elizabeth, it's like she made a wish and can't believe it's come true. *Get the fuck over yourself.*

She's having fun with the novelty of a boy toy.

She isn't yours.

You've got another three weeks of fooling around and playing games. Then, you walk away.

When I get home I have a text from her, asking the same question I did earlier.

Goose: *Still on for Tuesday?*

Me: *Sure thing, boss.*

* * * *

I don't text or talk to her at all on Monday. It's the first day in a week that we haven't seen each other. Good. I need a break from her.

I dodge Devin's call and flake on our regular gym session. I don't need another lecture from him.

At afternoon practice, I push myself harder than I have all season, throwing myself into drills. The coaches appreciate it. Montgomery doesn't since it gives them more time to ride his lazy ass.

"Pick up the pace, Montgomery. My grandma can run smarter routes!" our receiver's coach shouts across the field. He jogs over to me as we both catch our breath and wait for the next set of drills.

"Still chasing little Miss Never-gonna-give-it-up?" Monte quips. I ignore him. "No wonder you're hustling. Trying to take your mind off those blue balls."

"Why are you so interested in my balls? Maybe you should grow a pair of your own." I know I shouldn't let him rile me up. The reaction is what he's after.

"Oh, I got a pair, you prick."

"What's your problem?"

"No problem. Just being real with you. You're nothing, you know that, right? A nobody. A fucking stray dog that little weird girl feeds scraps. She's playing with you, man. Out of fucking pity."

"You'd know, being pitiful is kind of your thing," I snap at him before setting off across the field at a dead sprint.

For the next few hours, I work myself to physical exhaustion. Route running, ladder drills, releases, blocking, hot potato. I don't stop moving for three hours except to take a quick drink of water. By the end of practice, my legs are jello and I can barely stand up.

Through it all, my mind doesn't stop racing with thoughts of Elizabeth. I don't picture her naked body. I picture those chocolate eyes the moment before I ran out of there. It wasn't pity. It was something I've never felt before.

* * * *

I roll my shoulders and take a few deep breaths as I stare at the door to Elizabeth's apartment Tuesday night. It doesn't stop my heart from racing. For the first time in my life I'm fucking nervous about a girl.

Man up, Jacobs.

I knock on her door. She seems surprised when she answers it.

"Hi," she mutters, staring at me quizzically. I guess she was expecting me to saunter in again.

I don't own her and it's important I remember that. No more playing boyfriend. Tonight I'm going to keep things flirty and casual.

"Hi," I reply, waiting to be asked into the apartment. I let my eyes wander over her. She's back in her baggy jeans, but she isn't wearing the standard loose T-shirt. She's in a tight tank top that'd give even a blind man the chance to admire how well-endowed she is.

The lettering stretched across her chest reads *Sorry I'm late. I didn't want to come.* That's Elizabeth, adorable and sexy all in one. The thirteen-year-old in me wants to bury my face in her tits, motorboating until I can't breathe. The twenty-one-year-old in me wants to make sure she comes. All. Night. Long.

"Hi," she says again, biting her lip with a coy smile. This girl is casually delectable.

"You said that already," I simper. "Can I come in? Or did you add voyeurism to our sex-abus?"

She gives me a light gasp before grabbing my shirt and pulling me into the apartment. She closes the door, crosses her arms and glares at me. I can't help but chuckle. She's beautiful when she's pissed.

"Stop staring!" she demands.

"Am I staring?" I ask with a wolfish grin. I haven't taken my eyes off her tits since she opened the door, but there's no need to admit that without teasing her first.

"You know you are."

"What could I possibly be staring at?"

"My…" She gestures to her chest, moving her hand in a big circle before re-crossing her arms.

"Your?" I plaster a stupid expression on my face, holding back my smile for as long as I can.

"My…chest." She almost whispers the word.

"Well, crossing your arms in that shirt makes it impossible for me not to stare at your…tits." She uncrosses her arms with a scoff and storms off.

"I think we need to work on your vocabulary tonight." I follow her into the kitchen.

"My vocabulary is exceptional. I scored a seven hundred and twenty on my verbal SAT," she touts.

"Congratulations, but that's not the vocabulary I'm concerned about."

She shakes her head at me.

"Say cock."

"What? Why?" she asks.

"You need a reason?"

She crosses her arms and purses her sexy lips. When I lower my gaze to her tits again, she drops her arms with an eye-roll. Eye-rolls shouldn't be sexy, but damn if Elizabeth Wilde doesn't make them hot.

"Just say it to prove you can."

"That's stupid."

"Say it."

"I don't want to."

She's being a brat. So, I push harder.

"Don't want to or you can't?"

"Are we eating dinner?" she asks.

"I already ate." We aren't fucking dating. She can make her own damn dinner. She pouts. Weird how we've already established a routine after only a week. "And don't try to change the subject."

"So what if I can't say it? It's not a big deal." She turns away from me, a soft blush rising on her cheeks.

"Yes, it is. How am I supposed to teach you how to fuck if you can't even say the word?" The light blush turns to a deep red as her whole body flushes.

"Fine. COCK!" she shouts at the top of her lungs before slapping her hand over her mouth. We stare at each other for a minute. I don't know who is more shocked, her or me.

A chuckle rumbles out of my chest. "It's a start."

She smiles back with tight lips. I walk over to the couch and pat the cushion next to me.

"Sit down. We'll start easy and work up to it, okay?" I give her a comforting smile.

"Okay," she tentatively agrees as she sits down across from me.

"Repeat after me. Endowments." I give her a devious smile and gesture to her chest.

"Endowments." Snark drips from her tongue and I love it.

"Chest."

"Chest," she parrots back.

"Breasts. Globes. Boobies." I ensure my face is stoic, as if I were giving an elocution lesson.

"Breasts, globes and boobies." She follows easily.

"Good. Tits."

"Tits." Her voice is confident and clear.

Easy, tiger, we're just getting started.

"Vagina. Lady bits. Snatch."

She copies me without hesitation, although her nose crinkles at the word snatch, which is excruciatingly cute.

"Pussy." I keep my eyes locked on hers. She doesn't flinch.

"Pussy." Her soft voice takes a sultry edge and I'm desperate to hear more dirty words from those full lips.

"Penis. Junk. Crotch."

"Crotch?" She recoils from the word. "I'm never going to say crotch."

"You just did. Twice." I give her a taunting grin.

"You know what I mean, Ass." She calls me ass like it's my name. Like it's a term of endearment.

"Fine. How about cunt?"

"Cunt," she answers, eyes locked on mine.

Hearing naughty words come from that pouty mouth is my undoing. I lean back and exhale, my mind racing with filthy thoughts.

"Fuck me," I murmur, surprised at how turned on I am without even touching her. Just the sound of her voice has me rock-hard. What is this woman doing to me?

"Fuck me," she repeats my words.

My little Goose isn't done. The realization brings a devious smile to my lips as I meet the challenge in her eyes.

You asked for it, sweetheart.

"Tell me you want my cock deep inside your pussy," I say flatly.

She shuts her eyes, swallows hard and takes a deep breath. I'd put money on her chickening out, right until her lips twist up mischievously. Her words come out slow and tormenting, oozing raw sex. I savor each and every one.

"I want your thick, hard cock deep inside my tight, wet pussy, fucking me until I can't help but scream your name in ecstasy." She leans forward and crawls toward me on the couch, inching closer with every syllable. She is the single sexiest thing I've ever seen. Her words hypnotize me. I'm in a trance, unable to look away from those deep, dark eyes.

Every drop of blood in my body surges south to my throbbing dick. I can't think, I can't move.

"Austin," she moans.

She makes my name sound filthier than anything she's said tonight. By the time she finishes, her mouth is inches from mine. Temptation rages through me. I fist my hands at my sides and hold back the animal desire to take her. Rough and hard, I'm desperate to claim her.

"Who are you?" I ask, my voice gravelly. I'm in awe of her. Amazed. And painfully aroused.

"Elizabeth Wilde. Nice to meet you." She sticks out her hand, barely able to fit it in the tiny space between our hot bodies. That smart mouth breaks the last of my restraint. I can't help but grab her hand and pull her flush against me.

"Smartass," I seethe before seizing her lips with mine.

I greedily slide my hands up her tank top, pulling it up and over her head in one smooth motion. I graze the soft, exposed swell of her chest with my lips as I unhook her bra.

"Wait." Her voice is shaky and breathless.

It takes all the willpower I have to pull away. She tucks a loose strand of hair behind her ear and bites her lip. My chest tightens at the sight.

"Don't you want to see my homework?" she asks in a near whisper.

As much as I'm eager to see every bit of her right now, the excitement in her eyes and the temptation of seeing her in some sexy lingerie is too much to resist.

"I absolutely do."

I give the crest of her beautiful breasts one last kiss each before I let her go. She scampers off toward her bedroom with one timid glance over her shoulder at me. I give her a reassuring smile. This girl has no idea what she does to me.

"It's not black. Or lacy," she calls out from her bedroom. *Thank God.* Maybe I stand half a chance of not creaming my jeans tonight.

"So what? Does it make you feel sexy?" I ask dismissively.

"Yes."

"Then it's perfect. Now, get your ass out here!" I demand.

The door to her bedroom creaks open, followed by the pitter-patter of her bare feet gingerly traipsing across the living room until she comes into view. My jaw drops.

It's not black and lacy. It's red and silky.

I devour every inch of her body, hungry for the sight of her delicious curves. The thin straps of the red teddy expose her slim shoulders. Her hard nipples peek through the thin fabric, which is held on by two meager strings tied in a small bow in the front. One quick pull and she would be standing there in nothing but her panties.

I resist the urge to unwrap her like a present, savoring the teasing delight of her pale skin against the scarlet lingerie. The fabric flares at her hips, exposing her smooth stomach. My gaze sinks lower to the matching red panties and her creamy thighs.

I've never wanted anything as much as I want Elizabeth right now.

"Well? Do you like it?" she asks timidly, as if there's a chance in hell I wouldn't approve.

I fucking love it.

Thankfully, I catch myself before I say the dirty *L* word. I'm too distracted to worry about how easily that word comes to mind.

"You look amazing." I don't know if it's my words or the obvious desire behind them that makes her smile, but it's the last straw. I can't resist any longer. I need to have my hands on her. I cross the living room in three large steps and take her in my arms. The force of our bodies slamming together causes us both to gasp.

I don't kiss her.

First, I need to know she's prepared for what's going to happen tonight.

"I'm going to take you into your bedroom, strip you naked and worship every inch of your body. I'm going to make you come until you are so exhausted you beg me to stop." My expression is serious and my voice sober. I mean every word.

"But the sex-abus..." She pauses, her breath picking up. She licks her lips. Gazing up at me with those trusting chocolate eyes, she whispers, "Okay."

I sweep her up in my arms and carry her back to her bedroom. I lay her down on the bed before taking a step back, trying to slow myself down. I want to luxuriate in every minute with Elizabeth tonight. I stand at the end of her bed, taking a moment to admire the tantalizing sight of her milky skin against the red silk.

She rakes her gaze down my body. I pull off my shirt, enjoying the way she bites her lip at the sight of my tight abs. She wants this as much as I do. Her gaze follows my hands as I flick open the fly on my jeans, one button at a time. I ease them down my thighs and kick them aside.

My thin boxer briefs riding low on my hips don't do much to contain my hard cock. She can see the outline of every inch. She swallows hard as she stares up at me. Her breath is ragged and I know she's both scared and excited.

"It's okay, Goose. We can take this as slow as you need," I tell her, not sure how much I mean it, how much self-control I have left. She nods but doesn't speak.

I kneel on the bed at her feet and crawl up her body. My fingers, lips, and tongue dance along her skin as I go. I kiss the inside of her thigh and graze her panties with my thumb. I lick the crest of her hip as I trace up her stomach with my fingertips. I suck on her neck and caress her hard nipples through the thin fabric.

I pick up one end of the tie at her chest, twirling it around my finger with a smile. I pull slowly, undoing the bow that's holding the delicate silk together. Once released, it glides down her sides and I'm rewarded with the glorious sight of her bare tits. I cup one in my hand and bring my mouth to the perky nipple of the other. Her skin is hot and delicious.

I spread her legs apart as I settle between them, resting just enough weight on her to feel the friction of our bodies coming together. I'd be in heaven if it weren't for how rigid she is underneath me. She's not the confident woman who was talking dirty on the couch just minutes ago. She's flipped that switch in her head again. Anxiety overwhelms her. She's scared and vulnerable. I need her to relax and trust me. Trust herself.

"You're holding your breath."

"Am I?" she says with a soft exhale.

"Yes. And you've got a death grip on the comforter," I point out without taking my hands or mouth off her.

"Sorry."

"You don't need to be sorry. About anything. Just relax."

"I can't."

"Why not?"

"I don't know." She lets out a labored sigh. She sounds defeated.

"Tell me what you're thinking," I demand as I suck her nipple into my mouth, causing her to gasp.

"I can't."

"You can." I trace my hand down her arm and slip my fingers in between hers, giving them a light squeeze. I lift my head and peer into her eyes. More than pleasure, this is about her feeling safe, confident and in control.

"A million things," she answers weakly.

"Such as?" I stare up at her, riveted.

"Like, was I supposed to shave *down there*? I mean, I'm trimmed, but are you expecting shaved? Is there such a thing as being *too* shaved? Why should I have to shave if you don't? That's a sexist double standard. What other primping was I supposed to do? I know I need to trim my fingernails. I bite my nails. Is that something guys care about? Should I get a haircut? Did I use enough deodorant this morning? What if I smell once we get sweaty? I wish I changed the sheets. What am I supposed to do with my hands? Am I supposed to touch you?" She only stops rambling when she runs out of breath.

"Wow. Okay. So, a lot going on up there." I smile and give her hand another light squeeze. "How about you try to focus on how this feels?" I dip my head and take her nipple into my mouth again, swirling my tongue around it firmly. She lets out a soft moan, but her body doesn't relax.

"I can't... I can't stop the thoughts."

Unwilling to give up, I rack my brain for how to get her out of her head.

"Are you willing to try something?" I ask tentatively.

She bites her lip, stares deep into my eyes and gives a gentle nod. I roll over and sit up against the headboard. I slip the lingerie off her shoulders and pull her into my lap. With her hips nestled between my thighs, her back against my chest, and my arms wrapped around her, we are intimately connected.

"Close your eyes."

She does so without question, dropping her head back against my shoulder. Now I can see her sweet face contorted with insecurity. My chest tightens at the sight.

"I want you to ignore the thoughts. The doubts. Focus only on my voice and my touch. Understand?"

She nods.

"Take off your panties," I command.

She doesn't move.

"Don't think. Just do it."

She furrows her forehead and pinches her eyes shut tighter but doesn't argue. She hooks her thumbs into the sides of her panties and slides them off, keeping her thighs closed tight the whole time.

She's completely naked and exquisitely beautiful.

I whisper into her ear, "I'm going to say a word. Just answer with whatever is on the tip of your tongue. Don't think. Just answer."

Again she nods.

"Hot," I breathe into her ear as I brush my fingers over her exposed skin. With a featherlight touch, I begin at her naked shoulders, dip down her collarbone, tease her nipples and stroke down her stomach to her hips. The light tickle of my fingers against her skin causes her to shudder against me. My entire body reacts, calling out for more, as the sensation surges through me.

"Cold."

"Sweet." I nip at her neck.

"Sour," she answers.

"Soft." I trail my hands back up the center of her body and cup her breasts. I tease her hard nipples, rolling them between my fingers with firm pressure. She squirms against me with a moan.

"Hard," she answers.

I rock my hips into her.

"Wet." I glide my hand down her body, slowing just below her belly button. She grabs my forearm firmly but doesn't stop me. "Don't think. Just answer. Wet?"

"Eager," she moans out as she releases my arm.

"Amazing," I whisper and dip my fingers into her silky folds, circling her sensitive clit.

"Terrifying." Her voice is both aroused and strained.

"Safe." I hold her tightly against me.

"Home," she answers as her body finally relaxes in my arms and her hips grind against mine, the passion rising in her as our bodies and words collide.

Desire. Want.

Lust. Need.

Craving. Hunger.

Delicious. Devour.

Her breath is shallow and fast. She's getting close. I'm desperate to feel her come apart in my arms.

"Goddess," I whisper in her ear and the wave of pleasure overtakes her as she climaxes. She moans and trembles. I almost come from her body writhing against mine. I hold her in my arms, savoring every second.

"Worshiped," she replies as she settles and her breath returns to normal.

Chapter Ten

Elizabeth

Wrapped up in Austin's body and his words, I lose myself to him over and over again.

He wasn't kidding about those great hands.

He's relentless in his pursuit of pleasuring me. In between climaxes, he holds me to his chest, our hearts beating together, trailing figure eights across my body in barely-there touches. Sometime around midnight my body can't take it any longer, every inch of my skin hypersensitive. He wasn't lying, I actually have to beg him to stop.

"Austin, please. No more. I'm exhausted." The words come out hoarse and dry. Even my voice is overworked. Austin's chest rumbles with laughter underneath me, sending soft vibrations through my overstimulated body. It's almost enough for me to ask for one more go.

Almost.

But right now, all I'm capable of is sleep. I could sleep for a decade.

"Had enough, Goose?" Even after hours, his sexy voice and warm breath on my neck are enticing. All night I've been the object of his skillful ministrations. He's been devoted to me and asked nothing in return. It must be a certain kind of torture to go so long without a release.

Why hasn't he asked me to touch him? Hell, why hasn't he even touched himself?

Maybe he thinks I'd freak out. Quite the opposite. I've yet to find a part of Austin that I don't enjoy gawking at. Touching. Kissing. I have a sudden naughty idea. I act on it before I can chicken out.

"I think maybe…" I roll over to face him. I'm staring into his eyes as I move my hand down his chest to his boxers. "Maybe it's your turn." I'm hoping to sound confident and sexy.

You missed by miles. More like mousy and creepy.

My poor attempt at seduction has Austin pulling my hand away. I'm not going to lie, the rejection is the emotional equivalent of getting punched in the nose, equal parts deeply horrifying and excruciatingly painful. It even makes my eyes water, much to my growing embarrassment.

"Not tonight." He places my hand on his firm chest and covers it with his own. He must have caught the bewildered look in my eyes. "I want to. Believe me, I want to." He gives his hips a little thrust, grinding against me as proof of his interest. "But tonight is about you, Elizabeth. Just you." He gives me a light kiss on the top of my head as he pulls me against his chest. His skin is soft and warm under me. I want to object. I want to explain how much I crave touching him, but I can't find the words.

"I… I want… I'd like," I start and stop about three times, unable to find my voice. He's watching me with hungry, gentle eyes that are at once disarming and arousing. I wish he didn't have this power over me. I hate that he does, that I let him.

"Forget it. Never mind." I roll over with a sigh, pulling the sheets tightly around me, and make sure to put enough space between us so that no part of our bodies is touching.

"What the fuck just happened?" he asks in confused awe.

I don't answer. He reaches out to touch me, but I flinch and pull away.

"You went from crazy sexy to crazy *crazy* in two seconds flat."

I still don't answer.

Screw him.

I will not let him have this power over me.

I can reject him too.

"Help me out here, my head's spinning. Elizabeth?" His voice is tender, but it does nothing to assuage the anger in me right now. "Elizabeth." He shifts to a stern reprimand.

He sits up in the bed and stares down at me. The muscles in his arms are tensing. He's trying to control his breath, inhaling deeply and holding it before letting it out in a sigh.

He's annoyed.

Join the club, partner!

"Fucking talk to me or I swear to God…" He trails off, leaving his threat to linger in the air, letting my mind fill in the blank with my worst fears.

Or I'll walk out that door and never come back.

"Elizabeth!" he shouts, exasperated. Note to self, Austin can't stand the silent treatment. Maybe I do have a little power over him after all.

"Fine!" I shout back at him. The bed sheets are thin, but I make sure to keep them in place around me before I confront him. I shoot straight up in bed, squaring my shoulders, and glare at him. "You're such an ass."

We lock eyes with excruciating intensity. The tension between us is off the charts. Austin's fists are clenched at his sides and his nostrils flare with each angry breath he takes. I have no idea if he wants to kiss me or kill me. I know the feeling.

"I want to be sexy. Irresistible," I hiss.

"You are." His voice is frank, flat.

"Obviously, I'm not." I gesture between us, illustrating the blatant distance.

My resistibility.

His rejection.

His face shifts from anger to something closer to confusion.

"Jesus, do I have to spell it out for you? I *want* to touch you, all right! I want to make you come. I want to have the same power over your body as you so clearly have over mine. But you don't seem to care and begging to touch your *cock* makes me sound like some desperate slut. So, like I said, forget it. Never. Mind."

Embarrassing rant complete, I flop back down onto the bed again and slap my hands over my face to hide how red I know I must be. I don't make a sound. I don't move an inch. I don't even breathe. Every ounce of my being is focused on the giant man in my bed, trying to figure out what he's going to do next.

If he's smart, he'll run.

He doesn't.

Austin lies down in bed next to me, tracing the line of my jaw with his nose. His lips tease my neck as his sultry baritone whispers, "Goose, if you want to touch me, all you had to do was say so."

"I just did," I deadpan. My heart's about to beat out of my chest, but I'm sure as hell not going to admit it.

"Always such a smartass." Without warning, he pushes my hand down into his boxers and wraps it around his hard length. I gasp.

Holy shit.

Holy shit!

Holy FUCKING shit!

"Fair warning, I'm not going to last long. You've kept me hard as a fucking rock all night. All week, actually." He tightens my grip on him as he guides my hand up and down his length. "Listening to you moan, feeling you come on my fingers." His voice grows carnal in my ear as he rocks his hips in unison with the strokes of my hand. "You have no idea how badly I want you." He moves his hand to my breast, cupping and firmly massaging. "I want to be inside you, feel you come on my cock."

He caresses my neck with his lips as his sinfully dirty words heat me to my core. I moan and squirm against him. His shaft is slick with pre-cum and I glide over him faster in my excitement, imagining him inside me with every stroke. He slides his hand down between my wet thighs and the second he touches my clit, I explode, screaming his name.

Austin follows after, with a raspy, "Elizabeth."

After our bodies stop quivering, Austin leans over the side of the bed and grabs the tank top I was wearing earlier. He wipes off my hand then himself before tossing it into a hamper at the end of the bed.

Austin lies back down and pulls me into him. I rest my head in the delicious place where his shoulder meets his chest, a place so comfortable I think it was designed just for me. The last thing I remember as I drift off to sleep is him stroking my back in sweet figure eights.

* * * *

My brain vaguely registers some sort of beeping sound just before Austin stirs under me, pulling away. I only closed my eyes a minute ago. It can't possibly be morning.

"What time is it?" I mumble, only half awake.

"Early. Really early." He reaches for his cell phone in his pants on the floor and silences the alarm. "Go back to sleep. I've gotta head out or I'll be late."

"You're leaving?" I'm sulking, but after last night, how can he run out first thing in the morning? I pull the covers around my body, colder now without Austin lying next to me. Aren't we supposed to have breakfast, or cuddle, or at least talk?

He isn't your boyfriend!

It's getting harder every day to think of Austin as just some playboy jock.

An employee.

I know this is nothing more than a job to him, but I can't help feeling there is a connection between us. There has to be something here. He has to feel it too.

"I've gotta be in the gym by six-thirty. I'm already running late." Or, maybe not. I'm a sentimental idiot.

170

The sun is coming up. I watch as Austin pulls on his jeans. I can barely make out the hard lines of his muscled body in the darkness, but I stare just the same. He turns and catches me watching, so I snap my eyes away. Hearing Austin laugh at me, I pull my knees up to my chest protectively. I'm so exposed. He notices.

"I'll be back tonight. Think you can survive the next twelve hours without me, Goose?"

"Oh, are you still here? I hadn't noticed," I deadpan, rolling away from him. The bed sinks down as he crawls over to me, laughing lightly. His touch tingles my neck as he brushes aside my hair before he places a kiss below my ear. It's becoming his new favorite spot. I'm a fan too.

"Admit it, you're gonna miss me," he demands. He traces his hand along my side and grips my hip firmly.

"Parts of you," I quip. He laughs out loud. The rich, deep, sexy sound makes my heart beat faster. I love Austin Jacobs' laugh. And many, many other parts of him. How many individual parts of a person can you love before you just love *them*? Maybe I should start counting, just to be on the safe side.

Thing number one I love about Austin—his laugh.

"Smartass. Rest up, Goose. I've got a date with that pretty little pussy of yours in a few hours." He couples his naughty words with a chaste kiss to my temple. The combination has me desperate for him to stay. The words are in my throat, ready to beg him to come back to bed, but I can't make them come out. I don't move. I don't speak. I lie there and listen to the sound of Austin getting ready to leave.

I listen to him pull his shirt on.

Say something sexy.

I can't. I listen to him open my bedroom door and step into the living room.

Say something clever.

I don't. I listen to him put on his shoes and open the front door.

Say anything!

I've got absolutely nothing. I even hold my breath. Then he's gone. I miss him already.

How weird is that?

I have a couple of hours before my first class at ten, but it's impossible to get back to sleep. I roll around in bed, growing irritated and frustrated for no reason. My queen-sized bed is ridiculously huge with just me in it.

I give up on sleeping and get dressed. I aimlessly wander around my apartment, too listless to be productive but too wired to do nothing. I can't even focus long enough to play Rule Them All. Instead, I sit on my couch and count my movies. Fifty-six. I run updates on my computer. I take out my trash. I'm having a heated internal debate between organizing my sock drawer and cleaning my oven, two things I've never done in my life, when my father calls.

"Good morning, Beth. I was expecting to get your voicemail this early." He almost sounds disappointed that I picked up the phone.

"I was up early this morning," I explain myself cryptically, avoiding the mention of my sleepover with Austin. "How are things?"

"Fine. Fine. I wanted to remind you about the dinner this weekend."

"Dinner?"

"Beth," he says my name like an admonishment. Two minutes into this conversation and I'm already in trouble for not remembering some dinner. "We are hosting a dinner party for family, friends and a select group of business associates. Better to get these things out of the way before the holiday season is here and everyone's schedules become impossible to coordinate."

I hate how he says 'we', as if I have any interest in this stupid party.

"Right. *That* dinner." I roll my eyes, but try to keep the derision out of my voice. I hate going to these things. My mother used to be all about them. It was like we were gearing up to host the Queen of England with the way she obsessed over the smallest detail.

I always feel like one more decoration, and not anyone's favorite at that. I get dressed up, stand around awkwardly and try to make pleasant small talk. Most of the night consists of plastering on a fake smile while my extended family and my father's friends make condescending remarks about me. It's about as much fun as being the assistant to a novice knife thrower.

"I expect you both to be here early. Cocktail hour will commence promptly at six-thirty."

I hold back the sigh perched in the back of my throat.
Wait, did he say both?
Both who? He can't mean Austin.

"Wait, both of us who?"

"You and Austin, of course, dear. Are you feeling all right?"

Nope. Nuh-uh. No way. Not happening. Negative ghost rider, the pattern is full. Ix-nay on the arty-pay. Hell will freeze over before I take Austin to my father's dinner party. Even if I could convince Austin to come with me—and that is one hell of a *big* if—the last thing I need is him in a room full of my pompous family.

"Sorry, but I don't think Austin is going to be able to make it."

"Oh, and why is that?"

"He has practice." And by practice, I mean happily spending his free time away from his non-girlfriend-quasi-boss.

"Stop being ridiculous. Of course he will attend. This party is more important than some football practice."

"His scholarship is dependent on him playing football. His practices are important." At least, I assume they are, whenever they happen to be.

"Relationships are about compromise and sacrifice. I am sure Austin can talk to his coach, explain the importance and escort you to dinner this weekend."

Oh good, just what every young woman wants, relationship advice from her father.

"But I—"

"Elizabeth Marie Wilde, we are done discussing it. I expect you both here at a quarter past six on Sunday."

"Yes, Father." When he uses my full name, I've lost the battle. There's no point in arguing. I'd be wasting my breath.

"Good. Now, I have to go. I have a meeting."

"Bye."

"Goodbye, Beth."

I throw the phone down on the coffee table and collapse onto the couch in defeat. Would my father believe it if I told him Austin was in a freak accident? He couldn't come because he was struck by lightning? Abducted by circus clowns?

Couldn't be any less believable than the truth— Austin didn't come with me because he doesn't care about me. He's only hanging out with me because I'm pathetically paying him to teach me to have sex because I'm too weird and awkward to figure it out on my own.

I'm lost in my imagination, thinking of the most believable unbelievable thing that could happen to keep Austin from coming on Sunday, when my phone buzzes. My breath catches seeing his name flash across my screen.

Dork.

Austin: *Dinner tonight?*

Me: *Is that an offer or a question?*

I hope it's an offer. I love it when Austin cooks for me. There's something sexy about a man who can cook.

Thing number two I love about Austin—his cooking.

Austin: *Both?*

Me: *Then, yes?*

Austin: *That an answer or a question?*

Me: *An answer, ass*

Austin: *Good to know you're just as feisty digitally as in person*

Me: *Shut up*

Austin: *I'm not talking*

Me: *You know what I mean!*

Austin: *Almost never. See ya tonight*

The short exchange with Austin leaves me with a big fat stupid grin on my face. I'm happy for all of five minutes, right until I remember the conversation with my father.

* * * *

I log into my game when I get back from class. Before Austin, I used to spend a couple of hours every day working on Uforia. It takes a lot of effort to keep a country running, after all. A few days are a lifetime in game time. But now having Austin over almost every day, I haven't even logged on in a week, other than to talk to Jackie. The little firecracker doesn't let me forget it either. She hits me up in video chat as soon as I log on.

"Where the fuck have you been?" she screeches at me. "I thought about calling the cops in case you were trapped under something heavy, like Austin's cock."

I don't respond to her taunting. It only encourages her.

"Yeah, sorry. I've been out for a bit. School has been crazy lately."

"Bullshit. School isn't what's been keeping you up all night."

"Whatever, Jackie." I don't bother arguing with her. She's right. Austin is what kept me up last night. And I loved every earth-shattering minute of it. "What's new?"

"Nothing much. Same old douche canoes needing to be reminded what manners are. I don't want to talk about these jackholes. Let's talk about your sexy slice of a man."

"I'd rather not. Has The Federation lifted sanctions against Cordovia?"

"Well, I wish I could pee standing up and chocolate bars grew on trees. The secret to happiness in life is getting used to disappointment. And who the fuck cares about Cordovia? I want to hear about Austin's big, beautiful cock."

"Ewww, Jackie!" I can't keep my face from turning bright red. I hate it when Jackie pushes my buttons this bad. I wish I had better control over myself. "And technically speaking, chocolate does grow on trees. The cocoa plant whose scientific name is theobroma cacao—"

"God, you're such a nerd it hurts sometimes." She doesn't let me share my wealth of random plant knowledge. Guess we're done with that topic. "So, did you try on that sexy little negligee for him last night?"

"I did…" I trail off, hoping not to have to explain the rest of the night. My face will turn a whole new shade of red, previously not seen in nature.

"And?"

"And he took it off me and we fooled around." I'm vague, but more descriptive than I was hoping to be. I doubt it will be enough to appease Jackie.

"Tell me *everything*. Describe every girthy inch."

"I couldn't say."

"Oh, come one. Give a single girl something to get through those long lonely nights."

"No, I mean, I really *couldn't* say. He never got naked."

"Pump the breaks. You mean he's seen all your little bits, but you have no idea what he's packing underneath the hood? How's that even possible?"

"I don't know. I mean, I *felt* it. I just haven't *seen* it. He said last night was just about me."

"Fuck me, that's sexy. The last guy I was with came on my tits, rolled over and asked, 'You're good, right?' Selfish prick. Isn't it kind of weird you haven't seen him yet? I mean, you guys have been fucking around pretty heavily for almost two weeks now."

"I haven't really thought about it." I have. A lot. I wrote a sex syllabus, for Christ's sake!

"What if he's tiny?"

"Believe me, that isn't a problem," I say without thinking. Jackie stares at me with her mouth open. "I've, you know, *touched* it."

"Naughty Lizzy!" Jackie giggles into the mic.

"Shut up. This was all your idea," I snap, extra annoyed at being called Lizzy.

"Hey, no judgment here. I'm proud of you. And maybe a little jealous. I could use my own manwhore."

"He's not a manwhore. Jesus," I admonish her. I'm pissed. I don't know why I'm so defensive of Austin, but I can't seem to help it. "He's a really good guy, actually."

"Is that so?"

"He's sweet. And funny. And…" I stop myself when I see the goofy smile on Jackie's face. "What? What's that look for?"

"You like him, don't you?"

"Duh. That's why I picked him." I know what she's getting at, but I blow it off, trying not to dig myself any deeper than I already am.

"No, Lizzy. You *like* him like him," she taunts in a high-pitched girly voice.

"Don't call me Lizzy. And no, I don't."

Jackie gives me a knowing stare.

"Fine. A little."

She crosses her arms and keeps staring at me, boring holes into my soul through the screen.

"Okay. Fine. I like him. A lot. So what? It doesn't matter." I don't mention that I actually love parts of him. As long as I don't love too many, I'll be fine.

"Ha! I knew it!" She licks her finger and makes an imaginary mark in the air, keeping score of how many times she's right. It's a lot. "Just be careful, okay? Don't forget, this guy is a major player."

"I know. Believe me, I know. I'm not planning our honeymoon to Niagara Falls or anything. I'm not delusional. It's just..." I trail off, unable to explain how Austin makes me feel.

"Just what?"

"He's...not what I thought, you know? He's more than I imagined."

"Yummy. How many inches more we talkin'?"

"Jackie!" I drop my face into my hands.

"Whatever, you know you love me."

"I tolerate you," I tease with an eye-roll.

"Just remember, Lizbit, it's supposed to be easy, dirty fun, not happily ever after."

"I know..."

"I'm not just worried about you. I'm worried about myself. If he hurts you, I'd have to kill him. Then I'd end up in prison and I don't think delicate little me would do well behind bars."

I snort, laughing at the idea of 'delicate' Jackie. "Please, you'd be running the place within a week!" We share a laugh.

"True. But orange just isn't my color."

I startle at the sound of a knock on the door before a wide smile forces its way onto my face. Austin doesn't wait for me to open the door this time. He lets himself in. I have to admit, I'm happy he's back to acting like he owns the place. I turn away, so he doesn't see my excitement, which gives Jackie a clear shot of my eager expression.

"Told you," Jackie chides again at the sight of my smile and googly eyes.

"Yeah, yeah. You're always right," I tell her with a sigh as Austin's tall frame appears behind me.

"Hi, Jackie," his smooth voice calls out.

"Hi, man meat," she replies flatly. Austin chuckles. Yep, that's my favorite sound in the whole world.

"Bye, Jackie!" I chirp, closing the chat window.

"Man meat?" Austin asks.

"Yeah, that's Jackie. Subtle as a sledgehammer." I shrug noncommittally, which seems to be enough for Austin, who heads to the kitchen. "She asked me why I haven't seen your *you know* yet." I vomit up the words before I can think better of it.

"My what?" Austin's expression is stoic.

We're back to this. He knows exactly what I'm talking about, but he isn't going to let me get away with not saying it. I need to warm up to it. I can't just spit the words out.

"You know you've seen *all* of me, but I haven't seen all of you."

"You're seeing me right now."

"You know what I mean, Austin."

"How am I supposed to know what you mean, when you can't say the words, Elizabeth?" He locks his beautiful blue eyes on me in a challenge. That sexy little smirk crosses his full lips.

Thing number three I love about Austin, and also hate — his irresistible smirk.

"I thought we went over this last night."

"Fine. Penis. Penis. Penis. P-E-N-I-S. Penis. Why haven't I seen your penis, Austin?" I cross my arms, beyond annoyed. He's so exhausting.

"If you wanted to see my *cock*, Goose, all you had to do was say so." He walks past me into the living room and takes off his shirt. I'm sitting there, totally frozen, staring at him. I've seen it before, but his body is amazing. His defined arms, his firm chest, his chiseled abs — every inch of him is delectable.

"What are you doing?" I ask before kicking myself.

He's getting naked, you idiot! Now shut up before he stops taking his clothes off!

"Getting naked, as requested." He keeps his eyes locked on mine as he unbuttons his jeans. The slow tease has me in heavenly anguish, feasting on every newly exposed inch of his skin and hungry for more.

"Right now?" I ask, swallowing a lump in my throat.

Shut up! my brain screams at me. My heart is racing and there's a growing ache between my thighs at watching Austin Jacobs strip in my living room.

"Right. Now." He hooks his thumbs in his boxers before sliding them off slowly, making a show of his little striptease. I try to keep my eyes above his waist for as long as I can, which is all of half a second. Apparently I have no self-control when it comes to Austin. I lower my eyes to his manhood now on full display in front of me.

It is official. Austin Jacobs is a god and I've happily converted to the Church of Maverick.

Praise the lord and pass the condoms. Hallelujah!

"You doin' okay over there?" he asks. There are no words left in my vocabulary. I'm incapable of formulating a response for several agonizing minutes. He's undisturbed, confident as ever with his flawless naked self.

"Yep. Good for you." *What did I just say? I think I'm having a stroke. Is that burnt toast?*

"Your turn." Austin points at me with a panty-dropping smile while he literally asks me to drop my panties.

"I'm good." I spin around and face back toward the empty kitchen, desperately hoping he'll let it go.

Nope. He's a dog with a bone. And by bone, I mean extremely large...*bone.*

Austin wraps his arms around my waist and picks me up off the bar stool like I don't weigh a thing.

"Tonight's lesson is getting comfortable in your own skin," he says. He slips his hands under my shirt. I don't stop him. I'm too distracted by the fact that he's naked. And pressed up against my back.

And naked.

Thing number four I love about Austin—any time he's naked.

He makes quick work of my clothes. His nimble fingers unhook my bra in one motion, sliding it off my body with a soft moan in my ear. He cups my breasts, teasing the nipples for a minute before he trails down my stomach to the button of my jeans.

Austin undressing me from behind, as if he's an extension of myself, is incredibly sensual. I'm ashamed to think he's going to find out how wet I already am for him, but I'm not capable of stopping him at this point. I'm not capable of remembering my own name right now.

Yep, must have been a stroke.

He slides off my jeans and panties at the same time. When he reaches my ankles, I pick up each foot for him to peel off the last strip of clothing and toss it aside. His touch keeps us connected as he stands back up, trailing his fingers along either side of me. When he reaches my hips, he pulls my ass against his erection and I let out a whimper. He massages my breast with one hand and glides the other between my thighs.

"Did you miss me, Goose?" he coos into my ear. I can't formulate words, but I manage to nod. He sucks on my neck and I bite my lip. "I want to hear you say it."

"Yes," I moan as I lean back into him.

"Yes what?" he demands.

"Yes, I missed you."

"Good." He lets me go with a quick slap on the ass and struts back into the kitchen. Yes, struts. Austin does a naked strut into my kitchen like he just won the Nobel Prize for sexiness. In his defense, if that were a thing, he'd certainly be a contender.

I cover my girly bits and look around for my clothes on the floor.

"Don't you dare." My eyes snap up to him at the sound of his firm voice. "You heard me. Don't you dare cover up. You've got no secrets. I've already seen all there is to see. Plus, I deserve a nice view while I make us dinner." I don't put my arms down. Instead, I meet his challenging glare with a mischievous grin.

I stumble backward into the living room until I'm standing in the pile of his discarded clothes. Holding his undivided attention, I bend down gingerly, trying to avoid giving him too much of a show, and pick up his shirt off the floor. Before I can get it over my head, Austin is out of the kitchen and tackling me onto the couch. I know he's an athlete and all, but damn he's fast.

He's lying on top of me, chest to chest, a smolder in his eyes. We're both naked. For a moment I think he's going to claim me right here on the couch. Then his face lights up with wicked delight and the tickling begins. I'm not just ticklish. I'm I-might-actually-die-if-you-don't-stop ticklish. My hysterical laughter fills the entire apartment and I start begging.

"Austin, stop. I can't breathe!" I frantically plead in between uncontrollable laughing bouts.

"You gonna stop hiding that killer body from me?" He pauses long enough for me to answer.

"Just the shirt?" I try to bargain even though I have zero leverage.

"No deal." He grabs his shirt out of my hands and throws it across the room before resuming my torture.

"Please! Stop!"

"Not until you're begging for mercy!"

I try to worm out from underneath him, working every angle, but his solid body is everywhere. There's no escape except to give him what he wants.

"Fine. Mercy, Austin! Mercy."

Austin sits back, making a point of admiring every inch of my exposed body. It takes all the willpower I have not to cover myself under his intimate examination.

"Good," he declares with a sexy smile before strutting back into the kitchen.

Thing number five I love about Austin—that damn naked strut.

Chapter Eleven

Austin

Cooking naked has its challenges, especially with the raging hard-on I'm sporting after having Elizabeth writhing naked under me. That's not the way I'd prefer to make her scream my name, but it'll do for now. At least I get to watch her sexy naked ass all night.

She hasn't moved off the couch. She's doing some sort of breathing exercises. Either she's quietly repeating "Loosey-goosey" to herself or I'm going crazy. It's cute she uses the little catchphrase I taught her, but I don't dare let on I can hear her. Something tells me my Goose would rather die than admit I was right. She's a willful little thing. I thought she might actually pass out from being tickled before she finally caved.

"What's for dinner?" she asks from across the kitchen island, having finally walked over while my back was turned.

She isn't covering herself per se, but she's sitting down and leaning forward with hunched shoulders, clinging to as much modesty as she can. I'll let her get away with it.

For now.

"My favorite thing to put my mouth on, tacos," I answer, earning me an eye-roll. I can't help but laugh. That saucy eye-roll is even cuter when she's naked.

"Can I ask you something...personal?" She fidgets with a dish towel on the counter, folding and unfolding it repeatedly. My shoulders tense immediately, but I don't answer. "It's just that I'm feeling kind of vulnerable here. You know, all *exposed*. So I thought it might help if you felt a little exposed too."

"I'm as naked as the day I was born. How much more exposed do you need me to be, Goose?"

"That's different. You're comfortable with your body." Her hungry eyes eat me up and I have to smile.

"Let me get this straight. You want to ask me questions to make me uncomfortable emotionally? Because you're uncomfortable physically?"

"Yeah, basically."

"And you expect me to say yes to that?"

"Yeah, basically. Please?"

I'd rather pull my fingernails out with rusty pliers than stand here answering Elizabeth's personal questions, but how big of a pussy would that make me? She's sitting across from me butt-ass naked. It scares the shit out of her, but she's facing her fears. I owe her at least the same in return.

Fuck it. Let's do this.

I know I'm going to regret the shit out of this, before I even say, "Fine. Ask away."

She studies me with those chocolate eyes, scrutinizing my body. "Why don't you have any tattoos?"

I let out a nervous laugh. To be honest, I'm relieved. That kind of personal question I can handle.

"Why don't you?" I shoot back at her.

"I hate needles."

"You're going to make a hell of a doctor one day," I chide.

"Shut up. I'm afraid to get poked with them. I'll be fine doing the poking."

"I know what you mean," I deadpan.

She throws the dish towel at me with an exasperated, "Ass. Can you ever be serious? It won't kill you, you know!"

"Maybe it would. Maybe it wouldn't. Why risk it?" I love riling her up. I can tell exactly how much of her blushes when she's naked.

"Just answer the question, Maverick," she demands with a cross of her arms and a shake of her head. Maybe it makes me an idiot, but I enjoy that stupid nickname, even when I know she's using it to be patronizing.

"Sure, Goose. I don't have tattoos because I don't give a shit enough about something to have it stare me in the face every day. Don't do forevers, remember?"

"Not even family?" She waits for a reaction. I don't give her one. "Your mom?"

"We weren't close." My tone is clipped, but Elizabeth keeps going anyway.

"What was she like?" Her voice is gentle and caring, but I don't give a fuck. I don't want to play this fucked-up game anymore.

"What the fuck do you care?" I snap at her.

I shove aside the pan of ground beef I'm browning. It hits the stove's backsplash with a clang.

It's been over a decade since my mom died and even longer since the last time I actually saw her. I don't know how many times I've tried to forget her. Forget her face, her voice, her smell. Forget all the broken promises. Forget all the nights going to sleep cold, alone and hungry. Forget that she never gave a fuck about me, just her next high. I can't. That's the most fucked-up part of all.

I will never forget the woman who never remembered me.

"I care."

I feel the conviction in Elizabeth's voice deep in my chest.

"About you."

My chest tightens at her words. I tell myself she doesn't mean them. It's pity, not love. Funny how often the two get confused.

"I'm not a fucking charity case, Elizabeth. Keep your pity to yourself." I slam my fist down on the counter, seething.

"Are you serious?" She laughs at me, a sickening cackle. Every muscle in my body goes tense. My hands ball into fists. I'm so angry I can't see straight. How dare she laugh at me? Who the hell does she think she is? I'm two seconds from tearing the entire apartment to pieces when her words shatter me.

"I'm the charity case! I'm *fucking paying* you to take my virginity. How pathetic is that?"

It's the first time I've ever heard her really swear. I turn around in time to see the first tear stream down her cheek. She brushes it away quickly, as if ashamed. Her bottom lip is quivering with the struggle to hold back her emotions. She's as broken as I am. I'm too shocked to respond, so she continues, her voice choked with dejection.

"I don't have friends. You're the closest I have to…" She trails off for a minute and I can see her brain revving into overdrive. "I'm not delusional. I know you're only here because I'm paying you to be. But we could be more. Friends, I mean. I want us to be friends."

I want to believe her. Seeing the sincerity in her eyes, I almost do. I turn away again before I lose myself in them. Lose myself to her.

I'm quiet for a long time. We both are. I can't even admit to myself what I want to be to Elizabeth, but being her friend is at least the beginning of something real. I'm talking before I'm even really sure what I want to say.

"She was young. Beautiful. Fun. And a drug addict. And a shitty mother. Sometimes a shitty human being. I hope to hell I'm not anything like her."

"What was it like growing up in foster care?" Her voice is calm and even now. If she has a reaction to my confession, she doesn't show it.

"Shitty. And lonely." I grab the discarded meat pan and salvage what I can of our dinner. I'm desperate to have something to do with my hands, to have a goal to distract myself with.

"Did they hurt you?"

"No. It wasn't a joy ride, but I never had anyone put out lit cigarettes on my arms, if that's what you're asking." I think about the years I spent bouncing between the houses of strangers, some well-intentioned, some not. "I was luckier than some kids, I guess. Most of the people I stayed with were decent enough. They just didn't love me. In their defense, I was kind of a little prick. If my own mother couldn't love me, why should some foster mom?" There's too much pain in my voice to pull off my sarcastic joke.

Sack up, Jacobs! You're whining about ancient fucking history.

"I think my parents loved me. I just don't think they liked me. I was a mistake." Her voice is soft behind me. She's talking to herself more than anything.

"You mean an accident?"

"No, I mean a mistake. I don't think people as controlled as my parents ever do anything by accident. They had a kid because that's what people do, but I think they regretted it. I was more a life accessory than their child."

Her confession seems as painful as mine. She's hunched forward, her shoulders slouched as she curls into herself. My fingers itch to touch her. Shoving down the urge to wrap her in my arms and hold her until that tension releases from her body, I take a deep breath and focus on our food.

I finish putting together all the toppings of our tacos and spread them out in a mini assembly line on the kitchen island. I don't go to sit next to her. I stand in the kitchen, needing the distance. We eat in companionable silence, each lost in our own memories. We clean up the kitchen, working together without words. She doesn't even bother hiding her body as we do. Being naked together doesn't seem as big a deal anymore.

I'm able to admire all of her in a new light. Don't get me wrong, in both my shirt and her red lingerie, she's dead sexy. But simply naked, she's something different. Something more. Her luscious curves are sensuous rather than sexual. She has an intangible quality to her, something natural and pure that's captivating. We finish cleaning and she catches me staring at her. I don't look away or try to hide it.

"You're beautiful," I tell her, because she needs to hear it. And she is, inside and out.

She blushes from head to toe, flustered.

"Movie?" she asks.

"Movie," I answer.

She fusses with the TV and I get comfortable lying across the entire couch. When she turns around and sees me, she crosses her arms and taps her foot like an impatient child.

"And where exactly am I supposed to sit?"

I tap the sliver of couch next to me and tell her, "Right here."

She huffs but obeys. She sits on the edge of the couch cushion, reminding me of our first night together. That was a lifetime ago. It's like I've known Elizabeth most of my life. *How did she do that?* I wrap my arm around her waist and pull her down to the couch, nestling her against me snugly.

My behavior earns me a squealing reprimand. "Austin!"

"Cozy?" I ask.

"Not really," she answers with a smile in her voice.

"Good," I reply with a laugh.

Both of us lying on the couch is a tight fit, but we manage. She's short and fits perfectly against me, head tucked under my chin so I can see. I grab the blanket she keeps on the back of the couch and drape it over both of us as I wrap my arms around her. "What are we watching?"

"You'll see, Maverick." She presses Play and I know almost immediately what movie she chose.

Top-motherfucking-*Gun!*

The source of our stupid nicknames.

My Goose is a clever little thing.

The movie is playing in the background, but I'm not paying attention. I've seen it a dozen times. Who hasn't? That's not why I'm distracted. I can't stop thinking about the woman pressed against me.

This is easy, even though it's one of the most foreign things I've ever done. I've never cuddled on a couch and watched a movie with a chick. It's so weirdly domestic. Most of what we do feels this way. Weirdly *un*weird. I can't help but wonder what it would be like to be with Elizabeth. Not having sex. Well, I fantasize about that too. But right now, I want to know how it'd feel to call her mine.

"Why didn't you just ask me out?" I spit, not caring that I'm interrupting the movie.

"Ha ha. Very funny," she scoffs.

I give her a squeeze to let her know I'm waiting for an actual answer.

"Wait? You're serious?"

"Yeah. It couldn't have been any riskier than *propositioning* me."

She gives me a sharp elbow in the ribs, a friendly reminder that she doesn't agree with my characterization.

"Seriously, why didn't you just ask me out?"

"Easy. Because you would've said no."

"You don't know that." I can't see her face, but I'd bet my left nut she's rolling her eyes.

"Yes. I do." Her body tenses against me and I wait to see if she keeps going. "What the hell do I have to offer a guy like you?"

A guy like me? What does that mean? I'm the one who has nothing to offer.

She's quiet again for a minute before finally adding, "Other than money."

"You have no idea, do you?" How can she not know how amazing she is? I hold her close, afraid she'll slip away.

"About what, Austin?" The bleakness in her voice is a knife to my stomach. I want to tell her, but I won't say the words out loud. If she hasn't realized she's too good for me yet, I'm not going to be the one to mention it.

"Elizabeth, you're hot," I tell her instead.

She laughs awkwardly, not believing me.

"I'm serious. I mean, in a nerdy, naughty librarian sort of way, but yeah. You're pretty hot."

"Seriously?" she questions and I can't help but laugh. She's so much more than just hot. She's a weird little goddess I can't get out of my head. She doesn't have any idea of the power she wields.

"Yes. Seriously." There's zero doubt in my voice.

"So, if I'd asked you out, you would've said yes?" she challenges.

In all honesty, probably not. I don't date. And if I did, Elizabeth isn't my type. She's too…everything.

"I guess we'll never know."

I think back to the first time I saw her, sitting across from me at that table in the library, nervous enough to faint and not able to control that smart mouth of hers. I'd be lying if I said she took my breath away. But if I'm honest, there was something about her even in that first meeting that made me curious about her. Hell, I'm not even sure what I would've said if she'd asked me out. Maybe it's a good thing she didn't.

We're both quiet again, happy to pretend to watch the movie.

"Okay, fine. I might as well just say it," she blurts out as if she was in the middle of a conversation with herself that she just decided to include me in. "I need a favor."

She's fidgeting with the blanket, twisting it in her fingers over and over again. She has the worst poker face.

"Oh yeah? Another proposition?"

She takes a deep breath and all at once rambles, "Is there any way you'd think about coming to a dinner party at my father's house this Sunday? He's insisting you come, which is entirely your fault."

"Because I'm too charming for my own good?"

Cue another eye-roll.

"No. Because you barged in last weekend. Then pretended to be this sweet and loving boyfriend," she admonishes me. "Anyway, my father wants you to come. Seems he approves of us. I think he sees me differently with you around. He's realizing I've grown up." She's fidgeting again. "But whatever. It doesn't matter. I'm sure I can tell him you were killed in a freak weightlifting accident or drank a tainted protein shake or something." She crosses her arms and tries to pull away, almost falling onto the floor in the process. I pull her back into me to keep her from running away.

Tainted protein shake? Where does she get this stuff?

It's dangerous to play house with her again. Plus, let's face it, I'm not exactly 'dinner party' material. But it took a lot of courage for her to ask me. After everything we've shared tonight, I can't stomach the idea of saying no to her.

"I'll come." My response is curt.

"What?" she asks, somewhat shocked. I don't think she believes me.

"I said I'll come. After all, what are friends for?" I keep my voice light, giving her a little reassuring squeeze. "But I have my own favor to ask too." I take a deep breath before I ask, wondering how much I'm going to regret this. "I'll come to your dinner *this* weekend if you come to my game *next* weekend. It's family night."

"Family night?"

I don't think she's ever been to a college sports game, so I shouldn't be surprised she doesn't know what a family night is.

"Yeah, it's when the families of all the players come. We each have a reserved section. Mine's always empty because, you know, orphan." I'm glib, trying to downplay the whole thing in case she says no.

I've had three years of empty stands. The only person who's ever bothered to come see me play is Devin. It was the same in high school. For the most part, I'm used to it. I don't really think about it anymore. But it wouldn't suck having Elizabeth up in the stands cheering for me. She doesn't answer and I get nervous.

"Since you crashed our party last week, my teammates have been pretty fucking annoying. It would get them off my back if you were there." This has nothing to do with the guys. The pricks haven't said shit about my family — or lack of one — since I threatened to fuck James' mom freshman year.

"Okay," is her soft reply.

"Okay?" I'm not able to hide the excitement in my voice.

"Yeah. I'll come. It's a date." She catches herself and tries to backpedal. "I mean, not a *date* date. Obviously. I just mean, I'm in. It's a deal. A plan."

"Deal."

Chapter Twelve

Elizabeth

The now-familiar sound of Austin's alarm is followed by his gruff morning voice behind me streaming a few choice obscenities. We didn't even make it to bed this time, falling asleep huddled together on the couch. Austin moves to get up and I almost fall off.

"Shit, sorry." He catches me right before I faceplant on the floor. Thank God for those athletic reflexes. He manages to climb over me and gets up. He leaves me the blanket we were sharing, which means he's now standing in my living room completely naked.

This is a view I could get used to.

I gawk at him, my tired brain too busy taking in the sight of his glorious body to bother telling me to keep my mouth closed.

Austin catches my flagrant ogling and chastises me with, "My eyes are up here, Goose."

Way to go, Elizabeth!

I pull the blanket up over my head to hide my complete embarrassment. Austin laughs.

"No more sleeping on the couch. I think my neck is going to be jacked all day," he says with a yawn and a stretch.

"Sorry," I call out from my sanctuary under the blanket.

"For eye-fucking me? You're hardly the first."

I shoot up on the couch and shout, "I was not."

Austin dips his eyes to my chest, which I exposed in my rush to confront him.

Real smooth.

I pull the blanket up to cover myself. "My eyes are up here, Maverick." I use his own words against him.

He drags his eyes up to mine with a wink and smirk. "I know."

My insides melt.

"I meant I'm sorry your neck hurts." I look away and try to ignore the effect his heated gaze has on me.

"Not your fault. I should've figured we were going to fall asleep again. It's getting to be a naughty habit." He wiggles his eyebrows at me as he pulls on his boxers and jeans. I search the floor for my clothes and realize they're on the other side of the apartment. *Guess this blanket is it for now.*

"I should pack a toothbrush."

I hop off the couch, making sure to keep the blanket wrapped around me tightly this time.

"Follow me," I demand, walking toward the bathroom.

"I'd love to, but I really don't have the time," he objects but follows me anyway.

My cheeks flush at his insinuation. "Get your mind out of the gutter." I scold him with playful smack on his chest.

"I can take my mind out of the gutter, but good luck getting the gutter out of my mind."

I roll my eyes at him and skulk off into the bathroom. "Here." I slap a brand-new toothbrush into his chest.

"Oh, Goose. For me? You shouldn't have," he teases.

"A girl tries to be hospitable," I quip with a shrug and a nervous smile.

Stealing his line from when I crashed his party earns me a chuckle. I push past him into my bedroom and get dressed quickly. If yesterday was anything to go by, I know he's going to be out of the door in a few minutes and I want to be there when he leaves this time. For some reason, it seems important to say goodbye to him.

"I've gotta get going," he calls out to me as I'm leaving the bedroom. He's already at the front door. Was he waiting for me? I want to wrap my arms around him, give him a great big goodbye kiss, but I can't bring myself to step any closer to him.

"Okay," I squeak out from the doorframe of the bedroom. He doesn't leave. We're standing there staring at each other in some sort of awkward standoff. Austin sets down his bag and lets out a sigh.

"Come here."

"Okay." I keep my eyes locked on his as I stalk across the room to him. There's a friskiness in the way he's leering at me. I have to bite my lip to keep from smiling. When I reach him, he wraps me in his strong arms and pulls my body flush against his.

"I need to go," he murmurs into my neck as he peppers me with wet kisses.

"Okay." I tilt my head to the side, giving him better access. I wrap my hands around his hard biceps, not letting him pull away.

"Elizabeth, you're not making this very easy. In fact, you're making this very *hard*." His voice is sizzling and his touch scorching.

Burn, baby, burn.

"Okay," I whimper as his lips claim mine. Our kiss is more than passionate. It's intimate. Austin kisses me like he knows every part of me. Every dirty secret. Every insecurity. Every bad memory. Every embarrassing mistake. And it's all okay. When he finally pulls away, I feel safe and accepted.

"I'll see you tonight?" It comes out a question, like he's unsure.

"Okay," is my original response.

I'm Shakespeare.

Austin gives me a quick kiss on the forehead, grabs his bag and heads out of the door. Even after he leaves, I can't stop the fluttering in my stomach.

Austin didn't exactly agree to be my friend, but he answered my questions. He opened up to me and that has to mean something. Plus, he agreed to come to my father's this weekend. We may not be *together*, but we're friends. Or at least on our way to being friends.

I think.

I hope.

* * * *

I can't get Austin out of my head. I'm obsessing over every single second we've spent together, searching for hidden meaning. Looking for proof of something deeper growing between us.

Stop it. You're going to make a fool of yourself.

I need to stop thinking about Austin. I need to keep myself busy.

I jump onto Rule Them All to distract myself, admonishing myself when I see how much Uforia has suffered in my absence. I let a couple of key trade deals lapse, my gross domestic product shrank by ten percent and my populace are growing discontented. Not good. If I'm not careful, I could end up ruining what took seven years' worth of time and energy to build. I make a mental note to be better at logging in regularly. I need to play at least an hour a day just for upkeep. I know that sounds excessive, but I swear I enjoy it. Most days. Some days. Okay, so sometimes it feels like a giant chore that I wish I didn't have to deal with. But this game is the only thing that's mine, that I built. It's my only real accomplishment in life.

Wow. That's pathetic.

I'm online for a little over an hour before Jackie signs on. As per usual, she's pinging me for details about Austin within five minutes.

"What's new with you and Man Meat?"

I hate her nickname for him. It's so demeaning. Sure, I'll be the first person to raise my hand and say Austin Jacobs is the sexiest man alive. But he's more than that. So much more. He's smart and sweet and gentle and kind and maybe a little tortured.

Thing number six I love about Austin—he's complex.

"Nothing really."

"Boo. That's boring. I need gossip. What did you do last night? Or should I say what did he do to you?" Jackie asks, leaning into the camera and giving a mockingly torrid tinge to her voice.

"Nothing. Really. We talked. And watched a movie."
Last night was much more than a movie night.

"You're kidding? What a waste. What are you even
paying him for, Lizzy? I think you might be getting
taken advantage of. And not in a kinky fun way."
Jackie's dismissive and flippant. She may mean well,
knowing I'm too shy to stand up for myself most of the
time, but her comments piss me off something fierce.

"I'm not being taken advantage of in *any* way. I know
what I'm doing, Jackie! You have no idea what's going
on between me and Austin. So, just shut up about it."
I'm not yelling exactly, but I'm sure as hell not gentle.
I've never spoken to Jackie this way before.

"Wow. Okay. Sorry." We're quiet for a while and I
know she's waiting for me to apologize too. I'm not
going to. She had it coming and we both know it.
"Good for you, Lizbit. Nice to see you've got a little
bossy bitch in there!"

I can't help but laugh. "I learned from the best." I give
her a little nod.

"Yes, you did, little Padawan! Let the hate flow
through you," she mocks with her sinister emperor
voice. We both crack up laughing.

"So, you conquer any good countries lately?" I try to
shift the conversation back to the game.

"I've had to put a couple people in their place. This
new league is forming, Law of Superiority. Bunch of
dipshits and punks who think they can bully The
Federation just based on sheer numbers. Bunch of
noobs. They've been trolling the shit out of me. So, I
think I'm going to have to own a couple of their asses."

Jackie and I are both part of the same league, The
Federation, a group of people who work together in the
game. It's an online version of NATO. There are a

bunch of different leagues with different levels of strength or prestige, but The Federation is one of the largest and most influential. So, naturally we get targeted a lot by the new leagues or players trying to make a name for themselves quickly.

"I've never heard of them," I answer as I click around, seeing if I can find any Law of Superiority players near my country.

"Well, you haven't been around much."

"Yeah, sorry about that."

"Look, I don't care. But you should watch your ass. These guys are out to pick a fight. You get caught with your pants down and they'll make you regret it. And if The Federation drops you for inactivity, you're proper fucked."

"I know. I'm going to make more time to play." I mean it. As stupid as it may seem to some people, this game is important to me. It's a big part of who I am. "Shit, I'm going to be late for class. I'll be back on tonight, okay?"

"Whatever." Jackie tries to sound detached, but I know she cares. She's a big sister to me, both in and out of the game.

* * * *

As soon as I get back from class, I toss my bag down and get logged in. It's good to be back in my element. I've lost track of time when Austin strolls in.

He heads straight to the kitchen, but calls out a quick, "Hey."

"Hey," I call back.

I don't log out. I don't get up. I don't even look at him. Austin's the reason I've been so distracted lately. I need to finish before I let myself get lost in him. I'm ignoring him, something I know he hates, so he makes his way over to me. I tense with every step closer.

"What are you working on?" he asks from behind me. I desperately want to turn off my screen, to push him away, hide this part of myself. Would it change the way he sees me to know I've spent the past three hours reworking an imaginary tax plan for my imaginary country to make my imaginary citizens happy? Austin already thinks I'm pathetic. I don't need to add the final nail in the nerd coffin.

"Nothing. Just a game."

Just a game.

Yep, just a game that's an embarrassingly important part of my life. A game that someone like you would never understand because you've never had to hide behind a computer screen to feel powerful.

"A game? You seem pretty intense to just be playing a game," Austin challenges. "What's it called?"

"Rule Them All. It's something I've been playing for a while."

"How long is a while?"

"Seven years."

"Holy shit! That's a long time."

There it is. The judgment.

My cheeks flush with anger and a little bit of shame. I push back from my desk, stand as tall as I can, cross my arms and prepare to fight.

"I don't expect you to understand, but I need to finish this tonight. I didn't realize how late it'd gotten. You should probably go." My words are terse and it catches him off guard. I see a flash of something resembling pain in his eyes and my resolve is shaken. I don't want to quit my game, but I don't want him to leave either. I want to have my cake and eat it too.

"You don't want to watch me play a stupid game all night anyway…" I trail off in a pitiful pout.

He glances back and forth between me and the front door, as if debating if he wants to leave. My heart stops as I wait for him to decide this evening's fate.

"How about we make a deal?" he asks.

"A deal?"

"I'll make dinner. Even gamers eat, right?"

I blush at being called a gamer. I mean, I totally am, but I don't want Austin to think of me that way. I want him to think I'm normal. I swallow the lump in my throat and nod.

"And after dinner, you teach me how to play."

I can't control my scoff. "You want me to teach you how to play?"

"Why not?"

"Because it's boring." It's true. Parts of Rule Them All are painfully boring. Did I mention spending the past three hours rewriting a tax plan?

"You seem to enjoy it just fine."

"Yeah, well, I'm weird, remember?" My self-deprecation earns me a laugh.

"Weird, but not masochistic. Teach me how to play, you sexy little nerd." Austin steps into my personal space, kissing along my collarbone and up to the sweet spot on my neck, below my ear.

"Fine," I practically moan. "But don't say I didn't warn you."

After dinner, Austin pulls a chair up next to mine and I walk him through the details of Uforia, including our new tax plan. He brings up a few points he's learned in his business classes, helping me tweak both the tax plan and a few trade agreements.

He's paying attention.

He's engaged.

He's driving me wild.

I thought naked Austin was the sexiest thing in the world. I was wrong. Nerdy Austin is way hotter. He takes out a notepad and writes down the details of the game. When I describe a complex part of the game that makes him think, he makes this adorable little face where he furrows his forehead and purses his lips.

Thing number seven I love about Austin—his concentration face.

Chapter Thirteen

Austin

I've spent an embarrassing amount of time sitting in front of my laptop, trying to think of something clever to say to Elizabeth. Or, should I say, to Lizbit31415. I wrote down her username last night when she was giving me a crash course on the game and her country.

It took longer than I thought it would to install the game and an aggravatingly long time to set up a country of my own. But I've got the time to waste tonight. The team has to be on the bus at the ass crack of dawn tomorrow for an away game, so Coach gave us all a curfew.

My roommates are whiny little bitches, crying about being locked up on a Friday night, unable to add one more notch to their belt. I've decided the next thing I'm sticking my dick in is Elizabeth, which isn't on the *sex*-abus until the week after next. So, I don't mind the night in.

After about twenty minutes of debating between a few of my best pickup lines I go with...

ManMeat4Sale: *Do you know how to bake? Because I'd love to taste your cherry 3.14*

Lizbit31415: *Austin?*

ManMeat4Sale: *What gave me away, the username or the epic pickup line?*

Lizbit31415: *Username. You have no idea how many cheesy/bad/disgusting/inappropriate pickup lines I get...*

ManMeat4Sale: *ur breaking my heart... i thought i was special*

I'm teasing her, but with how long it's taking her to respond, I wonder if she's taking me seriously. I know I'm special to her. At least I know whatever the weird thing we've got going on between us is unique. I don't know what we are to each other, but I know it's got to be different from what she has with anyone else.

Lizbit31415: *You're "special" all right*

ManMeat4Sale: *Ouch...my little goose has claws*

Lizbit31415: *What are you doing on here?*

ManMeat4Sale: *Is that a trick question? Attempting to Rule Them All...duh*

Lizbit31415: *You're a dork*

ManMeat4Sale: *I know you are, but what am I?*

ManMeat4Sale: *I bet you $10 you just rolled your eyes at me*

Lizbit31415: *Shut up!*

ManMeat4Sale: *I'm not talking. And you owe me $10*

Lizbit31415: *No way. I never took the bet!*

ManMeat4Sale: *Fine. I'll make you a deal…*

Lizbit31415: *Another deal?*

ManMeat4Sale: *Yep. I let you welch on the bet if you give me some game pointers*

Lizbit31415: *While I still say I am under no such financial obligation, I'll help you out. What are friends for, right?*

ManMeat4Sale: *So, we have a deal?*

Lizbit31415: *Sure, Mav…we have a deal*

A few minutes later, my screen pings with a notification.

You've received a gift of foreign aid from Uforia *in the amount of –* ten dollars.

Guess Elizabeth can admit when I'm right after all.

I'm amazingly content spending my Friday night nerding it up with Elizabeth. The game is as complicated as I want to make it. I can set a lot of crap to be automatic, or I can micromanage the shit out of it. Elizabeth is clearly a micromanager.

She's right, the game is boring as fuck. It's more like econ homework than a video game. But how excited she gets about it is cute as shit. I swear, she gets turned on talking about her trade policy. Between her enthusiasm and having SportsCenter on in the background, the night goes by pretty quickly.

ManMeat4Sale: *I've gotta hit the sack, early game*

Lizbit31415: *ok*

ManMeat4Sale: *What's the dress code for Sunday?*

Lizbit31415: *Collared shirt and suit, tie optional*

ManMeat4Sale: *Ties are never optional. They're either required or they will not be worn*

Lizbit31415: *I'll try to remember that*

ManMeat4Sale: *Pick you up around 5:30?*

Lizbit31415: *Perfect. Good luck tomorrow!*

ManMeat4Sale: *Thanks. Sweet dreams, Goose*

Lizbit31415: *Night, Mav*

* * * *

Staring at Elizabeth's closed apartment door on Sunday evening, shifting my weight back and forth nervously from foot to foot, I can't decide if I should knock or just walk in. We've both gotten used to me waltzing in. But tonight I'm dressed up and taking her out. This doesn't have the comfortable feel of our normal nights together. It's more of a date. Jesus, I sound like a pussy.

Just knock on the damn door, Jacobs!

Elizabeth answers quickly. She must've been waiting on me. I run my gaze over her, taking in the sight. She's the epitome of understated class in a muted gray dress, conservatively ending at the tops of her knees. The cardigan she's wearing probably has more to do with downplaying her amazing tits than keeping her warm. Her hair is pulled back into a sleek ponytail, making me think for the first time that she might actually own a hairbrush.

All prim and proper, she isn't the shy girl I met in the library anymore. She is a woman. Someday she'll be someone's wife. Someone's mother. I shake away images of the future I'll never be a part of and focus on what I can have. I picture all the naughty things I get to do to her instead.

I snake my hand around her back and pull her close so I can whisper in her ear, "You're pretty enticing." I kiss the delicate spot on her neck, below her ear, that makes her tremble.

"Enticing?"

"The whole innocent modesty thing makes me want to get you a little filthy." I move my hand down to her ass and give a little squeeze. Her breath is ragged and all I want to do is shove her back into the apartment and help her lose control.

"You look nice," Elizabeth compliments me in a shaky voice. She's nervous, her hands adjusting various parts of her outfit, but I'm happy to see a sweet smile light up her face as she takes in my appearance. I admit it, I clean up nice. Looking at me now, she'd hardly be able to tell I'm poor white trash.

An alarm goes off on her cell phone, making us both jump.

She shoves me back with a dismissive, "We need to go. We're going to be late."

"I thought you said it didn't start until six-thirty."

"It doesn't. My father wants us there early."

"So, by *late* you mean not early enough," I chide. She's unamused. Anxiety rises back up in her features and I decide to cut her some slack. "Well, we better get going then. Wouldn't want to be just on time." I reach my hand out to her. She takes it and I lead us off to my truck.

When we pull into Elizabeth's driveway, I'm dumbfounded. I knew she was rich, but I had no idea how rich until we drove up to her family's mansion.

Yes, mansion.

The word *house* doesn't cut it trying to describe the four-story brick monstrosity the size of a full city block we drive up to. It's got massive windows, two-story columns and a water fountain taller than I am. It's literally a *mansion* on an *estate*. We passed tennis courts and a horse stable on the way in. A fucking horse stable! I've never even ridden a horse, much less needed an entire stable to keep a bunch of them in.

"Holy shit, are you a fucking Rockefeller or something?"

Elizabeth doesn't answer me. I don't think she even heard me. She's playing with the edge of her cardigan, fidgeting. She's jittery, like she's the one who's in way over her head rather than me.

"What's wrong?" No answer. "Elizabeth?"

She finally looks up at me when I call her name.

"What? Nothing. Why would something be wrong?" Her eyes are locked on the front door like she's expecting to see a horde of evil clowns come streaming out at any minute to murder us both. I grab her flittering fingers and give her a reassuring squeeze.

"You've got a shit poker face, Goose."

Elizabeth lets out a sigh and squeezes my hand right back.

"I hate these things. Everyone still sees me as some weird and pathetic eight-year-old. *Delicate.* That's what my mother always used to tell people." Her voice has an edge of terror to it.

Shit, she's seriously intimidated by the idea of going inside that house. Her house. To see her family. And I thought I was fucked up. I hop out of the truck, come around to the passenger-side door and pull her out of the cab.

"What are you doing?" she asks incredulously.

I take her hands in mine. "You need to shake it out."

"The hell I do. Not here," she snaps at me. I can't help but snicker at her indignation.

Delicate, my ass.

"You don't have to shimmy. Just shake out your shoulders. Release some of that pent-up tension. You'll feel better. I promise." I roll my shoulders to demonstrate. She rolls her eyes in response.

There's my girl.

After a few moments wasted in a staring contest, she rolls her shoulders and we mutter "Loosey-goosey" together a few times. She's on edge, but at least a little bit of the panic has subsided.

"Close your eyes," I urge her. She gives me a sideways glare, unsure of my intentions. "Please," I add before she complies.

I drop my forehead to hers and tell her, "You're not delicate. You're tenacious. You're fierce. You're wild. You're powerful. You're my weird little goddess." I tenderly kiss her lips before stepping back. Her deep chocolate eyes are watery with wonderment.

No one has ever looked at me this way before. If I didn't know better, I'd say it was love. But it can't be.

Not from someone like her.

Not for someone like me.

"Shall we?" She doesn't answer, just walks past me toward the front door. I can't help but notice she's standing a little taller now.

Opulent is the word that comes to mind as we walk around Elizabeth's house. The floors are a spotless marble. All the fixtures are polished gold without a single fingerprint. There are massive portraits lining the walls, all the Wilde forebears glaring down in silent judgment. It is a beautiful mausoleum. A mansion, but not a home.

This place is something out of a magazine and so are all the people. They have a staged quality to them. Their flaws have been airbrushed into obscurity before publication. Their smiles are wide but their eyes are empty. They see Elizabeth as an ornament, there to be seen, but not held. Admired, but never loved.

These people are courteous enough, but it doesn't escape my notice that I'm being judged. I'm used to not being good enough, I expect it. But I'm surprised they seem to be judging Elizabeth too. And not kindly.

Nearly every person we talk to makes some snide underhanded comment about her.

"She is majoring in biology," Richard tells a colleague as Elizabeth and I stand conspicuously behind him like some zoo exhibit. Elizabeth gives her father a genteel smile despite the fact he got her major wrong.

"She has done quite well, considering." Richard talks about Elizabeth as if she's not standing right behind him.

Considering? Considering *what*? That she's got a world-class prick for a father?

I take half a step forward only to be met with Elizabeth's small hand on my chest. I peer down at her, startled.

"Please, don't," she whispers so softly only I can hear. I swallow down my frustration and plaster on a fake smile that matches hers.

Who knew something called cocktail hour could be such a fucking nightmare? The worst part is standing by, watching Elizabeth smile through the insults. I'm not sure how much more of this I can take.

"Beth, darling," Patricia, the woman introduced to me as the best friend of Elizabeth's late mother, exclaims. "Richard tells me you have moved out?"

"Yes, I—" Elizabeth barely starts before Patricia cuts her off.

"Are you sure that's wise?" Patricia pats Elizabeth's hand in a patronizing reprimand. Elizabeth's eyes drop to the floor. My jaw clenches.

Patricia turns to me and adds in mock whisper, "She's *delicate*."

Fuck this chick.

"Excuse us, Patricia. Elizabeth promised me a tour of the house before dinner." I grab Elizabeth's hand and drag her away. We make ourselves scarce until dinner, wandering the empty rooms hand in hand without saying much.

Luckily, we're seated with a few of Richard's work colleagues for dinner. They are more than happy to talk about golf and the stock market. Our conversation is boring as fuck, but at least I don't want to punch their teeth in.

After dinner, everyone is having a drink and mingling. Again. I underestimated how much time rich people spend drinking and talking.

I'm keeping a close eye on Elizabeth, but I'm too annoyed at her meek demeanor to stay tied to her hip. Instead, I'm hovering by the bar. I've got to be sober enough to drive us home, but a drink or two is about the only thing that's going to help me finish this evening without losing my shit on one of these posh assholes. A Cruella-de-Vil-looking woman approaches me as I nurse my second whiskey.

She holds out her hand with an, "I don't believe I've had the pleasure."

I'm not sure if she's expecting me to shake it or kiss it.

"Claire Wilde. And you are?"

"Austin Jacobs. Elizabeth's boyfriend." I give her hand a firm shake before dropping it. I'm polite, but not friendly. Claire doesn't seem to notice.

"Elizabeth's boyfriend? Is that so?" Her pursed lips and questioning eyes tell me she's unconvinced.

This bitch would definitely make a coat out of puppies.

"Yes. That *is* so." I've introduced myself as Elizabeth's boyfriend about a dozen times tonight. I'm getting pretty comfortable with the title. Having Cruella here challenge it annoys the fuck out of me. It's not that she thinks Elizabeth is too good for me — that I'd understand.

Just look at this fucking mansion.

She casts a judgmental gaze across the room at Elizabeth, eyeing her with a slight shake of her head. She doesn't believe Elizabeth could have a boyfriend. These people are the reason Elizabeth can't see her own worth. I catch Elizabeth's eye. She gives me a nervous smile.

I hate this version of her, the quiet, timid little girl, letting herself get pushed around. I miss that feisty streak in her that challenges me when I push too hard.

Cruella puts a manicured hand on my forearm, dragging my attention away from Elizabeth.

"Well, then, as her favorite aunt, let me say thank you."

"Thank you for what exactly, Claire?" I ask, a little lost.

"For being with our little Beth, of course. It's really quite sweet of you," she answers as if it were some great sacrifice on my part.

Is she thanking me for dating Elizabeth? This woman's unbelievable.

"She's always been such an *odd* thing," Cruella says with a tinge of disgust in her voice. "Sweet enough, but so very shy and quiet. Rather *eccentric.*"

I down the last of my whiskey in an attempt to keep my mouth shut. I make the mistake of glancing back at Elizabeth. The deep blush on her cheeks and the tears she's fighting back leave me with no doubt that she heard every word her aunt just said.

That's when I lose it.

"Well, Claire, I'm sorry I'm going to have to disagree with you. I'd call Elizabeth captivating, not eccentric.

As far as being quiet goes, I don't have any complaints. She's always plenty vocal with me. Maybe she doesn't have much to say to condescending assholes." I try to give Cruella my most gentlemanly smile, but I'm struggling to keep my amusement contained as the affronted shock splashes across her face.

My pleasure's cut short by the sound of Elizabeth's shrill voice calling out my name. "Austin. Can I see you outside, please?"

"Of course, darling," I call back at her. "Please, excuse me." I happily make my escape from Elizabeth's 'favorite' aunt.

"What the hell is wrong with you?" Elizabeth starts in on me as soon as we're out of earshot of the rest of her family.

"Excuse me?" I ask in disbelief. How can she be pissed at me?

"You just called my aunt Claire a condescending asshole!" She crosses her arms and I try not to think about how sexy Elizabeth is when she's mad.

"First of all, I didn't call her anything. I was making an observation about you. And second, are you seriously pissed at me right now? For defending you?"

"You weren't defending me. You're being rude."

"I'm being rude? I get Daddy holds the purse strings and needing to kiss a little ass sometimes, but these people *are* condescending assholes and you've let them talk down to you all fucking night. How am I the dick in this scenario?"

"You think this is about money? *These people* are my family!"

"That doesn't give them the right to treat you like shit."

"They don't treat me like shit!"

"Oh, come on. You know better than that."

She has to know her family are a bunch of dicks.

She's giving me the silent treatment now, arms crossed and glaring at me.

"And you just sit there and play the demure, good girl. Maybe they wouldn't treat you like a fucking child if you actually grew up and stopped acting like one."

Her mouth drops open at the same time as her arms drop to her sides and her hands ball into fists. For a second, I think she's going to hit me. I'd deserve it. Instead, she does something much worse.

She walks away.

She stops at the threshold of the patio door, turning back just enough to tell me, "Go to hell, Austin."

Fuck. I fucked that up.

I take a few minutes to cool off before I go back inside and find Elizabeth. She's standing in the foyer saying her goodbyes to her dad. *I guess we're leaving then.* I offer a handshake and courteous goodbye to Richard before following Elizabeth out to the truck.

I try to put my hand on the small of her back to guide her across the driveway, but she picks up her pace to pull away from me. She's pulled away from me before when she's felt overwhelmed or scared. But she's never pulled away out of anger.

This feels shitty.

"Keys, please," she demands when we're a few feet from the truck. I stare at her confused. "You've been drinking. I'm driving home." She holds out her hand expectantly.

"I had two drinks in four hours. I'm fine." I'm nowhere near drunk. I'm not even buzzed. But she doesn't budge.

"Either I'm driving or I will call a cab."

I've never seen her so determined. I decide this isn't the hill I want to die on. If she wants to drive my piece-of-shit truck home, what the hell do I care? I toss her the keys and climb into the passenger seat.

Twenty minutes into the drive and she hasn't said a word to me. She's got a white-knuckle grip on the steering wheel. Her eyes are locked on the road, barely blinking. She's definitely still pissed. I can't take the silence any longer.

"Elizabeth—"

She cuts me off with a simple, "Don't."

"I just want to—" I swallow my pride and try again to apologize.

She doesn't say a word, but I'm silenced by her fucking death stare. If looks could kill, she'd be a WMD.

"This is total bullshit," I say. I'm done apologizing now.

She doesn't answer, eyes locked back on the road stretching out in front of us.

"I was the *only* one at that whole damn party who *didn't* treat you like shit, but I'm the one you're going to scream at?"

She stares at the road as her eyes narrow and her scowl deepens. The engine whines, telling me she sped up. The highway is deserted, but it's curvy, dark and lined with trees. She's too emotional to realize how dangerous it is to drive this road that fast.

"Slow down."

She speeds up again.

"Elizabeth!"

It's like I'm not even here.

"Be a juvenile brat. Sulk in silence all you want, but I am serious. You need to slow. The. Fuck. Down."

She glances in the rearview mirror before slamming on the brakes, bringing us to a near complete stop before darting off the road. The shoulder strap digs into my chest and my hands shoot to the dashboard to brace myself.

"What the fuck are you doing?" I ask, pushing the words past my stomach, which is currently lodged in my throat.

She shoves the truck into Park, turns off the ignition and throws the keys at me with a haughty, "Drive yourself home then."

I'm in such shock, the keys bounce off my chest and drop to the floorboards. I'm groping around for them stupidly when she jumps out of the truck. Playing catch-up, I chase after her.

"Where the hell are you going?" I yell.

"Anywhere but here!" she screams back, her voice cracking.

"You can't walk along a highway at night, Elizabeth." My voice is sharp, but I'm more worried about her than I am pissed.

"Leave me alone, Austin!" she shouts over her shoulder, but mercifully she stops walking when she gets about ten feet away.

I slacken my stride, hoping she won't take off again if I give her space. She's got her back to me, but her silhouette shows her arms are crossed and her chin is pointed defiantly in the air. We're engulfed by silence. The only sound I hear is the pounding of my heart.

I rake my hands through my hair and let out an aggravated sigh. I'm standing on the side of a deserted highway at night with this crazy woman who won't even talk to me.

"Would you fucking say *something*? I'm not staying out here all night."

"No one is asking you to stay."

"Like hell I'm going to leave you stranded on the side of the road."

"I am *not* a child. I can find my own way home."

"Oh, yeah? Throwing a tantrum is really mature."

She turns abruptly, charging toward me with her arms flailing. Her eyes are wild and fiery. Hands raised and fingers curled, she's a cat ready to claw my eyes out.

"You have no right to judge me. Or my family. Who the hell do you think you are? You don't know me. You don't know how I grew up."

"It must have been so tough for you, having to decide which of your ponies to ride and all. Real torture."

She stops short, just outside of arm's reach.

"Screw you. You don't have a monopoly on shitty childhoods. Do you know how many times I've heard my parents say I love you?"

She pauses. I don't answer.

"Twice." She holds up two fingers in my face. "My mother on the day she died. My father at her funeral. That's it. In my whole. Fucking. Life!"

Her body is physically shaking with rage, but tears gather in the corners of her eyes. I didn't realize how broken she is. The urge to hold her is nearly overwhelming. I clench my fists to keep myself from trying to touch her.

"Then fuck 'em," I say with a shrug.

"What?" She lets out a heaving sigh before turning away from me again.

"Fuck. Them. They don't want you? They don't love you? Then fuck 'em. You don't need 'em. You should be throwing up middle fingers till you sprain your wrist. Not smiling in the corner like a fucking idiot."

She scoffs.

"You're not a kid anymore, Elizabeth." My voice gets softer. "You don't need to waste your time trying to please *those* fuckers anymore."

"That's easy for you to say. You don't have any family left to disappoint."

Fuck, that was harsh.

She whips around to face me, slapping both hands across her mouth as her eyes go wide in terror. I stare at her in stunned silence.

"Austin, I'm sorry. That was... I shouldn't have said that."

She reaches out to me, but I'm too far away. Neither of us moves to get closer, so she drops her hands listlessly down to her sides.

"Why not? It's true. I don't have a family. Never really did. And even *I* know *that*" — I point through the darkness back toward her house — "isn't how a *family* should treat you."

She wraps her arms around her waist, hugging herself tightly, and drops her eyes to the ground for a few excruciating heartbeats. When she gazes up at me, the moonlight catches the glint of a tear rolling down her cheek.

"I know."

"Excuse me?"

"You're right, okay? I know my family are a bunch of assholes, Austin." She brushes the tear off her cheek and stares out into the black night. "I hate it, the way they talk to me. How they'll always see me. But they're all I have." Her voice is soft. Childlike. It breaks my heart because I get it. I was raised by disappointment and nurtured by neglect. I know deep down how it feels to love someone who can never love you back. How she's survived by telling herself she doesn't deserve better. But fuck that. She deserves the world.

"I'm sorry." My voice is awash with regret. I take a tentative step toward her, testing the waters. Her eyes snap to mine. They aren't angry, they're sad. A frown has replaced her scowl.

"I don't regret calling Cruella out on being an obnoxious twat, but I am sorry for what I said to you." I take another small step closer. She doesn't pull away. "I didn't mean to hurt you. It's just seeing them shit on you was driving me crazy..." There's a hint of a smile on her lips. "I shouldn't have gone off. I really am sorry. I guess seeing people I care about get shit on pisses me the fuck off."

"I guess so," she quips with a half-smile as she takes a small step closer to me. "I'm sorry too. I might've overreacted a bit," she says to the dirt as she kicks an imaginary rock. "With the whole brake-checking thing. You've got great brakes."

We share a quick chuckle before silence fills the shrinking space between us. I don't know who reaches out first, but suddenly she's in my arms and, however she got there, I'm grateful. I clutch her to my chest and gently kiss the top of her head. She squeezes my waist and buries her face against me with a relieved sigh.

"Seriously, you should tell them all to fuck off. Especially Patricia. I hate that chick," I hum into her ear.

"I know." She giggles into my chest. "I just can't."

I hold her in the silent darkness. Something broken is healing. She lets out a contented moan and I take it as my cue.

"Okay, let's go." I plant a kiss on her forehead and pull her along to the truck with an arm over her shoulder. "Now you get to help me find the damn keys."

She curls into my side as I pull back out onto the road. I slip my fingers in between hers, the connection somehow vital to surviving the night. We are quiet on the drive back, but I don't mind the silence now.

I'm tired enough when I pull up to Elizabeth's building that I let the stupid valet take my keys. Elizabeth doesn't bother asking me to come up. She doesn't have to.

She opens the door to her apartment and I guide us back toward her bedroom. She lets go of my hand and steps to the end of the bed. Keeping her eyes locked on mine, she slowly undresses. It's intimate. She's showing me all of herself. Standing completely bare in front of me, she says a single word.

"Stay."

It's part command and part plea.

As if there's anything in the world that could pull me away from her right now. I don't answer with words. I peel off my clothes and toss them in a pile next to hers. She takes my hand as she climbs under the covers, pulling me down next to her. I curl into bed beside her and pull her dainty body against mine, holding on to this special woman as if my life depends on it.

"I've got you, Goose." I keep myself awake until I'm sure she's asleep, wanting to know she feels safe.

Holding Elizabeth is better than anything I've had in a long time. It's what I've always imagined coming home could be. I drift off to sleep to the music of her soft snoring.

Chapter Fourteen

Elizabeth

Austin pulls away, the cool morning air replacing the warmth of his body next to me.

It's early.

Really early.

His alarm hasn't even gone off yet. I'm half-asleep but awake enough to know I don't want him to leave.

He's sitting on the edge of the bed when I grab his hard forearm and plead, "Stay." My voice is thick with sleep. I'm not sure he hears me, much less understands. Luckily, the kung fu grip I have on his arm is less subtle. I'm not ready to let him go. I need a little bit more of him. I think I'm always going to need a little bit more.

I might be addicted to Austin Jacobs.

"I'll be back," he answers as he extricates himself from my clutches. He steps into the living room and I hear him talking to someone. I can't tell what he says, but he's crawling back in bed with me in a few minutes. As soon as he's under the covers again, our bodies gravitate together like magnets. The sensation of his toned body engulfing mine is sublime.

"You don't have to go?" I ask timidly.

"Nah. Playing hookie today. Go back to sleep."

I cling to this delectable moment, holding him tight. He's on his back with his arms around me, my body curled into his side. The contact is not nearly enough. I let out an involuntary sigh, frustrated I'm not able to get close enough.

Without thinking, I climb on top of him, straddling him. He lets out a soft groan as I settle my weight onto him. I lay my head on his chest and the sound of his steadfast heartbeat echoes in my ear. I hum contentedly.

Austin lazily holds my waist with one hand and brushes my messy hair off my shoulder with the other. His fingertips tracing those figure eights across my naked back send a shiver through my body, making me rock my hips down against him. He gives me an appreciative moan.

He's hard.

I don't know if it's because I'm naked on top of him or just because he's a guy and it's morning.

Morning wood is a thing, right?

I lift my head and gaze at the glorious hunk of naked man under me. A half-asleep Austin is a whole new experience. His face is softer, and yet somehow more serious. Genuine. Awake he's always smiling, joking. Even when it's an act, which I'm starting to think is more often than not. Lying underneath me, with his eyes closed, he looks innocent. Vulnerable.

Thing number eight I love about Austin—when he lets his guard down.

I'm naked on top of Austin Jacobs. I should be terrified, but I'm not. I'm not overthinking it or freaking out. I'm just enjoying him.

I move my hands to either side of his head and slowly lower my lips down to meet the tip of his nose. Then, his forehead and each of his closed eyes. Finally, I press a slow, lazy kiss on his full lips.

A morning kiss.

A wake-up kiss.

With my forehead pressed to his, our lips barely touching, I whisper, "Good morning, Maverick."

He opens his eyes and peers up at me. The corners of his mouth twist up in a tender smile.

"Morning, Goose," he answers, sliding his hand into my hair, angling me for another kiss.

This one is deeper, more sensual. What started sweet turns heated when I hear a growl of desire from deep in Austin's chest. It sparks a fire between my thighs. The air between us turns thick, heavy with need. I can't wait another week.

I want this.

I want him. All of him.

Now.

I slip my hands into his hair and dip my tongue to taste his. I shift and center myself above his hard length. I sway my hips, brushing my core against his shaft, and let out a soft cry of pure ecstasy.

Austin draws in a sharp breath and tightens his grip on my waist. I grind against him, feeling empowered.

Feeling worshiped.

Feeling like a goddess.

I move my hands to his chest and I push myself upright. All I have to do is sink down.

Austin's eyes shoot open and he grabs my hips with both hands.

"Easy, Goose. Those hips are writing checks your pussy can't cash." He's wearing that taunting smirk on his lips, but his piercing blue eyes hold something more. There's desire in them, but also a hint of concern.

I swivel my hips, teasing him, showing him how ready I am.

"I want this." My voice is strong. I leave no doubt.

"Are you sure?" His voice is apprehension warring with craving. "Last night—"

I interrupt him. "This isn't about last night. This is about me."

I try to press down onto him again, but the grip he has on my hips stops me. His expression is pained, as if it hurts to resist. Call me a masochist, but it turns me on knowing he can barely hold back.

"Fuck," he grunts, the word laced with lust.

His eyes are locked on mine, searching for any doubt. He won't find it.

"I'm ready," I tell him. I've never been so sure of anything in my life. I trust him completely, with all of me. With my body.

With my heart.

He looks around the room before admitting, "I don't have a condom." He slams his head against the headboard with a frustrated thud.

"It's fine. I'm on birth control," I answer, aching for him.

He hesitates. After a moment he stills and locks his eyes on mine.

"I've never done it without a condom," he confesses.

"Me neither," I quip with a coy smile. I'm rewarded with his mischievous grin. I don't know what's gotten into me, but I'm a new woman. One who takes what she wants. And right now, I want Austin Jacobs.

"Touché." I watch the playfulness fade from his face, replaced by a gentle sincerity. "We'll go slow. We can stop any time you want."

I bite my lip and nod, not trusting my voice.

This is actually happening.

His firm grip on my hips relaxes, letting me slowly lower myself onto him, inch by inch. He's bigger than any toy I've ever used, but there's no pain. Only a sense of fullness and connection when he's finally seated deep inside me.

I close my eyes and take a breath.

So long, virginity.

I try to focus on my body, on this feeling.

Don't freak out.

Why did I think I could do this? *Ride* Austin, like it's nothing new. Like I've done this a million times before. I haven't. I'm not a new woman. I'm not a sexual goddess. I'm just me. And this is a big deal.

It's sex.

With Austin. I'm petrified. Frozen. Fossilized.

Am I doing this right?

Should I be making more noise?

Less noise?

Should he be on top?

Should we have waited?

"I need you here with me, Goose." Austin's voice rings in my ears as he sits up, pulling my chest to his with one of his muscular arms. "Just be here, now." He caresses my cheek and I lean into it while he peppers my neck with the softest kisses. "I've got you." The sound of his voice anchors me to this moment, to him.

I'm on top, but Austin has taken control. He lifts me by the waist, sliding out of me slowly. I rest my hands on his strong shoulders and follow the leisurely rhythm his hips set. With every stroke, pleasure builds in my core, coiling tighter and tighter like a spring under tension. "You're so beautiful." His breath is hot against my neck.

His words are velvet caressing my worried mind, soothing my anxiety and stoking my lust. "I've wanted you since that first night."

I focus on his words as he plunges into me faster, driving me to the edge.

"Since I saw you in nothing but my shirt. Do you know what you do to me?"

I shake my head, unable to form actual words.

"You drive me crazy," he grunts. He sounds desperate, consumed. I dig my fingers into his solid shoulders, reveling in the sensation of him. He captures my lips with his in a flood of devotion. He kisses me with everything he has, everything he is.

I've never felt so close to someone, so connected. We're moving together, breathing together, our hearts beating together.

He presses his forehead to mine. "I want you to come apart for me." So I do. He slides his deft hand between us, circling the most sensitive part of me in exactly the way I need. Pleasure explodes across my body, shooting out to the tips of my fingers and down through the ends of my toes.

"Austin," I cry out.

He steals my breath with a kiss as I ride a wave of ecstasy, cradled in his arms. He clutches me tighter, pulling me into him, as if worried I might slip away, then comes apart right after me. We cling to each other, hearts racing and out of breath.

"So, that was…" his sultry voice rumbles.

My heart catches in my throat. Was it as amazing for him? He has to feel the connection. It's palpable.

"Exquisitely weird," he finishes with a smirk.

The spell is broken. My heart plummets, shattering into a million pieces.

Weird.

Of course, how else could he describe being with me?

"You asshole," I screech in his face as I shove him as hard as I can, desperate to get away before the tears start flowing. He doesn't budge. Instead, he nimbly rolls us over, keeping our bodies intertwined, and pins me to the mattress.

"Come on, Goose. It was just a joke."

"Get. Off. Me." I glare up at him in furious contempt. I snake my arms between us and try to push him off. It's no use, he's solid as stone.

"Not a chance. Not until you calm down." He tries to lean down and kiss me, but I don't let him. I jerk my head to the side hard enough to give myself whiplash. I fight desperately to keep the tears out of my eyes.

"Hey, I didn't mean it that way." His voice is thoughtful. He's earnest and remorseful, but I don't care. It doesn't stop the black hole churning in the pit of my stomach, sucking away every ounce of my self-confidence.

"Goose," he prods. I don't react. I can't look at him. I want him to leave and never come back. "Elizabeth," he says my name sweetly, reverently. It's too late. He can't take it back. "I was teasing. I'm sorry." He sighs and drops his head to my shoulder.

His lips tease the sweet spot on my neck. I can't see his face, nuzzled against me. His body covers mine completely. What minutes ago felt safe suddenly seems dangerous. We lie here for a time, our wills warring in the silence.

"It was" — he takes a deep breath and holds it, as if steeling himself for his next word — "exceptional. It's never felt like that before." His voice drops to just above a whisper. "It was *weird* because that wasn't just sex. It was…" Even this close, I strain to hear him. "It was something…*more*." His words are labored and hesitant. I relax my body a fraction, resisting the urge to wrap my arms around him. To soothe him.

I'm desperate for him to keep going.

"I didn't mean to hurt you. I'm sorry."

There's a pregnant pause. There is more he wants to say, but he doesn't. He lets out a heavy sigh. It doesn't matter. He's said enough.

With his final apology, I relent, turning my face back toward him. I can't see his eyes, but we're now cheek to cheek. He trails kisses along my jaw and I wrap my arms around his neck. When he kisses me sweetly, I taste his atonement. I wrap my legs around his hips so he can feel my forgiveness. We spend the rest of the lazy morning kissing, touching. Making love.

* * * *

"Holy shit, she *lives*!" Jackie taunts me when I answer her video chat. I guess I had that coming. The past few days have flown by in a sex-filled haze. The sexual floodgates have been thrown open and I can't control the torrent from washing away everything that isn't Austin.

"Sorry. I know I've been kind of MIA this week."

"Ah, the demands of a wanton sex goddess," she jeers. I blush. "Where is your sexy man meat this evening, anyway? Thought you two were practically sewn together at this point."

"He has a curfew tonight. Big game tomorrow."

"Good. Finally get some rest for that poor vajayjay."

She's right, I'm a little sore. But I'm so not going *there* with her. I lie instead.

"It's nice to have the house to myself again." I miss Austin. I don't know how or when it happened, but suddenly he's become a part of my life. All week, when we weren't in class or he wasn't at practice, we were together. We make dinner together. We study. We cuddle on the couch watching movies. We even play Rule Them All. I've gotten used to waking up in Austin's arms. I'm comfortable there, with him. He fits into my life flawlessly. He drives me crazy, makes my heart race, but he's safe.

He's home.

"Fucking liar." Jackie calls me on my bullshit with a devious smile. "You miss that big dumb animal, don't you?"

The blush on my cheeks gives me away before I even answer.

"Maybe. Just a little. He's a good cook." I try—and fail—to sound detached.

"Something tells me you enjoy what he's eating more than what he's cooking." She gives me an exaggerated wink. "You know what I'm sayin'?"

"You're equal parts clever and disgusting, as always." I try to change the subject. "So, I got a package this morning without a return address. Is that from you?"

The way she lights up tells me that's a yes.

"Oh Em Gee, yes. I almost forgot. Open it. Open it!" she screeches at me with that mischievous glint in her eyes again.

"Please tell me this isn't some weird sex thing."

"Nah, I don't think you need any more help in that department. Although, I guess if you're into role playing, it might be useful."

I pause halfway through opening the box, skeptical if I want to open it at all.

"Oh, come on. Just open it."

I pull out a big red shirt with *JACOBS* printed in big block letters on the back. I stare at Jackie blankly.

"It's a jersey. You know, a *football* jersey. *Austin's* jersey."

"Yeah, I gathered that, what with the name and all. What exactly am I supposed to do with it?" I hold up the jersey like it's a dirty dish rag.

"Wear it. To the game tomorrow. Duh."

"No way. I'm trying to *avoid* the creepy fangirl vibe, remember?" The last thing I need is for Austin to think I'm reading too much into being invited to his game. It isn't a sentimental gesture—it's just to get his teammates off his back.

"Where the hell is your school spirit?" she mocks. "There's more."

There *is* more. A lot more. I now have enough school swag to open my own gift shop. In addition to the jersey, I've got sweatpants, beer koozies, stickers, a hat, a blanket and pom-poms.

"You don't think this is a little over the top?" I deadpan.

"It's probably the only college sporting event you'll ever go to. You should do it right."

I roll my eyes at her.

Why bother arguing? We both know how this is going to end.

* * * *

I'm wearing every damn piece of school swag Jackie sent me, including the idiotic stickers under my eyes. I'm a poser, but no one seems to notice. I blend right into the sea of red that is our grandstands. The place is packed, hardly an empty seat in the house. Except for the ones Austin reserved for me. In his *family* section. My heart flutters.

A woman in her sixties smiles at me and points to one of the empty seats next to me with a paper sign that reads "Reserved for Jacobs family."

"Is this seat taken?" she asks. "Mark said he could only reserve ten seats and we're busting at the seams over here." She seems sweet, so I let her take the seat. There aren't any Jacobses to fill them anyway.

I look around me at the stands full of big, happy families, ready to cheer on their sons, and my heart breaks for Austin. He deserves so much more than this. So much more than just me.

The general buzz of the stadium turns into full-volume cheering as the team comes charging onto the field. I can't help but get swept up in it all and scream along with the horde.

I'm able to pick Austin out of the rest of the crowd of uniforms as he jogs out onto the field. He's imposing in general, but in all those pads, he is positively god-like.

Yep, I've tapped that.

Oh, God. I've been friends with Jackie too long.

I haven't seen him since he left my apartment Friday morning about thirty-seven hours ago.

Yes, I might be counting.

And suffering from withdrawal.

I bite my lip and try to push aside the memories of what's under those pads. It's pointless. I've got a stupid, goofy grin on my face when Austin glances up into the stands. His eyes are scanning the crowd.

Is he looking for me?

Before I can think better of it, I lift my arms up and wave stupidly to get his attention. And to my horrifying embarrassment, it works. A wide smile spreads across his handsome face as he takes in my ridiculous outfit. His eyes widen and he makes an up-and-down gesture. Even without words I know he's asking, "What's with the getup?"

I treat him to a shake of my pom-poms—not a euphemism, my actual red-and-white pom-poms. With a shoulder shrug and a smile, I don't need words to give him my response, "When in Rome." He gives me a wink before turning his attention back to the field. I can't wait to get him home tonight.

It's a ways into the game and I'm almost relaxed when I get a tap on my shoulder. I look up, up, up, into the dark eyes of a giant. This guy's huge, bigger and broader even than Austin. His size is intimidating. Plus, he's scowling down at me. *What'd I ever do to you, dude?* I stand up and lean back against the seats, thinking he's trying to get by me. He doesn't budge. Even now that I'm standing, this guy towers over me. His eyes are a deep brown, almost as black as his hair, and they are studying me intently.

"Elizabeth," he declares, as if he decided that's what my name will be. It isn't a question.

"Yes?" How does he know who I am? Am I in some sort of trouble? Has someone hired this guy to come rough me up for some offense I didn't know I committed?

"Devin." He holds out his hand. When I just stare at it, he adds, "I'm a friend of Austin's."

There's a slight sting at the knowledge that I wasn't the only person Austin invited to sit in his family section.

Told you, you aren't special.

I shake his hand and we take our seats in silence. We're both happy to watch the game and ignore each other. I can tell Devin's glancing over at me occasionally, observing me like an animal in the zoo.

And here we have the awkward gamer girl. As she is outside of her natural habitat, you will see she has adopted the native colors in an attempt to camouflage with the environment and improve her chance of survival.

It grates on my nerves. I peek over at him, catching him staring. He doesn't look away. A few weeks ago, I would've ignored him, tried to make myself as small and invisible as possible. Now, I want to give him a piece of my mind.

"Can I help you?"

"Nope." He takes his time returning his gaze to the field.

"How did you meet Austin?"

"Same place, same time." Well, that's about as noncommittal as you can get with an answer. He keeps his eyes on the field, dismissing me with his body language as much as his words.

"How long have you known each other?"

"A while."

You don't say, how informative.

I decide to turn up the heat, knowing he'll react if he knows Austin at all.

"Did you ever meet his mother?"

Devin turns his large body toward me, reading me with those charcoal eyes. I'm proud I don't flinch under the scrutiny.

"Once," he finally answers before turning back to the field. It's enough for me to know that he isn't family, but he must've known Austin since they were both kids. Maybe from foster care.

Outwardly, they're complete opposites. Austin has a bright smile, beautiful blue eyes and sandy-blond hair. He's always joking, teasing, up for a good time. Devin is dark, black hair, olive skin. He's brooding and menacing. Inside, there's something similar between them. A certain level of detachedness. They're both used to being on guard.

Despite how off-putting Devin's demeanor is, there's something familiar about him too. I wouldn't go so far as to say I'm comfortable sitting next to him, but I'm not as uncomfortable as I would be sitting next to a stranger.

Practically the entire school is up here in the stands. It shouldn't surprise me when I catch a glimpse of Jessica a few rows in front of me, but it does. Remembering my drunken ridiculousness makes me ashamed. I owe her an apology. Before I have a chance to chicken out, I hop out of my seat and make my way to her.

"Ahhh, hi," is my awkward introduction.

"Hey," is her cool reply.

"I'm Elizabeth. I'm not sure if you remember me. We met at a party about two weeks ago. At the football house." I'm fidgeting, dragging my hands through the strings of the pom-pom, trying to avoid eye contact.

"Oh, I remember you."

Yep, she's not a fan.

"Okay. Yeah, so I wanted to come over and say sorry." I chance a look up at her to see surprise flash across her face. "I was really drunk and *super* obnoxious. I didn't mean to be rude. With the whole Barbie thing."

She cocks her head at me quizzically. Since I don't know when to leave well enough alone, I let the word-vomit spew out, unhindered by good sense.

"It's just that you're so pretty. You know, tall. Blonde. Beautiful. You reminded me of a Barbie." Her eyes narrow on me.

Shut up, Elizabeth. Quit while you're behind.

"Not in a bad way. You're not stupid or anything. I'm sure you're super smart. Beautiful and smart. The whole package."

Great, now she thinks you're hitting on her.

"Okay, well. Anyway, sorry." I turn to walk away, but only get a few steps before I find myself turning back to clarify, "Just so you know, I'm not hitting on you. I'm not gay." Now people around us are staring.

Walk away, Elizabeth. Just walk away.

"Not that there's anything wrong with being gay, I'm just not. I just think you're pretty. And smart. And—"

"Elizabeth," she cuts me off, holding up her hand. "You really don't know when to quit, do you?" she asks with a smile. I nod, shrugging my shoulders in acknowledgment of my awkwardness. "Apology accepted."

"Thanks, Jessie." I give her a wide smile in return, genuinely relieved.

I finally listen to my brain and turn to walk away. I get a few more steps before she calls out to me one more time.

"Hey, nice shirt," she adds with a nod.

"Thanks," I reply, my cheeks burning.

I saunter back to my seat.

"Who's that?" Devin asks as I sit back down, nodding to Jessie, who's watching us with a smile.

Who's a curious little cat now?

I can't hide my surprise, knowing there's only one reason he'd be asking. Not that I would blame him, Jessie's stunning.

Yep, definitely have a girl crush.

"Just someone I owed an apology," I answer dismissively, happy to be the one to withhold information this time. Devin stares at me for a few minutes, waiting for me to say more. When he realizes I'm not going to, he scoffs and turns his attention back to the field without a word. I don't even bother containing my smug smile.

Devin and Jessie sittin' in a tree...

The game is close to being over, a victory within our grasp. I can't say I understand much of the rules, but I can read the scoreboard and the game clock. I keep my eyes focused on Austin, regardless of where he is on the field. I'll admit, I do a fair share of ogling. I can't help it. He is a sexy, sexy man.

I watch him sprint down the field and block a pass effortlessly. The home crowd cheers as he dashes our opponents' last hope of victory. Out of nowhere, another player hits him at full speed, the most vicious tackle of the night. There are yellow flags flying everywhere and both sidelines clear. It's pandemonium, but all I focus on is Austin.

He doesn't get up. He isn't moving. My heart stops. My mind goes blank. My body goes rigid. I reach out and grab Devin's forearm in a panic, squeezing with everything I have. I can't breathe. Tears are forming at the corners of my eyes. The crowd is buzzing at a near-deafening roar and the announcer is rambling about something, but I can't focus on any of that. My vision tunnels and all I can see is Austin's body laid out on the field. I shoot out of my seat, the need to get to him the only thought I'm capable of processing.

I can't move. Something's holding me back, pulling me back down. I drag my eyes away from Austin to find out what's stopping me. It's Devin. He has a tight grip on my arm. I meet his eyes, pleading.

Let me go. I need to get to him. Please.

"You can't go down there. It's practically a brawl." The words don't register. I try to tug my arm away to no avail. "He's all right. Look." Devin nods to the field where Austin has gotten up and is already jogging back to the sideline, albeit a bit gingerly. I'm able to breathe again.

The surge of adrenaline is wearing off, but my hands are shaking. I sink back down into my seat and try to slow my racing heart. Devin eyes me nervously. It's his job to make sure I don't do anything too embarrassing for Austin. I try to ignore him and his judgmental gaze.

Austin gives the crowd a smile and a wave when he makes it to the bench, earning him a round of applause. His stare lingers on me and, before I can catch myself, I stupidly give him a wave back. He gives me that sexy smirk and my heart flutters.

"He cares about you." Devin's voice breaks me out of my reverie.

You wouldn't say that if you knew I was paying him to be with me.

A dismissive laugh dies in my throat when I see the honesty in Devin's eyes.

"It's not… We're not…" I swallow hard, unable to find the words.

Devin doesn't wait for my explanation. "Be careful."

"Careful?" *Oh, great. What did I do wrong now?*

"Austin's going to let you get close, then he's going to pull some bullshit." Devin's eyes are on the field, on Austin.

"What do you mean?"

"It's what he does. When someone gets too close, he fucks it up. It's a test, pushing you away to see when you'll break. So, when you leave, he can say he was right. There's no such thing as love and everyone's an asshole." Those few sentences are more words than Devin's said to me the entire rest of the night combined. I'm trying to take them in, to really understand them. Austin pushes people away because he's scared. I know that feeling.

"He's going to make it hard, but don't give up on him too fast."

Give up on Austin?

Not possible.

Chapter Fifteen

Austin

My body aches and I'll have some nasty bruises in the morning, but seeing Elizabeth waiting for me after the game makes me forget the pain and smile like a fucking idiot. She's standing across the field wearing a sweet smile and my jersey. I haven't touched her in a day and a half and my body is screaming that it's been too long.

When I'm about fifteen feet away, I charge at her. She squeals when I pick her up, wrapping her arms around my neck. I set her down but don't let her go. First, I lean down and kiss her, slipping my tongue into her open mouth. My little Goose missed me too. I pull back and take a moment to appreciate the flush on her cheeks.

"Austin," she admonishes me, glancing over at Devin with embarrassment. I was so focused on Elizabeth, I didn't even see him. He's missing out on some much-needed work hours to be here. It means a lot to me, it really does. But right now, all I can think about is Elizabeth.

"Afraid of a little PDA, Goose?" I tease. Devin doesn't give a fuck about a kiss, as the usual indifferent scowl on his face can attest. "Nice school spirit." I put my hands on her hips and push her away to get a good look.

"Jackie," she offers by way of explanation. Bless Jackie and her influence over Elizabeth's wardrobe. I'm not sure which I appreciate more, that black dress or my jersey.

Turning my attention to Devin, I give him a quick fist-bump.

"Thanks for coming, man. You heading to the after-party with us?" I ask him as I wrap my arm around Elizabeth. He never comes, says it isn't his scene, but I always extend the invite anyway.

Elizabeth answers before he can. "After-party? It's kind of late. I was just planning on going home."

No way is she weaseling out of this one. I played an awesome fucking game and I'm in the mood to celebrate. And I want her by my side while I do.

"Oooooh, no, you don't. You owe me after ripping my curtains off the wall," I tell her with a teasing grin.

Devin gives us both a confused look. Elizabeth doesn't seem the destructive drunk type, but, alas, my wall tells a different story.

"Don't worry, we can pretend you aren't invited if that makes you more comfortable," I chide her, earning me a playful slap on the shoulder.

"Princess!" Montgomery's voice booms across the field, souring my mood. "Glad you could make it."

I move to confront him, but Elizabeth holds me back, clinging to my side.

"I'm glad I made it too," she chirps before turning to me and adding, "You were amazing out there tonight."

Monte chuckles. "Yeah, you really know how to take a pounding, Jacobs." He winks at Elizabeth.

I'm going to end this fucker. Right here. Right now.

With more precision than the finest surgeon, Elizabeth tells him, "Jealousy isn't attractive. Seems the rumors are true." She looks over at Devin and with mock pity deadpans, "Giant ego. Tiny penis. Couldn't make a woman come with both hands and a map where G marks the spot." Devin nods with a smile and I can't hold back a laugh, pulling Elizabeth tighter against me. Turning back to Monte, whose jaw is in the dirt and eyes are wide with shock, she adds, "Word of advice — you can *either* be an asshole *or* be shit at sex. Not both. A man has to have *some* redeeming quality, after all. Now, if you will excuse us, we have celebrating to do and an after-party to attend."

With a hair-toss and defiant strut, Elizabeth makes a grand exit leaving Devin, Montgomery and me dumbstruck. So long Dr. Timid. Ms. Feisty just gives me a raging hard-on.

* * * *

The house is packed tonight, busting at the seams. There's always an extra buzz after we win one at home. Everyone is a bit more pumped, more eager to let loose. A drink in one hand and a tight ass in the other. These nights it's stupidly easy to get laid. Half the girls on campus are here, wearing next to nothing and giggling like lunatics. They're on the hunt for jock cock.

Three sorority chicks have cleared a bit of space in the middle of the living room, dancing as half the team watches. The music is cranked up, some obnoxious pop shit that has them shaking what their mama gave them. They eye-fuck the shit out of me as I push through the crowd of gawkers on my way back from the kitchen. I could have any one of them if I wanted. Maybe even all three. I don't bother giving them a second glance.

I hand Devin a beer, eyeing the front door. I let Elizabeth drive herself home with the promise that she'd catch an Uber over to my place for the party. That was about forty-five minutes ago. She should be here by now and I'm getting pissy about it. This party has all the pussy and booze a guy could ask for, but sitting here waiting on Elizabeth it's just a hot, crowded, noisy prison.

"What's up with you two?" Devin asks. I don't need to ask who he's talking about. The only reason he agreed to come tonight was to grill me about Elizabeth.

"Nothing. She's just a friend," I answer, forcing myself to drag my eyes away from the front door.

"You sticking your tongue down your friends' throats now? Fair warning, I had onions for dinner."

"Fuck off. It's complicated."

"No shit. You need to be careful with that girl," Devin warns in his big brother voice.

"Still afraid I'm going to break her? Don't worry, she's tougher than she seems."

"No doubt. I'm more worried about her breaking you, bro. I saw the look on your face when you caught her in the stands tonight."

I'm in no mood to have this conversation with him. Luckily, Jessie decides to interrupt us. Unlike most of the other girls, she is fully clothed, albeit in a tight T-shirt with the school's mascot and jeans that hug her in all the right places. She doesn't need to play it up and I can respect that.

"Hey, Austin. Who's your friend?" she asks me, but her eyes are devouring Devin. He takes a long drag of his beer, happy to let her get an eyeful but not bothering to introduce himself.

"This is Devin. Rhymes with heaven, but he's closer to the devil," I sing with a wide grin. It's not the first time I've used that line. Devin fucking hates it, which is about ninety-nine percent of why I say it. He glares at me and I can't help but laugh. Jessie is oblivious. She hasn't taken her eyes off Devin.

I'm yesterday's news.

"I'm Jessica. Jessie," she coos with a sweet smile. "Are you a transfer? I don't think I've seen you on campus before."

"Not a student." His answer isn't even a complete sentence. He stares at her impassively. He's my friend, but he's also a prick.

Jessie is undeterred. "Just visiting? It's an awesome campus. I can show you around sometime if you want. How long are you going to be here for?"

Devin shrugs. Jesus, he's impossible. How the hell does he ever get laid?

"Devin's a local boy. But I'm sure he'd love to be shown around some of your sights."

Devin doesn't appreciate my insinuation, judging by his glare, but Jessie doesn't seem to notice. A loud crash draws our attention to the center of the living room where some guy just took a swan dive off the pool table. In the packed space, it causes a chain reaction of people falling like dominoes. The human wreckage sends Jessie tumbling into Devin's lap. He wraps a steadying arm around her, pulling her against him and sheltering her from the spilt drinks raining down where she was just standing.

"Thanks," Jessie purrs at Devin as she tucks a strand of blonde hair behind her ear. She's smiling from ear to ear, a total goner.

Devin just huffs, but he hasn't taken his hands off her. He glances at me, catching the satisfied smile on my lips. I'm about to spit out another one-liner when a quick nod from Devin sends my gaze searching the other side of the room. I spot Elizabeth quickly. Some guy has his arm wrapped around her waist, whispering in her ear. What's fucking worse, she's smiling.

Fuck no.

I cross the room in a matter of seconds, not caring who I shove out of the way to get to her.

"Austin," she calls out happily as soon as she sees me. It's too late, my blood is already boiling.

I turn to the guy, who wisely drops his arm from her waist and takes a step back.

I step into his space and growl, "Fuck off." Thankfully, he does. I don't need to go to jail for cracking some guy's jaw tonight.

Elizabeth glares at me. I snake my arm around her waist and pull her against me. I don't just kiss her, I claim her. It's rough and dominant. She bends to my will, following my lead.

Over the loud music I hear the din of voices surrounding us. Whisper-shouts of "Who's she?" and "Are they together?" swirl around us. The crowd has cleared a small space, everyone keeping a distance. Watching. We're on display. I've made us a spectacle.

A spike of guilt shoots through me when I see Elizabeth wilting under so many questioning eyes. She hunches her shoulders and curls into me, trying to hide. Her face is flushed and her eyes are pleading.

"Follow me," I command, jealousy swirling in my veins. I take her hand and lead her back to my room. She doesn't object.

I close the door and pin her against it, caging her in my arms.

"What took you so long?" I temper my harsh words with soft kisses on her neck.

"I got a call from my father." There's a fragility in her voice that calms me a bit.

"What did he want?" I ask.

"To scold me for taking off last weekend."

I stifle the groan rising in my throat. Richard Wilde is a dick. I change the subject, not wanting to rehash the fight about her family.

"And who was that guy?" I demand, pulling her bottom lip into my mouth.

I grab her thighs, lifting her off the ground. She doesn't miss a beat, wrapping her legs around me. Her hips are even with mine now. I grind against her, making sure she feels how hard my cock is.

"No one. Just a guy from one of my classes." Her voice is shaky from desire. She's breathing heavily.

"You seemed chummy," I push.

"The room was loud…" Her explanation trails off as my hands roam her body, teasing her nipples through the fabric of her shirt. She moans in my ear, driving me crazy.

"I missed you," I accidentally confess. "I love seeing you in my jersey."

"I can tell," she says with a giggle that goes straight to my dick.

"Fuck, I need to be inside you. Now." I pull away from her, setting her back down on her feet, but keeping her pinned to the door. She kicks off her shoes and I kneel, peeling off her pants and panties all at once. The hem of the long jersey is the only thing between me and her naked pussy. I drag it up slowly, revealing heaven before my eyes. I kiss her hip as I drag my fingers up the inside of her thigh. She grabs my shoulder and moans.

My desire to fuck her takes a back seat to wanting to taste her. I glide my fingers along her silky folds, feeling how wet she is. Fucking drenched. I slide two fingers inside her tight pussy, curling them against the spot that drives her crazy.

"Austin," she whimpers. The sound of my name on her lips make my cock harder. Kneeling in front of her, I lift her leg onto my shoulder, opening her more for me.

"Did you miss me too, Goose?" I ask, working her pussy with my fingers. She nods. "Say it."

"I missed you."

I reward her with a slow lick, ending at her clit. I tease her with lazy circles, making her desperate.

"Please, Austin." I love the sound of her need.

I relent and flick the little bundle of nerves with my tongue while I keep pumping my fingers in and out of her. It only takes a few seconds for her to come against my face, screaming my name. It's the sexiest thing in the world. I will never get sick of making this woman come.

I don't wait for her to recover from her first orgasm, knowing she's not done for the night. I stand up, unbuckle my belt and drop my pants to the floor. I grab her hips and spin her around. Her hands slap against the door as I press a hand into her back to bend her forward. I kick her feet apart and glide a finger against her overstimulated clit.

I'm rougher than I've been before, but her heavy breathing and gentle moans tell me she's enjoying it. I need her to know she's still in control.

"It's okay to tell me to stop."

"I know," she acknowledges but doesn't say more.

Game on.

I grab her hips and in one hard thrust I bury myself balls-deep inside her. I pull out slowly, knowing she loves my head dragging against the walls of her pussy, before slamming back into her.

Her moans get louder as my pace gets faster. I should tell her to be quiet, but I don't. I love knowing anyone in the hallway can hear her calling my name. That they know she's mine.

I grab a fistful of the jersey, getting leverage to take her harder and faster. The bedroom is filled with the sound of our bodies slamming together. I lose myself in the ecstasy of her tight pussy wrapped around me.

I lean forward, pressing my chest to her back, and tell her, "I want to hear you come. I want to feel you." I slip my hand between her thighs, and a few quick strokes on her clit is all it takes. She's writhing against me, moaning my name, her pussy squeezing my cock. It's fucking glorious. I grab her hips and fuck her with everything I have. I claim her, coming inside her until my knees go weak.

I drop my head between her shoulders, trying to catch my breath.

I kiss her neck, below her ear, and whisper, "That was amazing."

Wrapping my arm around her waist, I lift her tiny body and carry her to the bed. I pull my shirt off and clean myself up.

"You're amazing," she hums, catching her breath.

"Yeah, worth every penny?" I quip as I climb into bed next to her. She winces at the comment.

Jesus, I'm an asshole.

"I didn't mean…" Her embarrassed voice trails off.

"Make sure to leave a positive review on scoreyourscore.com." I can't shut up. "Best boy toy on campus."

She cringes.

"You're more than that."

Our heads share a pillow as I stare into her eyes. Lying next to her, but not touching her, is a strange new kind of intimacy.

"Oh, yeah? And, what's so *amazing* about me?" I ask softly, legitimately curious.

"You're everything I'm not and wish I were." She places her hand over my heart and it beats faster in response. "You're fearless and strong. You're confident and clever."

I shake my head in disbelief. I search for the sarcasm in her voice but can't find anything but pure sincerity. I place my hand over hers and try to swallow past the knot of self-doubt in my throat.

She nods with a smile and continues, "Life gave you nothing. You're here through sheer willpower. Do you know how intimidating that is? You're kind of my hero." Her cheeks flush and she bites her lower lip. She drops her chin to her chest, but I've already seen the tears forming in her chocolate eyes.

I'm nothing special. A nobody. I've spent most of my life just trying to get by, surviving with the mangled pieces of myself I could cobble together. Now this weird little goddess crashes into my life and calls me her hero. Suddenly, I'm standing on the edge of a cliff, staring down into the abyss. The fear of falling is as exhilarating as it is terrifying. I know in my head I need to step back, but I can't force myself to pull away.

Reaching out, I wrap my arms around Elizabeth. A bizarre warmth radiates from where her palm presses into my chest. Not the fleeting burn of passion or lust, but a searing ache deep inside. Something is changing between us. She's reaching into me, exchanging one of my broken pieces for a pristine one of hers, and stitching us together in some permanent way. I didn't let her in, but she made it here anyway.

I brush back a strand of hair and lift her chin. My gaze traces up her beautiful, innocent face, pausing at her soft pink lips before settling on her gentle eyes. My heart soars at the simple acceptance I find in them. My breath catches in my throat. I trace the curve of her full bottom lip with my thumb, my pulse quickening as desire surges through me. I want to be her hero. I kiss her fiercely, with everything I am. With everything she believes I could be.

This girl shatters me.

She gives me hope that the world isn't exclusively pain and shit.

* * * *

This time when I wake up with Elizabeth curled up underneath me, I shamelessly cuddle the shit out of her. I squeeze her into my chest and nuzzle against her neck until her grumpy morning voice chastises me.

"It's too early. Go back to sleeeeeeep," she whines.

"Too late. I'm up. And I'm hungry." I hop out of bed, toss off the covers and give her naked ass a quick slap.

"Aaauuustiiiiin," she cries.

"Damn, you are whiny in the mornings! Come on, Goose. Get up. I'm going to teach you how to make breakfast."

After fifteen minutes of cajoling and another fifteen of making out and groping while trying to get dressed, I finally get Elizabeth Wilde right where I want her. In my kitchen.

"Crack two eggs into a bowl and whisk them together," I instruct from behind her, lazily holding her hips.

"Like this?" she asks, tapping the egg on the side of the bowl.

"A little harder," I sing into her ear as I brush my lips against her neck.

"Austin..." she murmurs as she twists slightly to have her lips meet mine.

"Aren't you two domestic as fuck," Drew groans, making his way into the kitchen.

Startled, Elizabeth gasps, jumps a foot in the air and crushes the egg in her hand. I pull away from her and lean against the far counter. Elizabeth rushes to the sink, dripping yolk across the floor. I cross my arms and glare at Drew. *Three's a crowd, dick.*

Swallowing a mouthful of milk straight from the carton, he elbows me and asks, "This going to be a regular thing then?"

I gaze at Elizabeth, scrubbing her hands like she's preparing for brain surgery. I take her in, head to toe. Her hair is a fucking mess. She's wearing my jersey, wrinkled from being tossed on the floor last night. The pair of gym shorts she borrowed are rolled over half a dozen times and still fall to mid-calf. One sock is pulled up to her knee and the other is slumped at her ankle. They're black with strings of white ones and zeros. She's a beautiful disaster. Yeah, I could get used to this being a regular thing.

Drew doesn't need to know that. I hide my grin and give him a noncommittal shrug.

He grabs a banana and a jar of peanut butter before heading to the living room with a dismissive, "Whatever, man. Better keep her away from Monte."

I growl. *Monte better keep away from her.*

Elizabeth dries off her hands and faces me now that Drew's gone. Tucking a nonexistent hair behind her ear, she gestures toward my bedroom and says, "I should get going."

"Why?" I shove off the counter and step in front of her, blocking her retreat.

"Your roommates. I don't think they want me here."

"Who cares what they want?"

She tugs at the hem of her shirt and doesn't look at me. "Don't you care what they think?"

"No." My answer is harsh. I'm annoyed that her demeanor has changed. *Is she ashamed to be seen getting domestic with me?* I cross my arms and glare at her. "Do you?"

She bites her lip and glances off toward the living room. Toward Drew. "I'm...in the way. I'm not... I don't want to make things complicated."

"They're not."

She mutters, "Not for you. You fit in everywhere."

"What does that mean?"

"Nothing." She sighs, brushing past me and beelining it for my bedroom.

I stalk into the living room and smack Drew in the back of the head with a, "Thanks for that, asshole."

"Does this mean there isn't any breakfast?" Drew calls back at me as I make my way to my room to figure out what the hell's wrong with Elizabeth.

"Fuck off," I call back before the sound of Elizabeth's horrified voice makes my blood run cold.

From the bedroom I hear her scream, "No. Oh God, no! Please."

My heart is racing and my only thought is to get to her. I'm at a near-dead sprint by the time I make it to my bedroom. I hurdle the bed like it's the last blocker between me and the game-saving tackle.

She's sitting on the far side of the bed, glaring at her phone and shaking her head. She slumps her shoulders and drops her head into her hands. Cowering in defeat, her small body trembles as she weeps. Kneeling at her side, I examine her for some injury. She's broken, but not hurt. The sight twists a knife in my gut. I wrap her in my arms and her cries get louder, her tiny frame shuddering as I press it against mine.

"It's okay. I've got you," I tell her in the softest voice my frayed nerves can produce. She sniffles and pulls away, wiping at the tears on her face with the back of her hand. She would hate me for saying it, but right now she looks like a little girl.

Small, vulnerable and broken.

All I want to do is hold her. I have an undeniable urge to keep her safe. She peers up with those chocolate eyes that are now red from crying. The pain in them breaks my heart. I would cut my own arm off to take that sadness out of her eyes. I know unequivocally that I would do anything for her. Realization strikes me like lightning, brilliant and violent.

I love her.

Terror hits me harder than a semi-truck, knocking the breath out of my lungs. I love this exquisite, feisty, damaged woman in a way I never thought possible. And it scares the fucking shit out of me. My chest constricts. I can't breathe. For half a second, I seriously think I might be having a heart attack.

Every fiber of my body is telling me to run. Don't pass Go. Don't collect two hundred dollars. Just get the fuck out before it's too late.

Before she destroys me.

It's already too late. My heart is hers to break.

Instead of running, I tuck a strand of her frizzy hair behind her ear, wipe away the tear trailing down her cheek and place a tender kiss on her forehead, hoping she doesn't realize the power she has over me.

"What's wrong, Goose?" I ask as I rub her back in slow circles.

"It's all gone." I stare at her, not understanding. She holds up her phone and gets choked up, "It's gone. Everything I've worked for."

"Take a deep breath. I don't understand. Your phone died?"

"No. Not my phone," she snaps, exasperated. "Uforia. My country. It's gone. Someone's destroyed it. Jackie just texted."

I let out a sigh of relief, my body releasing some of its pent-up tension.

"This is all just about your game? You scared the shit out of me. I thought someone died," I tease with a soft chuckle. The daggers shooting out of her eyes quickly shut me up.

Fuck. That was the wrong thing to say.

"*Just* my game?" she scoffs, giving me a shove as she stands up. "Just a game," she repeats again, more to herself than to me. She paces around anxiously like a caged tiger.

"It is *not* just a game. It is my *everything*. Do you know how many hours I've spent building Uforia? Do you know how hard I've worked?" Her hands are flailing wildly and there is a terrifying fire in her eyes I've never seen before.

Standing up, I tell her, "Okay, calm down," I know the second the words are out of my mouth it's the wrong thing to say. Again.

She charges at me with her sweet face contorted in fury. She goes from broken girl to rampaging hulk in two seconds flat.

"Calm down? Calm. *Down!* Oh, why didn't I think of that? My world is crumbling around me, but Austin says to calm down, so I'll just say loosey-goosey a few times and everything will be okay."

"Glad to see your sarcasm is intact. I get it—"

"No. You don't. Clearly." She walks away from me, throwing her hands up in the air. "How could you? How could I possibly expect *you* to understand?"

Ouch. Her words are a punch in the stomach.

Her tone is detached and her gaze is dismissive.

"You have no idea what it's like. This is all I have. And now it's gone." Her whole body freezes in place, hands still in the air mid-gesture, eyes glazed over. Someone hit her Pause button.

"Elizabeth?"

Her eyes snap to me and understanding washes over her face. "And it's all your fault."

What. The. Actual. Fuck?

"Excuse me?" I ask. I may be in love with her, but she can't shit on me just because she's having a bad fucking day.

She starts back with her pacing but has exchanged her wild gesturing with tugging at her messy hair.

"God, I'm such an idiot! Jackie warned me. I've been so distracted with this" — she gestures between us — "with *you* that I let myself forget what's really important. I've got to get home. I need to log in and try to salvage what I can." She's talking mostly to herself as she scrambles around the room searching for her shoes. She can't get out of here fast enough.

For a moment the world goes silent. Everything is blurry and warped. I'm underwater. Drowning. All I can hear is the rushing beat of my heart pounding in my ears. My chest is tight, an unseen weight crushing my heart. I can't draw a full breath. I gasp, sucking in as much air as I can. I hold it for the count of three before I'm able to say a word.

"You can't be serious right now," I snap.

It's not until I taste blood that I realize I've bitten a gash on the inside of my cheek. I realize I love this girl and she tells me I'm not important. Even worse, I'm nothing but a distraction. Something deep inside me breaks.

Fuck this.

Fuck her.

"Grow the fuck up, Elizabeth. You think some game is what's important? A bunch of fucking strangers on a screen? It's not fucking *real*. Maybe if you spent more time in the *real* world, instead of wasting your life playing make-believe like a fucking six-year-old, you wouldn't need to pay a guy to fuck you!" I want to hurt her and I do.

Her mouth drops open. Her body tenses like I slapped her. Her eyes are glassy with unshed tears. We stare at each other in bitter silence. Neither of us moves, but she's further away every second that ticks by. Just before the tears fall, she turns her back to me. She stalks across the room to her shoes and furiously throws them on.

"I can't do this anymore," she says to the air. To no one at all.

My mind is racing. My heart is breaking. I didn't realize my life was a house of cards.

I'm dead silent as she grabs her things and heads for the door. I want her to turn around. I want her to reach out to me. I want her to stay.

She doesn't.

This feels like the end. Like that stupid fucking egg, it's shattered into so many pieces it can never be whole again. I knew it couldn't be real. It wouldn't last. That doesn't make it hurt any less.

"Have a nice life, Elizabeth," I call out as she slams the door behind her.

Chapter Sixteen

Elizabeth

Back at my apartment, sitting in front of my computer, I should be entirely focused on Uforia, but I'm not. I can't. Thoughts of Austin plague me, smothering me with their demands to be heard. *Why do you miss him? Why can't you stop thinking about him? Why do you want him here with you?* When I stop and listen, a wave of satisfaction washes over me.

I'm in love with Austin Jacobs.

Realizing you're in love is like remembering the name of a song that's been stuck in your head forever, driving you crazy. You know you *know* it, but you just can't name it. Can't make it real. I finally have a name for the tune my heart has been singing for weeks. Suddenly everything makes sense. I love him. I want to be with him. Not because of the sex, but because he makes me feel like a woman. He makes the bad days livable and the good days unforgettable. He makes me feel like I can do anything, be anything. And now he's gone.

Realization hits me harder than a slap across the face, sharp and painful. My heart breaks, because I know I'm too late. Tears trail down my cheeks at the memory of my last words to him.

I let myself forget what's really important. I can't do this anymore.

My head knows what happened, but my heart can't understand. I close my eyes and all I see is his face, contorted in pain, disbelief and betrayal. My game forgotten entirely, I collapse into a blubbering heap on the floor, tears and snot streaming down my face.

How could you be such an idiot?

This game used to be the only place I could be myself. But that's not true anymore. Austin saw me in all my weird, awkward glory. He saw me and he didn't run away. Our fake relationship is the realest one I've ever had. Losing Uforia felt like losing myself, but it's not. It was the end of a fantasy. Austin helped me find who I am. Losing him hurts more than losing a million Uforias.

I reach for my phone and dial his number, not knowing what I could possibly say to him.

Don't leave me.

You are the only thing that's important.

I want to be with you.

I love you.

I can't find the words. It doesn't matter, he doesn't answer anyway.

I've lost him.

I make my way to my bed and throw myself into the sheets. They smell like Austin. I slam my eyes closed tight, but the tears come anyway. I remember his smile, his laugh, his words. Phantom tingles torture me with the memory of his touch. I crave the safety of his arms. The feeling of home.

I want to crumple up into a ball. I want to hide and cry and pretend the world doesn't exist. Austin's voice rings in my head, tormenting me in the darkness. *I need you to be brave.* I bury my face in the pillow. I can't. *Yes, you can.* I shake my head, my sobs subsiding into quiet, deep breaths. *Silly Goose. Don't you know you're a goddess? You can do anything.*

I sit up and wipe away the remaining tears. If Austin believes in me, I sure as hell should be able to believe in myself. It's time for me to grow up and deal with the real world. I can't keep running away from my fears, hiding behind a computer screen and avoiding anyone who might be able to hurt me. I need to make this right. I can do this.

* * * *

I plop down in front of Austin, same as the first time we met. That was another lifetime. Just a few weeks ago I didn't know who he was or how much he would teach me about life. About myself. Sitting across from him again, I'm even more terrified than the first time. I know what I have to lose now.

His beautiful blue eyes meet mine and I launch right into my rambling. "So, here's the thing. I'm an idiot. And a jerk. And I miss you. A lot. Like so much I can't sleep."

Time slows down when you're in hell. It took me twenty-seven hours and seventeen minutes—give or take a few seconds—to work up the courage to talk to him, but those hours without him were excruciating. I was a fish scooped out of the ocean, terrified and suffocating, only able to flop around uselessly until I eventually die.

Despite the fact that we haven't talked since I stormed out of his house, he doesn't seem surprised to see me. His face doesn't even hint at recognition, much less show any sign of missing me. I won't let his indifferent stare deter me. I have a point around here somewhere and if I keep babbling, I'm sure I'll find it eventually.

"I've been trying to think of why. I mean, it was just three weeks, right? No big deal. I should be able to go back to my life." I'm staring down at my hands, flailing as I talk. Stupid things have a mind of their own. "But I can't. And there are a lot of reasons, I guess. I miss watching you cook dinner. I miss talking to you about my day. I miss the way you touch me. I miss the sound of your laugh. I even miss that stupid, smug smirk of yours. I miss all of you."

There's only one thing left to say, the only thing that matters.

I take a deep breath and spit it out, "And I'm pretty sure it's because I love you."

I risk glancing up into his piercing eyes and that's when I know beyond any shadow of a doubt. "Yep. I'm totally, idiotically, obsessively in love with you."

It's a relief to say it out loud. His mouth drops open at my words, but he doesn't seem to have anything to say. It makes my heart stutter. I wasn't expecting him to say it back, but at least some form of acknowledgment would be nice.

"I know you don't believe in the whole love thing and you don't do forevers," I add quickly, making sure he knows I'm not expecting the romantic happily ever after. I just want to be with him. To go back to how it was before I told him he wasn't important and ruined everything.

"You are important to me. And I was hoping we could go back. To how it was before. We're still friends, right?"

His stoic face reveals a hint of something I can't quite read.

Longing?

For a brief moment, his eyes search mine and I think I have him. Then something shifts. He's pulled a veil down between us. I don't recognize him anymore. His expression is hard and his eyes are cold.

A chill runs up my spine when he says, "Fifty thousand dollars."

"What?" I gasp, pulling back and shaking my head.

He plasters a cruel sneer on his beautiful lips. "For the rest of the school year, it'll cost you fifty thousand dollars. Don't get me wrong, you're a halfway decent fuck, but it's a job, right?" He gives me a lackadaisical shrug as if he ate the last donut in the box instead of ripping my beating heart out of my chest.

My stomach's one giant knot. I'm physically ill. I might throw up.

"I'm not delusional. I know you're not in love with me or anything. I just thought..." He's not looking at me. He's watching something over my shoulder. Someone. I turn to see the leggy brunette across the room smiling at him. He gives her his trademark sexy smirk. My smirk.

I want to disappear. To spontaneously cease to exist. I'm torn between the desire to run as far and as fast as I can à la Forrest Gump or to slink away into a dark hole where I wallow away the rest of my life muttering about losing my precious like Gollum. I make a list of the pros and cons of my two potential futures, Gump vs. Gollum.

"I...I thought there was something...*real*...between us." My voice is a broken whisper. Having him so close and yet completely unattainable forces the first tear to roll down my cheek. He turns back to me, but he doesn't see it. He doesn't see me. I'm invisible.

"There's nothing between us. Never was. Never will be. If you want to keep playing this *weird* little game of house, it's going to cost you. Nothing in life is free."

Gump wins. I turn and sprint out of the library as fast as my feet will carry me.

Run, Elizabeth, run.

Chapter Seventeen

Austin

The same nightmare has been torturing me all week. I'm seven years old again, reliving the worst day of my life.

I try to be a big boy, take care of myself. I make my bed, change my shirt and brush my teeth before school. Ms. Kathy asks me why I don't have any lunch again today. I don't want to get Mom in trouble. I shrug and say I don't have it.

Ms. Kathy keeps me after school so she can talk to Mom. Only, Mom never comes.

My butt falls asleep in this stupid orange plastic chair. I sit on my hands for a cushion and kick my feet to wake it up, but it doesn't work. School's over. It's dark out and quiet. I wonder how I'm going to get home.

I want to go home.

Ms. Viola says she's a social worker. I don't know what that means. She is trying to get me in trouble. She asks when I last saw my mom and I lie. I tell her I don't know, but I do. It was five days ago.

Ms. Viola says she's going to take me to stay with some really nice people for a little bit. I don't want to go and I cry. I tell them I can take care of myself, but they don't listen. I wish my mom was here. She'd tell them I've been a good boy. I'm always a good boy.

I'm in a strange house full of other kids in a neighborhood I don't know. The place smells like old socks and window cleaner. The kids are loud and some are mean. I stay awake wondering how Mom will find me. I'm scared I'll never see her again and it's all my fault. I should've lied. I hate it here. I want to go home. I want my mom.

What if she never comes back?

'Come here, my sweet boy,' Mom calls to me.

I run into her arms.

'I missed you so much, baby. I love you. I'm never leaving you again.'

I want to believe her. She smells like sweat and cigarettes. It reminds me of home. The other kids told me she doesn't love me anymore. That she doesn't want me. I don't want to believe them. I want my mom to love me. I'll try harder. I'll be so good she'll never leave again.

When I open my eyes, I can almost smell the cigarettes and disappointment. You can't count on anyone in this life. My past haunts my dreams, but Elizabeth torments my days. I should've known better. It's good Elizabeth walked away from me. We're both delusional if we think we're in love. It wasn't real. None of it was real. I don't matter to her any more than some stupid game.

And she doesn't matter to me.

It's time to get back to my life, what's really important. I've got one more semester before I graduate. I've got applications to submit to MBA programs and scholarships to apply for.

My alarm goes off, reminding me I have a fucking life to keep together. Fuck if I care. I hit Snooze, but instead of drifting back into my nightmares, I stare at the ceiling. I have a million things to worry about, but the only thing running through my head is Elizabeth's face when I told her what we felt wasn't real. Her lips quivering. Her eyes welling up with tears. The confused wrinkles on her forehead. She looked like I told her someone she loved died. And I guess I did. The guy she thought I was.

I pull myself out of bed and try to get out of my head. I open the drawer on my nightstand and grab the fifth of vodka I bought a few days ago. It's half empty. I take a long pull, closing my eyes to focus on the feeling. The burning down my throat is a welcome momentary distraction from the ache in my chest. I toss the bottle into my gym bag and head to the shower.

* * * *

"Jacobs," the assistant coach shouts at me from across the field. "Coach's office. Now."

I jog back into the locker room, knowing there's no way this is going to be good. I've been half-assing practice all week, showing up buzzed and not giving a fuck. I'm in no mood for this shit. If I didn't need this scholarship, I'd be off this field in a heartbeat. Two weeks and the season will be over.

I knock on the door jamb. "You wanted to see me, Coach?"

"Close the door."

I take a seat across from him and wait for the ass-chewing. He stares down at the paperwork in front of him like it insulted his favorite grandmother. He's more angry than usual, his lips pursed and his eyebrows pinched together so tight they're nearly touching.

He doesn't even bother looking at me when he says, "Jacobs, you're off the team."

"What? I know I've lost focus this week—"

Standing up, he pushes back from his chair and slaps the folder down in front of me. "You tested positive for HGH."

"Human growth hormone?" I laugh. That's how ridiculous this is. I actually laugh at him. "That's not possible."

"Think this is funny? You just flushed your scholarship—your fucking life—down the toilet."

"Coach, you can't be serious." I open the folder, flipping through the pages of lab results that don't make any sense. There are numbers, percentages and drug names I can't even pronounce. "There's gotta be some kind of mistake. You know I'd never touch this shit."

He crosses his arms. "That's what I would have said at the start of the season. Now, I have no idea who you are."

"I don't do drugs." My tone is sharp. I'm getting pissed. I'm a lot of shitty things, but a fucking drug addict isn't one of them.

Coach shakes his head. "You used to be the hardest-working guy on this team. Now, you show up to practice late, reeking of alcohol and tripping over your own damn feet. You're lazy, unfocused and have an attitude the size of Texas. Doping isn't going to make up for half-assing your training, son."

"I don't do drugs. And I'm not your son." I throw the folder across the desk and pages go flying.

He sighs. "This will go on your permanent record."

"Fucking fantastic. Is there anything else or can I go?" I stand and stalk toward the door.

"You need to be out of the football house by this weekend."

A dry laugh escapes me as the hits just keep on coming. "Of course I do."

"I thought you were better than this."

"Apparently not."

I storm out of his office, slamming the door hard enough to rattle the windows. I almost rip my gym locker door off its hinges and throw everything into my gym bag. I'm not coming back here. I'm done with this place.

Three and a half years of pushing myself, of putting my ass on the line for this team, and it all means jack shit. A piece of paper tells them I'm injecting poison into my body and that's what they all believe. Perfect record and all they see is where I came from. I'll only ever be some loser druggie's bastard.

I make it out to the parking lot before reality sets in. Sitting in my truck, I take an inventory of my life. I'm off the team. No more scholarship. No more roof over my head. Even if by some miracle I manage to finish this year and graduate, I'll never make it into an MBA program with this on my record, much less get a scholarship.

"Fuck!" I scream at the top of my lungs and punch the steering wheel until blood is dripping from my knuckles and I can't feel my fingers. The pain is a welcome distraction from the rest of my life crumbling around me.

* * * *

I stumble through finals week half-drunk. I have no idea if I passed any of my classes and at this point I don't fucking care. I'm sleeping in my truck with everything I own piled in the back under a tarp. *So this is how rock bottom feels.*

Knuckles rap on my driver's-side window, followed by Devin's gruff voice. "Wake up, sunshine."

I rub the sleep out of my eyes and shake the foggy dreams of Elizabeth's smile out of my head.

"It's early, man." I don't know what time it is, but I must've only passed out a few hours ago. I sit up and comb my fingers through my hair. Someone poured a bucket of sand in my mouth. I need a drink. I open the door and climb out of the truck, stretching my aching back.

"You look like shit." Devin hands me a cup of coffee.

"Thanks," I growl. We walk around to the back of the truck, I drop the tailgate and we both take a seat. I take a sip of coffee, happy for the warmth in my empty stomach. "How'd you find me?" I've been ignoring his calls.

"Only a handful of places in this town you can park overnight without getting hassled. Wasn't hard."

He hands me a takeout container and I nod in thanks. The scrambled eggs make me think of Elizabeth for the millionth time in half as many minutes. I remember my lips on her neck as I tried to teach her how to make eggs. *Domestic as fuck.* The last time I was happy before it all went to shit. That memory can go fuck itself. All of them can.

"You about done with this shit?" Devin asks.

I lift my hand and flex my fingers. Nothing is broken. My knuckles are swollen and bruised but healing. I miss the pain. I deserve it. "Not yet."

"Have you talked to her?"

I glare at him. My stomach twists.

"No."

I haven't talked to Elizabeth since she ran out of the library. It's been two weeks. I thought it would get easier, that I'd forget about her, but I haven't. I've never let myself want anyone before. Now I need her. I never knew I was lonely until she walked out of my life. I've lost everything, yet nothing seems to matter more than her.

Devin nods and asks, "Going to finish school?"

I shake my head. "What's the point? I was born a white trash piece of shit. I'll die a white trash piece of shit. Everything in between is just a delusion."

"Whatever you say, man," he grumbles. "This piece of shit is going to work."

I hold up the food. "Thanks."

He nods and walks off.

Fuck, I want a drink.

Chapter Eighteen

Elizabeth

I walk out of my biochem final in a haze. I'm mentally, physically and emotionally drained. I've been functioning on autopilot since I left my heart and my dignity back in that library with Austin. I barely managed to drag myself out of the apartment for finals. I can't quite bring myself to care about anything.

I miss him.

I miss him so much my chest aches from it. Most people don't realize a person can actually die from a broken heart. Stress-induced cardiomyopathy, or broken heart syndrome, is when the heart literally decides to stop pumping. The muscles weaken and give up. It occurs almost exclusively in women. *Surprise, surprise.* Men are selfish assholes. Every one of them.

My head knows Austin will never love me, but my heart yearns for him. Love sucks.

"Elizabeth!"

I snap out of my stupor and glance around the busy quad to find Jessie waving at me from a few feet away. She comes charging up, flailing a newspaper in her hand like she's a duckling trying to take flight.

"Do you believe this bullshit?"

"Yes. No. What?" My brain is fuzzy. Since Austin, I haven't been sleeping much. Every ounce of energy I've been able to muster has been funneled into studying for finals.

Jessie grabs my arms and pulls me over to a bench. She shoves the paper in my lap as we sit down.

"This article about Austin." Jessie points to the top headline. I shake my head as my eyes strain to focus and make sense of the words. Seeing me struggle, Jessie explains, "He was kicked off the team. They said he was using performance-enhancing drugs."

"That's not possible."

"I didn't think so either, but he's been so different lately. Irritable, on edge."

"Austin would never use drugs," I say unequivocally. "He just wouldn't."

Jessie shakes her head. "He's not even going to fight it."

"What? But won't he lose his scholarship?"

"Yep. I told him, if it's not true, he needs to fight it, and he bit my head off. Said there wasn't any point."

I mutter, "Why wouldn't he at least try to fight it?"

Jessie shrugs. "He doesn't care about anything these days. Monte has been such a loudmouth too. Bragging to everyone about how the only reason Austin's been beating him all season is because he's been doping."

"I hate that guy."

Jessie chuckles. "Me too. He always seemed sketchy to me." Her cell phone goes off and she jumps up exclaiming, "Shit. I'm late. What else is new, right?"

She darts off in long, graceful strides.

I stare at the newspaper, befuddled. I can't figure it out. I know he didn't do this. Why won't Austin fight for himself?

* * * *

This game isn't my escape anymore. It's a chore. I've poured myself into it, hoping I could turn myself back into the person I was before Austin. The girl who was happy playing make-believe and living online. But I'm not that girl anymore. I'm not sure this ever made me happy, but it certainly can't now. I know what happiness is. I know how love feels. *Home.* This game can't give me what I felt with Austin.

I hate it a little more every day. It taunts me with what I lost. Who I was stupid enough to give up. If it weren't for Jackie's constant ranting about "teaching the bastards a lesson," I would've quit by now. It's not about trade deals and peace treaties anymore. It's all war and embargos. Jackie loves every second.

"Eat shit, punk. Think you can invade one of us and get away with it?" she taunts the latest Law of Superiority player she's targeted for destruction. "Vendetta, bitch!" she screams into the mic like a crazy person. She's on a bit of a havoc bender.

My country isn't mine anymore and I honestly don't care, but Jackie's made it personal. They came after me because the rest of The Federation was too strong. Earned myself a big fat told-you-so on that one. Funny how things can seem so important one day, and not matter the next. Without Austin, this game is just a game.

"Lizbit, you take the southern border. Make sure they can't resupply. Another week without alcohol or sugar and we won't need to invade. Their people will tear them apart for us." Jackie's sinister laugh fills my ears.

I unenthusiastically reply with, "You got it, boss." I go through the motions, her reluctant sidekick for another forty-five minutes before I beg off. "Jackie, I'm about ready to call it for tonight," I sulk into the mic.

"It's only eight-thirty. Come on. We can take down at least one more city."

"I'm really not up for it."

"Hey, what's up with you?"

She stares at me in our video chat. I keep my eyes focused on one of my other screens, refusing to meet her eyes as I lie. "Nothing."

"Nothing my ass. You're beyond distracted. I thought you were done with finals."

"I am."

"Then what is it?"

I shake my head. "Nothing."

Jackie busts out her warning tone. "Lizbit, lie to me again and I'll hack your Facebook and post pro-Apple memes."

I gasp. "You wouldn't"

She quirks an eyebrow. "Try me."

I let out a deep sigh. "Fine. Austin is in trouble."

"Who gives a shit?"

"I do."

Jackie groans. "Why? The prick deserves it."

"He's getting framed for using performance-enhancing drugs. He got kicked off the team."

"Good. I was hoping he'd get rectal cancer, but I guess this works too."

"Jesus, Jackie!" That's pretty harsh, even for her. "Rectal cancer? You're awful."

"No, *he* is awful. He broke your heart."

"Just because he doesn't love me doesn't mean he deserves to have someone ruin his life. Austin grew up with nothing and no one. My family isn't perfect, but at least they're a safety net. Austin has no one in his corner, but he's clawed and scraped and cobbled together a life. And now he's losing everything. Over a damn lie. He must be devastated. It's not fair. It's not right."

Who would do such a thing? My heart is pounding and the bitter taste of adrenaline coats my mouth. Austin may be too disheartened to fight, but I'm not. I'm furious for him.

Jackie's got a wicked smile on her face and my suspicion is growing by the second. I snap at her, "You didn't do this, did you?"

She gasps dramatically and places her hand over her heart in mock shock. "Who, me?"

"Jacqueline Meredith Ryan, tell me you didn't do this." I wag a disapproving finger at the computer screen.

She holds her hands up in surrender. "I wish I could take credit for it, but no. I didn't."

I glare at her, not believing her denial.

"I didn't! I swear. Besides, those lab systems are super secure and even my genius has its limits."

That gets me thinking. Who would have the skills to pull this off? "You're saying only a leet hacker could do this?"

"Yeah. Well, no."

I shake my head, confused.

"You don't need to hack shit to fake lab results. The weakest link in any network is always the people. I can't imagine handling piss pays that great. I guarantee someone in that lab is on the take. If you know the right guy and have a lot of cash to throw around, you're golden."

The lightbulb flicks on in my head and it all makes sense. "Monte!"

"Who-sy, what-y, huh now?"

"Austin's teammate. Former teammate, Montgomery. King of the Douchebags?" I use the nickname I gave him after our classroom confrontation and Jackie finally remembers who I'm talking about.

"Tiny penis. Giant ego."

"That's the one." I chuckle. "It has to be him. He hates Austin. And he's always bragging in class about how his dad is some big-time plastic surgeon for celebrities." My hands fly around wildly and my mind races a mile a minute. "If I can prove it was him, that he set Austin up…"

"Why would you do anything to help that asshole?"

I ignore Jackie as I construct my masterplan. "Maybe if I steal his phone or hack his laptop —"

"Woah, pump the brakes there, Jason Bourne. You realize that shit is illegal, right?"

"Which is only a problem if I get caught."

"Elizabeth, don't be stupid. He's not worth it."

I take a sharp breath and stare dead into the camera. "Yes. He is."

Jackie studies my face and sighs. "God damn it. You're going to do this no matter what I say, aren't you?"

"Yes."

"Fine, then let's do this the smart way. I bet this guy's stupid enough to write his email password down. What are the chances you can get into their house?"

* * * *

This is a bad idea.
This is a really bad idea.
This is a really terribly bad idea!

I stare up at the football house and push down the painful memories of Austin. The last time I came to one of these parties, it was to be with him. Now, bumping into Austin is my worst nightmare. I don't want to see him. And I don't want anyone to see me. I take a deep breath and try to remember the plan.

In and out. Quick and quiet. Ninja-style.

I glide in through the open door, making my way between the drunk coeds celebrating the end of the semester and the football season. We lost our last two games, the ones we played without Austin, but that doesn't stop everyone from getting drunk. The party is in full swing, music cranked up and wall-to-wall people. It's claustrophobic, suffocating. My heart is racing. I don't belong here. I can't believe I thought I could do this.

Calm down. You haven't even done anything yet.

I roll my shoulders and mutter "Loosey-goosey," under my breath. I can do this. No big deal. I'm just hanging out at a party. *Nothing suspicious to see here.* I bob my head along to the music, searching the room for Monte. If I'm going to search his room for a password, it'd be better if he wasn't in it. I'm in luck. He's lounging on the couch in the center of the living room, luxuriating in the attention of the rest of the team. He really is King of the Douchebags.

I wipe my sweaty hands on my skinny jeans and glance around to see if anyone is watching me. *Nope. Invisible as always.* For once, it's a blessing. The music softens to a dull roar as I inch my way toward the bedrooms.

I stare down the never-ending hallway. *Well, shit.* There are about a million and one rooms and I have no idea which one belongs to Monte. This might take all night.

A giggling couple connected from lips to hips comes tumbling down the hallway. They're walking by Braille, bouncing off the walls as they stumble toward me, refusing to break their kiss long enough to even watch where they're going. I pretend to be looking for the bathroom, in case they notice I exist. They make it to the last room on the right and practically fall inside. *Note to self – skip that room.*

My palms are sweating and I'm desperately trying not to seem nefarious as I slip into the first bedroom on the left. It is a mild disaster. It smells like a used gym towel and dirty clothes are covering about three-quarters of the floor. I do my best to step over them, but give up when I have to choose between stepping on a sweatshirt and trying to jump the five feet to the next open spot. I search the room, looking for anything that might have someone's name on it. There's a backpack on the ground by the desk and I dive for it. Pulling out an old essay, I read the name. Andrew Edwards. *Damn.* Wrong room.

I crack the door and peek out into the hallway. The coast is clear, so I slip out. *Nerd ninja powers, activate.* I move on to the next room. The door is locked. This plan isn't working out so well. I move on to the third door and am relieved when the latch opens. I shut the door behind me and lean against it. I don't know how James Bond does it. My hands are shaking from the adrenaline at this point. I close my eyes and take a long, ragged breath in through my nose and out through my mouth. *Breathe, Elizabeth. Just breathe.*

A pungent scent burns my nostrils. It smells like a can of body spray exploded in here. I cough, covering my nose and mouth with my hand as I choke on the faux manly smell. Yep, this has got to be Monte's room. It reeks of douchebag. I make my way over to the desk where his laptop is charging and flip through the textbooks and papers littered there. Nothing. I search the bag on the ground. Nothing.

In a panic, I text Jackie.

Me: *There's nothing here!!!! I'm screwed.*

DominaTrix: *Take a deep breath and keep looking...desk drawer? Check for Post-its.*

A deep breath is not possible in this cologne fog, but I keep going. I search his desk drawers. Still nothing. Desperate, I search his nightstand. Only a half-empty bottle of lotion and a box of condoms. Trojan Extended Pleasure. *Guess little Monte's got a hair trigger.* Gag.

I've searched every nook and cranny in this room and there's no password. I'm typing out a defeated response to Jackie as frustrated tears fill my eyes. *This isn't over.* There has to be something else I can do. Something more I can try. I stare down at Monte's desk. I know the evidence I need is somewhere on this laptop.

"Fuck it," I say out loud to myself. My battle cry as I grab the laptop and dive head first into the world of petty crime.

That's when I see it. A bright yellow Post-it sitting right where the laptop was. I snap a quick photo and shoot it to Jackie with one word.

Me: *Jackpot!*

DominaTrix: *Pu$$y_Slaya??? what a douchecanoe*

Me: *Told you…his highness, king of the douchebags*

I laugh at myself, at the ridiculousness of this situation, as I carefully put the laptop back exactly where it was. I'm relieved and have a wide smile across my face. Already thinking about the next step in the plan to rescue Austin, I'm not careful enough when I leave Monte's room. I didn't notice someone standing at the end of the hallway, staring at me.

"What are you doing, Elizabeth?" Austin growls.

I jump about three feet in the air and let out a sharp yelp. Austin's blue eyes are on fire as he scowls at me, one eyebrow raised in contempt. I press my hand to my chest and will my heartbeat to slow down. My mouth has turned into the Sahara. I try to swallow, but I can't. I try to breathe, but it's more of a pant. I haven't seen him since the library. Since he shattered my heart into a million pieces. He's even more beautiful than he is in my daydreams.

Of all the people to catch me coming out of Monte's room, it has to be Austin? Why, God? Just why? What the hell did I ever do to you?

"I…uh…I was…looking for…uh…the bathroom?"

Smooth, Elizabeth. Real smooth. At least I didn't tell him I was gassy.

Austin shakes his head, crosses his arms, and says, "Liar. Try again."

His glare is molten on my skin, searing into me. I can't stop my gaze from roaming over his body. He's wearing a long-sleeved black Henley pushed up to his elbows, dark jeans and black boots. He hasn't shaved recently and his jaw is covered in hair a shade darker than his golden locks. He makes devil-may-care disheveled sexy as hell. He's dangerous and alluring. *Of course he has to look amazing.*

Lying to him didn't work, so I try the truth. "I needed something."

"From Monte?" He takes a long pull of his beer, unfazed.

I tug at the hem of my shirt and bite my lip, desperate not to cower under his scrutiny. "Yes."

Austin steps toward me, encroaching on my personal space in the way he does. The scent of his sweet and spicy cologne fills my senses, along with the new smell of alcohol. He hides it well, but he's drunk. Usually that's a complete turn-off, but Austin is different. I'll never *not* want him. The heat from his body makes my skin tingle. My heart aches for him. I want to touch him. I'd give anything to have him hold me again.

He snarls, "I thought you were smarter than that." His contempt slices through me.

Tears sting my eyes. I stand as tall as I can, pull my shoulders back and snap at him. "What do you care?"

Austin shrugs. "I don't." He brushes past me into the bathroom, slamming the door.

I Forrest Gump my way out of the party, not stopping for anything until I've put a safe distance between me and Austin Jacobs.

* * * *

I go through my masterplan checklist. It's been a long week. But, with a bit of help from Jackie and Jessie, everything is set for Austin's hearing tomorrow. All I need Austin to do is show up and he'll have his life back. Vindication. Picturing his face, the relief and excitement, makes me smile. I want him to have everything he wants, even if that doesn't include me.

Three loud knocks on my door startle me out of my daydream. I wrap my sweater around me tighter and glance at the time on my computer. Quarter past ten on a Thursday. Three more harsh knocks echo in the apartment. I creep over to the door, trying not to make a sound. I check the peephole and find my father standing there, seething.

"Father?" I ask, not trusting my eyes even after I've opened the door. I rub them vigorously, but my father is still standing in my foyer, more enraged than I've ever seen him. "What are you doing here?"

He holds up a piece of paper and waves it at me. "I am here so you can explain yourself."

I take the paper from him and he paces anxiously. I spend a few minutes examining it while he fumes at my side. "This is an invoice from Mr. Phillips."

He nods and points to the description of services provided. "Care to explain this?"

Despite his rancor, I stay calm and answer, "It was for legal fees."

"Not your legal fees."

"No. Not directly."

He snatches back the paper, whips off his glasses, and glares at me. I've never had his undivided attention before. If I'd known spending a few thousand dollars was the way to get it, I might've bought a sports car on my sixteenth birthday or a yacht on my eighteenth. I might've spent the money when his attention mattered to me. I couldn't care less what he thinks now. I know what I did and I know why.

"Was it for that Austin character?"

"Yes," I answer flatly. "What do you care? It's my money, isn't it?"

"What do I care? I thought you were smarter than this." He puts his palms on my shoulders, one of the most tender gestures he's ever made, and I resent him for it. "It was bad enough when he was rude to your aunt at our Christmas party, but now you are paying his *legal* bills. What sort of trouble has he gotten you into?"

I cross my arms and bite back a sigh. "It was a school hearing, not a criminal one. And not that you asked, but Austin is innocent."

"Beth, this man is not innocent. He is using you, trading on our good name and fleecing you for money."

He is condescending and obtuse, same as always. But it doesn't make me cower or feel small. Something is different this time. I'm different. Now, it makes me angry.

I chuckle at the irony. "You've never cared about me or what I do before. But now that it involves a little money or potential embarrassment, you want to play the concerned father?" He drops his hands to his sides and stares at me as if I'm speaking in tongues. "Sorry, but that ship sailed about a decade ago with my self-worth and idealism on board."

My father slips his glasses back on and tips his nose up in the air. "You may think I was not present for your childhood, but I assure you I care about your wellbeing more than this sycophant."

I take a sharp breath and calm myself down before I answer, "His name is Austin and he has never asked me for anything."

My father sighs. "Of course he would never outright ask. He is manipulating you to believe it was your idea. He is praying on your naivety for his own personal advantage."

I stand my ground. "He's not manipulating me. Hell, he doesn't even know I was the one who helped him. Mr. Phillips kept me anonymous."

"Beth, I am your father and I am not accustomed to—"

"Father?" I interrupt him. Years of neglect final boil over in my veins. I lash out at him. "You've never been my father. You are a figurehead. A misanthrope."

"You will waste our entire family's fortune and ruin our good name before that man will love you. What would your mother say?"

There is venom in his words, but I don't feel the sting he intends. Something inside me snaps at the mention of my mother, the one I tried in vain to make love me.

"Who cares! She was a selfish woman who made me think I wasn't worthy of love," I shout at my father for the first time in my life. My hands shake as rage fills my heart. I am done being treated like a child. Done being patted on the head and patronized. I point an accusatory finger at him and add, "And you let her. Because you were either too busy to notice or too heartless to care."

He gasps and stumbles back a few steps. He recovers quickly, straightening his jacket and standing tall. But I don't let him mount a defense. I press forward, unshackling myself from the illusion that he'll ever be the father I deserve.

"For once in my life, you are going to listen to me. Austin broke my heart. But I helped him get justice anyway because he's a decent human being. And because I love him, whether he loves me back or not. That's how love works. It doesn't matter if someone deserves it. It's not conditional. Love is not a currency. Mother belittled me my entire childhood and I loved her anyway. You're a foolish old man who ignored me my entire life—" I stare up at him and my voice cracks with emotion. "And I love you anyway."

"Elizabeth—" He says my name gently, the word itself an apology.

I'm not ready to forgive him. "But if you think I'm going to waste one more second of my life trying to be what mother wanted or what you think I should be, you are sorely mistaken. I'm not perfect, but I'm your daughter. The only one you'll ever have. I'm not going to change. You can love me as I am, or you can fuck off. At this point, I really don't care."

"I only want what is best for you. You were not raised to know how treacherous the world can be."

I shake my head, exasperated. He isn't listening to me. "I know exactly how disappointing people can be. I think it's time for you to leave."

My father doesn't fight me for the last word. He turns tail and leaves in a huff. I hear the door close and I collapse on the floor in a pile of mush. I've used every inch of backbone I have and maybe even some I don't. I feel empowered and a little sad. I've irrevocably broken my relationship with my father. Maybe it's always been broken. I hope someday it can heal.

Chapter Nineteen

Austin

I sink down into Devin's couch. He's got a giant smile on his face, but I'm in shock.

"This attorney took care of everything?" Devin asks, handing me a beer.

"Mr. Phillips. Yeah. Looks that way." I take a long sip, gulping down the cold alcohol. "He called me out of the blue on Monday. Said he heard about my case and wanted to provide his services pro bono. He got his hands on evidence, emails or some shit, showing Monte paid off one of the lab techs to falsify my results. I guess he's been paying the guy all year to cover up his own results too."

I laugh at the memory of Monte being kicked off the team and out of the house. Tampering with a drug test is apparently worse than failing the damn thing in the first place. Drew invited me over to watch him pack up his shit. Half the team was there, giving me apologies and bullshit excuses about how they knew all along I was innocent. Even Coach called to apologize. Fuck all of them. They're full of shit. Not a damn one of them was there when I was in the gutter. None of them would lose any sleep if that's where I ended up tomorrow.

"You going to be able to finish your degree now?"

I nod. "Scholarship's back and that attorney even got the school to cough up extra cash for me to get a place of my own." I stick out my bottom lip in a mock pout. "For all my pain and suffering."

Devin shakes his head in disbelief. "Lucky little shit…"

"Better to be lucky than good." I clink my beer with his. "Can I crash here until I find my own place?"

"Anytime, man," he answers with a satisfied nod. He sips his beer and hides a smile.

His door is always open if I want it. I know it was killing him to watch me spiral, sleeping in my fucking truck and drunk off my ass. But we both know we can only help someone who wants to be helped. And I sure as fuck didn't. Even if he'd offered, I would've shut him down. I needed to be alone, wallowing in the gutter. To lose everything.

It wasn't until I saw Elizabeth coming out of Monte's room that I let myself feel anything other than self-pity. Before that, I'd resigned myself to the shit life I knew I was meant for. *Hello minimum wage. Goodbye self-respect.* Long hours at a shit job, living in a trailer park, barely scraping by until I die. But the idea of someone like Elizabeth ending up with that worthless piece of shit Monte made me want to burn the world down. It lit a fire under my ass.

She deserves better. I'm not good enough to be her forever, but Montgomery isn't even worthy of her right now. When I sobered up the next morning, I took my laptop to the library and used the free Wi-Fi to log into Rule Them All. My country was destroyed and I had a fair amount of hate mail, almost all it from Jackie. Nothing from Elizabeth. She didn't care enough to tell me to go fuck myself.

I created a new account, CuratorofLostSouls. I told myself I only wanted to know she was doing okay, to keep her away from assholes who didn't deserve her. But I don't need to spend every waking hour playing to do that. My heart rate picks up each time I log on, waiting to see if Elizabeth is online. I close my eyes and picture those deep brown eyes of hers. I remember how soft her skin is. The shape of her lips. The taste of her. I'm desperate to touch her again, but I know I never will. I'll settle for just hearing her sweet voice.

* * * *

"That fucking game is worse than the damn drinking," Devin grunts at me after emerging from his bedroom.

Maybe he's right. I was up all night again. I don't give a shit about the game, but the hours of bullshit are worth it for the few minutes I get to see Elizabeth's beautiful face in the group video chat. Most of the time it's Jackie barking out orders, but when Elizabeth speaks, it's like she's sitting right beside me. She's with me. I don't talk to her. She'll never see me. I just listen.

"Seriously, do we need to have a gamer intervention?" Devin calls from the kitchen, turning on the coffee pot. I haven't told him the game is about Elizabeth.

"Nah. I'm caught up in some stuff right now. It won't last much longer. "

Last night was huge. Elizabeth finally got her country back. Law of Superiority is far from gone, but they're crippled for now. I've joined forces with Elizabeth's league, The Federation, to help her get back what she lost because of me. What she really wants. The only thing I can give her.

I'm about to log off and take a nap when my screen lights up with a new message.

DominaTrix: *I know who you are.*

Fuck. It's Jackie. I stare at the screen, wondering how the fuck she found out and what the hell I'm supposed to write back.

DominaTrix: *Leave her alone, Austin. You've done enough.*

CuratorofLostSouls: *I don't know what you're talking about.*

I choose to go with denial.

DominaTrix: *Prove it.*

My screen lights up with a video chat request. *Fuck.* So much for denial. I plug in my headphones and accept the request, knowing I'm about to get flame sprayed by Elizabeth's best friend.

"How's it going, Jackie?" I ask nonchalantly.

"Die in a fire, shithead," she jeers with a sweetly evil smile. "Are you going to leave my best friend alone, or do I have to come cut your balls off?" Her voice is unnervingly charming.

"I'm not doing—"

"The fuck you're not. I see you, scheming, manipulating with your little band of dickwads."

"I'm just helping her out, Jackie."

"Thanks for that. She's got her country back, now you can fuck right the fuck off."

I'm used to her brutal honesty after the hours of gaming, but knowing she could take away the only part of Elizabeth I have left makes me cringe. I can't lose this.

"You're done fucking with her head, Man Meat."

My heart stops. "Does she know?"

"That you're the one helping her? No, not yet. And not ever if I have anything to say about it. That's why you need to back the fuck off. What do you think you're playing at anyway?"

"Nothing. It's not a big deal," I lie.

"It is. To her it is. You know she loves you, you piece of shit. Even though it's killing her."

Jackie's words plunge a knife into my heart, but I don't show it.

"She doesn't love me. It was just a stupid crush. She'll get over it." And so will I. Someday. "Isn't she with Monte now?" Rage surges through my body at the idea of his hands on her.

"Monte?" Jackie makes a gagging sound and mimics vomiting off camera. At least, I think she's faking. "Were you dropped on your head as a baby? 'Cause you're a fucking idiot. Even if Lizbit wasn't completely in love with you, she'd never have anything to do with that douchecanoe."

A weight lifts off my chest and my heart expands tenfold. "She's not seeing anyone?"

"Are you listening to me at all?" Jackie throws her hands up in frustration and shakes her head violently, her bright red hair flying around the screen. "You've given her penis PTSD. You're *literally* her worst fear. You didn't just reject her, you eviscerated her."

"She walked away first." She didn't just walk away, she ran. I wasn't the only one who put up walls.

"Whatever you have to tell yourself, prick. But we both know that's bullshit. She laid her heart at your feet and you stomped on it."

My stomach knots up remembering Elizabeth's face that day in the library. The pain of watching her walk away aches in my chest.

"If you pulled that shit on me, you better believe I would've let you twist in the wind. And *loooooved* every minute of it. But no. Not Lizbit. That girl loves like it's going out of style. Even after you devastated her, she's still defending you."

I let out an aggravated sigh and ask, "What are you talking about?" Elizabeth wants nothing to do with me.

"I'll admit it's awesome she finally told that absentee jackoff of a father to go screw himself—"

"No fucking way," I interject confidently. "It'll be a cold day in hell before Elizabeth would ever talk back to her dad."

Jackie deadpans, "Better get the Devil a parka and some mittens then, because it's a fucking blizzard down there."

I shake my head, not believing. Jackie rolls her eyes at me.

"It was over you. She told him off *for you*."

A pinch of shame twists my gut.

"He found out about the five grand?"

I should have given it back to her. I have most of it. What I didn't spend on food and basic survival has been sitting untouched in a bank account for weeks. I don't deserve it. Loving her isn't a job. Fuck, it wasn't even a choice.

"Five grand?" Jackie scoffs. "Who cares about money? It was about you using her to beat a drug rap. Not exactly on-brand for Richard 'The Dick' Wilde."

"Are you high right now?" I ask in all seriousness. Elizabeth didn't even know I was in trouble. And if she did, she wouldn't care.

"Christ on a cracker! You may be hotter than the sun, but you really are a dim fuck."

I stare at Jackie blankly, waiting for an explanation.

"She's the one who broke into Monte's room and got the evidence to clear you. Idiot." Jackie's tone is condescending as shit, but all I can focus on are her words. "It was totally badass by the way." Her eyes dance with mischievous pride.

The room is spinning. My heart rate is jacked. Hope springs up in the back of my mind, but I beat it down. I can't believe it. I wouldn't survive being wrong. She hates me. I know she hates me. She'd have to after everything I said. There's no way she'd help me out, save my life. What would she get out of rescuing me and losing her father? Nothing.

"That's not possible." My head is a jumbled mess. Goose broke into Monte's room? She put herself on the line. For me? Without asking for anything. Without even telling me.

"Clearly, we've already established hell has frozen over. Who do you think paid for that lawyer?"

The guy said it was pro bono. I should have fucking known. No one has ever helped me out without wanting something in return. No one except Elizabeth. Even when I had nothing, when everyone thought I was a drugged-up loser, she was there for me.

"What the actual fuck?" I manage to stammer in complete shock. My heart is racing faster than if I'd mainlined an energy drink. I have to see her. I have to know.

"Wait, you didn't know?" Jackie's surprised voice rings in my ears. "I thought that's what all this Curator of Dark Douchebagness bullshit was about. You trying to pay her back."

"It's not."

"Then what—"

I don't bother answering Jackie. I'm already out of the door.

I manage the twenty-minute drive to Elizabeth's in ten and storm into her apartment without knocking. She launches off the couch like it's electrified.

"Why would you do it?" I practically scream at her.

"Austin," she screeches in terror, just about jumping out of her skin. I caught her off guard. Serves her right. She should've locked her door.

I stalk closer to her, my chest heaving from basically running here. I need to know the truth. "Why?" I demand.

She's staring at me, completely dumbstruck. The silence is killing me.

"Elizabeth," I say her name as a warning and she finally snaps back to reality.

"Why *what?*" she asks, throwing her arms up. Between her pinched forehead and clenched jaw, it's obvious she's royally pissed.

"That lawyer. Why did you save my ass?"

There's an entire apartment between us, but I'm suffocating. Being in the same room with her again takes my breath away.

"How did you find out?" she asks, avoiding answering my question. Her eyes shoot to the floor and her shoulders slouch.

"Jackie."

Elizabeth lets out an aggravated huff. "That stupid blabbermouth. It was supposed to be anonymous."

"So it's true?"

She nods. I dig my nails into my palms to keep from reaching out for her.

"That night at the party, why were you in Monte's room?"

She purses her lips, angry that she has to answer when I already know the reason. "To get his password. Prove it was him. That you're innocent."

"All of it. It was all you?" She shrugs, like it was nothing. I take a deep breath, trying to calm myself down. "Tell me why you did it."

She bites her lip, drawing my eyes down to her beautiful mouth. Jesus, I want to kiss her.

She crosses her arms, juts out a hip and declares, "You know why."

"No, Elizabeth. I don't. I have no fucking idea." My words are dripping with irony. I can tell by her ragged breath and the longing in her eyes that she still feels something for me. But she's too scared to say it. After what I put her through, I can't blame her. I'm desperate to hear her say the words. "Why? Why would you help me?"

"You know *why*, you smug bastard. You know *exactly* how I feel about you." Her short, choppy breaths surge through her flaring nostrils. I know her heart rate is pegged and her adrenaline is off the charts, same as mine. She's beyond pissed now, flailing her arms and pacing. I don't care. I love this fierce woman, so I keep pushing her.

"Why don't you give up on me already?"

"Oh, why didn't I think of that!" She knocks herself in the head with her palm. Her anger doesn't seem to affect her sarcasm. "Thanks for the suggestion. Do you think I *could* even if I *wanted* to? I can't *choose* to stop loving you any more than I *chose* to start."

She doesn't realize she's said it. She's too busy yelling at me to catch it, but I do. Her accidental admission of love sears my chest, etching itself into my soul. She's mine. She loves me. After everything, she still actually loves me. She's pissed as fuck, but she loves me. I want to hold her, whisper in her ear how much I love her too, but Ms. Fiesty's determined to keep her distance.

"Happy now? Does that make you feel better? Don't worry, I'm not going to go all *Fatal Attraction* on you if that's why you're here. I know you couldn't care less about me." She stalks over to the front door that I never bothered closing and asks in mock civility, "Now, can you please get the hell out of my apartment and never come back?"

Her chocolate eyes lock on mine, fury making them sparkle. Even in her baggy pajama pants and ratty sweatshirt, she's never looked more beautiful to me. My Goose. My weird little goddess.

"Not a fucking chance." I close the space between us in three quick steps and have her in my arms before she can run away. I crash my lips on hers, pouring out all the years of doubt and hurt. Letting go of all the pain so I can grab on to her love with both hands and never let go.

"Don't," she cries, shoving me away. Walking away, she lets out a tortured laugh that breaks my heart. When she turns back to face me, she's on the verge of tears. I make a silent vow to never be the cause of those tears again. "I can't do this again. No more games. No more pretending. I want something real."

I don't hesitate before I answer, "This is real. It's always been real. I love you. I think I have since the first time I saw you."

"Oh, yeah? You have a real shitty way of showing it," she quips. She doesn't believe me and I don't blame her.

"I know. Fuck, I know. This scares the hell out of me and I've been a pussy. I'm sorry." I reach out for her, but she pulls away. She's slipping through my fingers and the idea of losing her again is ripping me apart. "I'm so goddamn sorry."

"Don't for a second think I'm trying to buy your love." She crosses her arms and glares at me. Her words are vicious, but her tortured eyes are filling with tears. I can't break through the wall she's built between us. "Helpful tip, don't make the next girl pay for it."

Every instinct I have is telling me to cut my losses. Turn around and never look back. But I ignore them all. If I leave now, I will lose her forever. Instead, I dig in, determined to hold on no matter the cost.

I take a deep breath. "This isn't about money and there isn't going to be a next girl. You're it for me. I love you." Anger drains from her face, replaced by stoic nothingness. There is no recognition in her blank expression. I say it again, silently begging her to hear me. Believe me. "I. Love. You." She stares at me, right through me. I use her name this time. "Elizabeth Marie Wilde, I love you. So fucking much."

She's dazed. Her eyes are wide and her mouth agape. I might have fried her brain.

"That's not... But you said... You can't..." She can't form complete sentences.

"I can. And I do." She doesn't believe me and there is only one thing I can think of to convince her. "I got a tattoo."

She blinks at me and shakes her head. "What?"

I pull up the cuff of my sweatshirt and take a few steps toward her so she can see the silhouette of a feather on my left forearm. Thank fuck she doesn't pull away. "I got it last week. I realized that even though my goose flew away, she left a mark."

She reaches out, her delicate finger tracing the thick lines across my skin. The sensation is soothing and exhilarating. Her beautiful dark eyes drag up to mine and something unlocks deep in my chest.

"I love that you wear T-shirts three sizes too big. I love that you think pizza is fine dining. I love that you snore louder than a grizzly bear." I take a small step toward her with every sentence. Thank fuck she's too entranced to pull away. "I love that you use movie references at least two decades old. I love that you have a favorite human organ. I love how I never know what's going to come out of your mouth. I love the way your smile can light up the room. I love that your laugh is the happiest sound in the world." One last step and I'm in her space, chest to chest. I lean down and tickle the sweet spot on her neck with my lips, whispering, "I love the way you shudder underneath me when you come." I lean back and with a smirk, add, "Or on top of me."

Her knees buckle, but I catch her in my arms. I hold her tight, pinning her against my body. Taking in her beautiful face, I push aside the jokes and get serious. For once in my life, I'm not going to hold back.

I drop my forehead to hers and vow, "I will feed you when you're hungry. I will keep you safe when you're scared. I will hold you when you're hurt. I will find you when you're lost. I will tell you that you're my goddess every single day. And I will love you no matter what." I kiss her with what I can only describe as unending devotion. The kiss is soft but excruciatingly passionate. I let my lips linger on hers, pleading and taunting.

Her eyes are pinched closed when she asks, "You love me?"

I kiss her again before I answer, "Yes."

"Are you sure?" she asks again, not willing to look at me.

I squeeze her tight and kiss her again. "I'm fucking positive."

"Well, that's weird."

Chapter Twenty

Austin

I take my jacket off and drape it over Elizabeth's shoulders before wrapping her up in my arms. She's a breathing ice sculpture. It's got to be in the forties out tonight and the valet is taking forever. The three of us finally made it to La Rouge, Elizabeth, her dad — who I've continued to call Dick despite how many times he calls himself Richard — and me. After a frosty few months when Elizabeth and I first officially started dating, he finally made an effort and invited us out to dinner. He insisted on choosing the place and here we are.

The food was decent, but not worth wearing a jacket and tie all night for. In his defense, Dick hasn't said a word about Elizabeth's outfit. It's not her usual baggy T-shirt and jeans, but it's also not the ninety-year-old librarian getup she used to wear around him. It's a flowy silk dress in dark green that clings to her curves and is tastefully, but teasingly, low cut in the front. A new image she's trying out that I wholeheartedly approve of, especially as I stand behind her and stare down into the deep ravine of her cleavage. She's shuffling back and forth on her feet, trying to keep warm. The sway of her hips plus the sexy little bounce of her amazing tits is doing it for me. I can't wait to get her home.

"Ugh," she sighs. "I can't hold it any longer. I've got to pee. Hold this. I'll be right back." She hands me her purse and disappears back inside the restaurant.

I glance over at Dick, clear my throat and make an effort. "She had a nice time tonight."

Dick looks me up and down. The coward peeks behind him into the restaurant to make sure Elizabeth is out of earshot and says, "You know she deserves better."

I tuck Elizabeth's purse under my arm and turn to face him like a man. "Yes, she does. Better than both of us."

He does me the courtesy of meeting my eyes and nods. It's almost imperceptible, but he does.

I give him a hard slap on the shoulder. "Thankfully, she loves us anyway."

"Then I suppose we will both have to be better." He puts his hands in his pockets and scowls.

"Yes, we fucking will."

We stand in the cold silence until Elizabeth comes back.

I pull her against me, neither of us caring that her father is watching. Kissing her neck, I murmur, "I missed you."

She giggles at the tickle of my lips on her skin and hums, "Seventy-nine."

"Seventy-nine what?"

"Things I love about you. I keep count. That you miss me when I'm gone, even for a little bit, is number seventy-nine."

"Fuck, you're weird." My grin is a mile wide.

"And you're an ass," she chides with a smack to my chest.

"Yeah, I know. But you love me anyway."

"Yeah, I do. Weird." She gives me a wry smile.

Fuck, I love this woman.

Epilogue

Austin
Seven years later

Elizabeth is fidgeting, fixing the collar of her shirt unnecessarily for the millionth time this morning. Some things never change. She twirls her wedding ring, the telltale sign that she's close to a panic attack. She doesn't get this way often these days, but today is a big deal.

I grab her hands and pull her against me. "Calm down, Goose. Everything's going to be fine."

She lets out an uneasy sigh. "You don't know that. You can't know that."

I take her face in my hands, gently kiss her sweet lips and whisper, "Have I ever been wrong?"

That earns me a much-deserved eye-roll, along with the laugh I was hoping for. I kiss her again. This time it isn't sweet. It's dirty and delicious. I wander my hands down to her ass, giving a little squeeze, as I slip my tongue into her mouth. She's still the sexiest woman I've ever met.

"Jesus, get a room," Jackson calls out across the waiting room, the little cock blocker.

"Don't be an ass, she's nervous," I retort.

"Don't call him that," Elizabeth reprimands me with a slap on the shoulder before wrapping Jackson in her arms. He's not even thirteen yet, but he's already a few inches taller than her. It doesn't stop her from babying him. I swear, sometimes I'm worried she'll smother that kid. But that's Elizabeth. She doesn't know how to love halfway.

"I wasn't *calling* him anything. I was *telling* him to amend his behavior. And, besides, it's your fault for being irresistible," I counter in my own defense. Elizabeth and Jackson roll their eyes in unison. If I didn't know any better, I'd swear he was her biological kid.

"Gross," Jackson scoffs at me. Wrapping his arms around Elizabeth, he adds, "Sorry." Jackson hugs her, squeezing tightly, making sure she's real. I know the feeling. Some days I think I dreamed her up too.

We've been fostering the scrawny punk for three years. At nine, Jackson thought he was tough enough to take on the whole world by himself. Within the first five minutes of meeting him, Elizabeth was determined to make sure he'd never have to. It took time for Jackson to trust, to believe us when we said I love you and promised we'd always be there for him. I can't say I blame him. We all have our own baggage in life, but Elizabeth is a hard woman to ignore. She has a way of worming into a person's heart and earning their trust before they're able to resist.

"Don't listen to him. I'm fine." Elizabeth tries to make her voice sound calm, but underneath she's frazzled. I flash her a knowing smile, just so she doesn't think she's fooling anyone.

Jackson clears his throat, drawing both our attention. "In that case, can I talk to Dad for a minute? Alone." I'm still getting used to that word, but I've never felt prouder than the first time Jackson called me his dad.

"Yeah, sure," Elizabeth says hesitantly. Her mind must be working overtime right now. I'm sure she thinks whatever the problem is, it's her fault. She's terrified of not being enough. I try every day to prove her wrong, but old habits are hard to break.

I give her a quick kiss on the temple and a light smack to her backside before I follow Jackson down the hall. I can hear her muttering "Loosey-goosey" to herself as I walk away and it makes me smile.

"What's up? Having second thoughts about becoming a Jacobs?" I tease Jackson. The intensity in his eyes makes me realize he just might be. My stomach twists into knots. That would break Elizabeth's heart. Fuck, it would break mine too.

I try not to get ahead of myself. "What's wrong?"

"I just can't shake this feeling. Like, I shouldn't be here. Like, someone's going to come running into the courtroom at the last minute and say it was all a mistake."

"It's not. We love you." I mean that with every ounce of my soul.

"Why?" he asks with a wry chuckle. "I'm such an undeserving shitbag. Why are you and Elizabeth wasting your time with me? You guys should adopt some perfect, unfucked-up baby. Seriously, I'm not worth it." Staring at Jackson is like peering into my past. I was that broken, before Elizabeth.

"First of all, watch your mouth. If Elizabeth hears you swearing, she'll have both our asses." I take a deep breath and pause for a minute, thinking about what I want to say.

I've never been so glad Elizabeth talked me into pursuing social work instead of an MBA. I've *literally* got a master's degree in this shit, and I'm struggling with the words. How do I convince this kid it's not about being good enough? Blood or not, he'll always be my son.

"Listen, Jackson, the weird thing about love is you don't get to decide if you're worthy of it. The other person does. And let me tell you, from one undeserving shitbag to another, when Elizabeth decides to love someone there's nothing you can do to stop her. Believe me, I've tried. Look at me."

He brings his eyes up to meet mine, tears building at their edges.

"We're all a little broken. But that doesn't matter when someone loves you. I don't care what you do, or what this court says. You're my son and I love you." I pull him into my arms and hold him, hoping it's enough.

"I love you too, Dad."

Now I'm crying. I let him pull away first, and we both wipe away the tears in our eyes.

I make several manly grunting noises to shake the emotion out of my voice. "We should get back to Elizabeth before she has a panic attack."

I can hear Elizabeth's terse voice around the corner before I can see her. She's obviously upset and my body tenses. I glance over at Jackson and realize with a smile that he's ready to take on whatever's upset Elizabeth right beside me. He really is my kid.

"Stop. Just *stop*. I'm not going to listen to any more excuses. Let me be perfectly clear, *Father*," Elizabeth says it like it's a curse word, leaving a bad taste in her mouth. "He is becoming your grandson today. If he mattered to you — if I mattered to you — you'd be here. I love you, but if you want to be part of this family, you have to make an effort. The choice is yours. I've got to go." I doubt Dick had a chance to answer before Elizabeth hung up on him. Their relationship has its ups and downs. It's hard to change after a lifetime of being a selfish prick. He tries, but not hard enough.

She turns around to see me and Jackson standing there, just staring at her. I step into Elizabeth's personal space, rubbing her tense shoulders. "You okay?"

"Yes. I won't let him not being here ruin this day," Elizabeth answers with a bittersweet smile. She never ceases to amaze me.

I lean down to make sure Jackson can't hear. "For the record, you're sexy as fuck when you go full-on momma bear." I kiss the sweet spot on her neck, knowing for a few seconds at least, I'm all she'll be thinking about.

"Mr. and Mrs. Jacobs? We're ready for you," a clerk with a clipboard calls out, making Elizabeth jump.

"Doctor." The clerk, Elizabeth, and I all turn to Jackson. "Mr. and Dr. Jacobs," he corrects with a smirk, looking quite proud of Elizabeth and pleased with himself. Elizabeth blushes.

"He's not wrong. Shall we, Dr. Jacobs?" I open the door for Elizabeth and Jackson before following behind them into family court.

We're only in front of the judge for about fifteen minutes then it's done. Jackson is legally our son. Elizabeth jumps for joy with a loud squeal. Jackson crushes her in a hug. I can't stop smiling. No, seriously, it's a problem. My face actually hurts.

I was terrified when Elizabeth said she wanted to adopt. What the hell do I know about being a dad? But, seeing the two of them, my *family*, I can't imagine my life without them. I wrap my arms around my wife and son, squeezing tightly just to make sure they're real. They are. And whether I deserve them or not, they're mine.

So, love is weird.

And I wouldn't have it any other way.

Want to see more like this?
Here's a taster for you to enjoy!

Happily Ever Austen:
Pride and Pancakes
Ellen Mint

Excerpt

Why isn't the car spinning out in the snow? Nothing dramatic that'd require an ambulance or the jaws of life, just a minor hiccup in her travel plans. Anything to delay her from this coming storm. But, no, Beth couldn't be that lucky.

Wringing her hands over the rented Civic's steering wheel, she glared out at the stark white landscape. It'd started muddy and drab, dawn hours away when she'd left New York City. Six hours later, deep in Vermont's snow-capped mountains, the azure skies did nothing to evaporate the dread in her heart.

The road was little more than dirt and snow packed down by wide wheels, increasing the throbbing headache Beth knew wouldn't vanish once she reached her destination. At the sign for the Honeymoon Cabin — *charming* — she turned right to follow an even thinner trail. The tiny car barely made it into the ruts dug out by a monstrous SUV, Beth listening to every *chunk-chunk* of snow splatting out of the wheel wells.

As a twist of smoke pierced the snow-peaked horizon, her editor's parting words rang through her skull. *'Land this damn interview, Cho. If you don't...'*

He didn't need to finish his threat—everyone in journalism was well aware of the always-looming cutbacks. It didn't matter how much money their website pulled in, it was never enough for investors. And the easiest way to line their pockets was by sending yet another reporter to the breadlines.

While the six-hour-plus drive in inclement leaning to suicidal weather didn't endear her, it was the subject of the interview that had Beth chewing glass. If it had been a fickle actor known for being handsy, she'd have brought her friend Bruno as an assistant. If it had been a mealy-mouthed politician—not that her employer cared about politics beyond if one was caught without pants—she'd have kept a slew of previous soundbites at the ready.

But this? This was...

Her thought snapped away when the ever-rising ground finally leveled out and she emerged before a picturesque cabin. It looked like a Victorian Christmas card had come to life. The cabin of massive red logs boasted a single chimney puffing perfect clouds of smoke into the air over snow-capped shingles. Quaint green shutters hung off the three windows she could make out. There was clearly a picture window for the living room, but it was frosted over from the encroaching cold. Pine trees lined the driveway, each one dusted in white snow as if a designer had painted them.

It'd be a lovely place to vacation or hide away in for a week while trying to hammer a book out. But that wasn't what awaited her inside.

Pulling a cleansing breath into her lungs, Beth snatched up her purse and laptop and struck out into the cold. Her leg sunk a foot into the snow, the freezing air punching into her chest and a gasp escaping her mouth. Cruel, frozen water tumbled into her shoes.

Damn it! Damn it! Damn it!

With each step she took to the cabin, more plummeting snow filled her ankle-high boots. They were cute for the city in winter but pointless this deep into the wilderness. It was doubtful anything short of a whole bearskin would keep someone warm up here. Thanks to her having turned up the heat in the car, the snow quickly melted to slush, seeping up her socks and leaving her crankier.

Despite dreading what awaited her inside, Beth dashed for the cabin. At least it'd be warm and snow-free. She grabbed onto the wooden railings with their woodland animal carvings and leaped up the three front steps. The door was a firehouse red with a wreath of cedar and holly hanging from it. Breathing in the smell of hamster bedding, she pushed on the handle and let herself in.

A flash of lightbulbs from by the fireplace interrupted Beth's entrances. Orange flames danced inside the stones there, three stockings without names dangling off plastic greenery above the fire. And standing beside it, an arm lazily draped over the mantel, was what had had her grinding her teeth for six hours.

"Tristan?" the photographer called the stone man glaring through space. "Can you turn and raise your chin?"

If he raised it any higher, all her shots would be directly up his nose.

Tristan Harty. Once a teenage heartthrob sporting floppy hair that dusted over those striking blue eyes, he'd climbed the charts with a handful of songs plucked out on his guitar. The trajectory of his career followed the majority of those who began in the same way. He'd grown older, teenage girls had moved on, his star had faded. Now, he was trying a comeback thanks to the rise in '90s nostalgia and his PR team had finagled an exclusive interview with her magazine.

Instead of the leather jacket overtop an expertly distressed T-shirt, they'd dressed him like Father Christmas. A black suit coat, tailored tight to his thin frame, lay unbuttoned over a crimson vest. A pocket watch, of all things, dangled off the vest. *Does he intend to recite some Dickens to the photographer as well?* Time had thinned the soulful mane of his younger years. Locks shorn to an inch revealed more of his forehead than any had seen in a decade.

While most men his age would have wrinkles piling up across that vast brow, the cold demeanor of Tristan Harty kept his face nearly as preserved as if he were a botoxed socialite. Somehow, his record company had convinced an entire generation of fifteen-year-olds that he was the deepest, most soulful man in existence. Beth wanted to laugh at the thought when the man in question focused away from his photographer to where she stood dripping at the front door.

Eyes bluer than a sapphire burned into her soul. She tried to swallow, but her throat constricted. Even turning her head was proving impossible as ten thousand watts bore down upon her.

"You!" a voice shouted, evaporating the confounding spell. Beth blinked, glancing back at the once bewitching man. With the glare broken, he transformed back into a snooty aristocrat hoisting up a guitar.

From the mess of photography equipment that claimed the cabin's entire living room bustled a wide man. He wasn't fat, at least not in that lovable oaf way, but his rectangular build easily fit into a doorway. He was the comedic opposite of the thin man pretending to play a song for the camera.

"Who are you?" he shouted at Beth.

She flexed her lips in a not smile. "The interviewer."

What had to be the manager scoffed. "You're late. What took you so damn long?"

"I'm afraid transporters haven't been invented yet, so I had to rely upon the old-fashioned horseless carriage," Beth snapped, in no mood to be shouted down by the reason she was in this mess. There were a dozen more interesting concerts and art house movies she could be reviewing at home instead of wasting an entire weekend in Vermont.

The manager pinged his beady eyes skyward. "What? You never heard of airplanes?"

She chewed on her tongue, keeping the caustic comment at bay. There was no chance of her company splurging on an airline ticket, seeing as how they couldn't ship their reporters as freight.

"Barry…?" A voice of reason stepped into the fray as the very subject of the interview spoke up. "Let it be," Tristan whispered. His speaking voice was soft and drifted in the tenor range, a surprise for anyone who knew his songs.

Barry the manager was in no mood to do such a thing. He was clearly incensed there was no underpaid intern to boss around and had to take all that anger out on someone. "Listen here…" Whatever derogatory term floated in his brain remained there, though he stared twice as hard at her eyes. "We ain't got time to waste here. So get this little Q&A session done fast. Got it?"

"Mr. Barry." Beth unlatched her purse, picking up her phone. "This little 'Q&A session' is part of the deal. I have full access to your…talent, and we host a release for his album." She should have been surprised at having to remind him of the back-scratching contract, but it was a wonder sometimes that most managers had the wherewithal to work a bed.

His annoyance at her tripled in strength. Beth internally smiled at her barbs when Barry pointed toward an open room. "Fine! Set up in there. I'll send Tristan in once he's finished."

"Thank you ever so much." She hefted her bag closer to her side. Just before she turned her back on the primping and posturing, another cobalt glare burned across her sights. For a foolish breath, her cheeks burned.

So I'm to work in the bedroom? While grateful she wasn't being forced to conduct her interview in the bathroom, she'd done worse. Once, she'd had to question a football player while crammed inside a food truck while an untended open fire singed an inch off her hair. Though, as she gazed around the room, a new unease settled in her gut.

While the living room and small adjacent kitchen were rustic and woodland themed, this was where the honeymoon adjective came from. The bed was gigantic, with four posters painted like birch trees, and a damn canopy, of all things. Red and pink silks hung off the posts and a shimmery duvet covered the bed itself. Perched between the ordinary pillows was one in the shape of a heart. There were no bottles of wine in a bucket on the nightstand, but a remote sat there instead. Beth was both curious and terrified to see what it was for.

She glanced at the oval-shaped mirror set in the vanity, finding in the glass an exhausted woman who'd been awake since three a.m., driven up a mountain and still had to crack this damn introvert. At least she'd thought to check in at the hotel first, knowing she'd be exhausted by the time this was over. A warm bath and a night of typing in her terrycloth pajamas was as good a reward as she could count on.

Unbuttoning her blazer, Beth set to work. There wasn't much in the way of seating in the bedroom, so she picked up the vanity's chair and placed it in the center. Hopefully, Tristan would feel just comfortable enough to be uncomfortable. Laying out her tools of the trade the way a warrior would before battle, Beth inspected the batteries' lives. Her phone was holding strong—she'd learned to keep her apps to a minimum lest she miss a vital picture or be unable to record a pivotal quote. The laptop was at seventy percent. Not great, but she'd only crack into it once she was back at the hotel.

The room felt too bright and cheerful. For some subjects, that'd be perfect. The candy-coated-sprinkle types loved nothing more than to bake cupcakes and divulge all their secrets while frosting. But not Tristan Harty. He'd been in the spotlight for over fifteen years, then out for eight. In all that time, the most people'd gotten out of him was his name, date of birth and current hit song. He was a black hole of personal information, and in order to keep her job, Beth had to get this vacuum to sing.

Cracking her knuckles, she took one last look at her reflection. Instead of the fretting thirty-year-old reporter, she saw a little girl. With her neon-pink unicorn notebook in hand, that girl in pigtails had been prepared to ask dictators and humanitarians alike the hard questions, and wouldn't stop until she got them. This Beth could handle some has-been musician.

Home of Erotic Romance

Sign up for our newsletter and find out about all our romance book releases, eBook sales and promotions, sneak peeks and FREE romance books!

About the Author

Amelia Kingston is many things, the most interesting of which are probably California girl, writer, traveler, and dog mom. She survives on chocolate, coffee, wine, and sarcasm. Not necessarily in that order.

She's been blessed with a patient husband who's embraced her nomad ways and traveled with her to over 30 countries across 5 continents (I'm coming for you next, Antarctica!). She's also been cursed with an impatient (although admittedly adorable) terrier who pouts when her dinner is 5 minutes late.

She writes about strong, stubborn, flawed women and the men who can't help but love them. Her irreverent books aim to be silly and fun with the occasional storm cloud to remind us to appreciate the sunny days. As a hopeless romantic, her favorite stories are the ones that remind us all that while love is rarely perfect, it's always worth chasing.

Amelia loves to hear from readers. You can find her contact information, website details and author profile page at https://www.totallybound.com

Made in the USA
Las Vegas, NV
21 July 2021